The
Black Swan

Ana Seymour

JOVE BOOKS, NEW YORK

THE BLACK SWAN

A Jove Book / published by arrangement with
the author

PRINTING HISTORY
Jove edition / June 2001

The Penguin Putnam Inc. World Wide Web site address is
www.penguinputnam.com

ISBN: 0-515-13063-X

A JOVE BOOK®
Jove Books are published by The Berkley Publishing Group,
a division of Penguin Putnam Inc.,
375 Hudson Street, New York, New York 10014.
JOVE and the "J" design
are trademarks belonging to Penguin Putnam Inc.

PRINTED IN THE UNITED STATES OF AMERICA

10 9 8 7 6 5 4 3 2 1

The Black Swan

The harp that once thro' Tara's Halls
The soul of music shed,
Now hangs as mute on Tara's walls
As if that soul were fled.

No more to chiefs and ladies bright
The harp of Tara swells;
The chord alone that breaks at night,
Its tale of ruin tells.

One

"I'm not afeared of curses, Cormac," Niall Riordan said with a wave of his big hand. "Let *me* marry the wench."

" 'Tis the eldest Riordan who must wed the eldest O'Donnell," Eamon pointed out gently, "else the feud will continue." Eamon had always been the peacemaker among the three Riordan brothers, though in battle he was known to be every bit as fierce as Niall and Cormac. The mere sight of the robust trio had caused more than one enemy to throw down a sword and beg for mercy.

Niall looked over at the oldest brother, Cormac, who sat with his feet propped up on a crude bench, staring into the fire pit with a glowering expression. "You've not the aspect of a bridegroom, brother," he said with the crooked grin that was a Riordan trademark. "Can't you even muster a smile in anticipation of the wedding night? If I remember rightly, the O'Donnell daughter's a comely lass, and they say 'tis a lusty thing to play for the first time on an unplowed field. Myself, I've never had the pleasure, since I prefer my women seasoned."

Cormac turned a dark gaze on his youngest brother. "There'll be no lusty play this wedding night. I'll plant no Riordan seed to split apart another hapless bride at the birthing nine month's hence."

Niall's grin died, and the three brothers fell silent. Each of their mothers had died in just such a way, giving birth to the three brawny sons of Ultan Riordan.

"Not all Riordan brides have died in childbirth, Cormac," Eamon said finally.

"Nay, some have fallen off cliffs or been eaten by wolves or taken ill with the bitters, but all have died, haven't they? Within a year and a day of the wedding, just as the blasted curse foretold." Cormac got up from the bench and started to pace the small tent that had been set up as the headquarters of the groom's family prior to the wedding feast.

The ceremony was to take place at Tara Hill, the ancient seat of kings, as Riordan weddings had for generations, though even this Cormac had tried to protest. "If this thing is to be," he'd told his father, "let no tradition be followed, no pattern repeated."

But Ultan Riordan had overruled his son, and the ceremony had been planned to duplicate those that, if the legend was to be believed, had proven tragic for so many Riordan brides through the generations.

" 'Tis almost sunset," Eamon said, rising to lay a hand on his brother's shoulder. "We should be going out to the ceremony."

Cormac shook off the comforting hand and snatched angrily at the cloak that his father had worn to wed all three of his doomed brides. His gaze fell to the black swan carefully stitched into the thick linen. The black swan, frozen in midglide, the badge of the Riordan clan. Some said the beautiful bird represented a silent cry of mourning for the lost Riordan loves.

"Aye," Cormac said, throwing the cloak around his shoulders. "We'd not want to do anything to break the druid's hex. Riordans always wed with the dying rays of the sun, don't they? I'd not keep my bride waiting to begin her last year of life."

"Do you really intend not to bed the maid?" Niall asked.

"Aye."

Niall shook his head. "If she's to live but another year, 'twould seem all the more reason to be enjoying her fruits as often as you can."

Eamon rolled his eyes in exasperation. "Perhaps you should keep your comments to yourself, Niall."

The three brothers stooped their heads to duck through the tent flap and emerge into the cool, moist air. "Let him babble, Eamon," Cormac said. "Nothing he says will alter my course this night. As soon as the priest pronounces us wed and the feast is done, I'll be riding off to the farthest reaches of the isle, and I don't intend to return until my first year of matrimony is well past."

"Have you informed the lovely Claire of this plan, brother?" Niall asked dryly.

"I haven't spoken to the lass since she was ten years old."

Eamon reached over to straighten the scarlet wedding cloak on his brother's shoulders. With the flat of his hand, he smoothed the embroidered swan across Cormac's broad back. "It might be a good idea to confide in her why you're leaving."

"So she can mock me like my own brother? Even if Father hadn't forbidden us to speak of it, I doubt I'd want to confess such a tale." Cormac shook his head. "Nay, 'tis not so rare for an arranged marriage to remain barren, especially when the bride is but a young girl."

They were striding toward the assembly of people who were gathered at the base of one of the ceremonial mounds of the ancient city, which was now nothing more than a windblown plain with only a few odd stones and ruins to mark what had once been the center of Celtic civilization.

"Is that the little girl you speak of?" Niall asked, pointing, his low voice rich with humor.

Cormac stopped abruptly and peered ahead through the slight mist. In the center of the group of people who had gathered for the ceremony was a tall woman with raven black hair that hung loose to her waist. Her silk wedding clothes molded around slim curves. From a distance, she had all the appearance of a beautifully carved statue. She was looking his way, her perfect features aglow with happiness.

He stood still for too long, and Eamon tugged at his sleeve. "Everyone's waiting, brother," he said in an undertone.

Cormac gave himself a little shake. *Jesu,* when last he'd seen Claire O'Donnell she had been a child, but she would now be . . . *how old?* Nineteen, perhaps? He blinked to see if the vision standing at the base of the mound would disappear into the mist, but it just stood smiling at him, seductive as a siren.

Niall leaned over to whisper in his brother's ear, "Are you doing some rethinking on that matter of the wedding night, brother?"

Cormac frowned, then stepped out from between his two brothers and stalked toward his bride.

It was not the wedding day Claire had imagined, but at least the bridegroom was everything she'd always wanted. Though it had been nearly ten years since she'd seen the oldest Riordan brother, the passing of time had done nothing to lessen her certainty that she could be happy with no other man.

She'd been enthralled with him years before, when he'd ridden at his father's side to arrange the peace between their warring families, and she was no less fascinated now as she watched him coming toward her with quick, long strides. His dark eyes were somber, and he didn't return her smile, but she wouldn't fault him for remembering that the wedding was a solemn occasion. She, herself, would do well to adopt a more serious demeanor, though she was having a difficult time restraining the outward signs of her joy.

Eileen slipped to a place beside her. "I hadn't remembered that your Cormac was so"—she hesitated and gave a quick, sideways glance at her slender older sister—"so *big*," she ended.

"Likely he was not that big when last we saw him, Eily. He was but seventeen. Now he's a man grown."

"He surely is," Eileen agreed. Her light blue eyes, identical to her sister's, grew wide. "The younger brothers, as well. What a trio they make."

Claire had no eyes for the younger Riordans. She was interested only in Cormac. As Eileen had said, he was big, with powerful shoulders and brawny arms, but it was his face that drew her attention. Her childhood memory had not prepared her for the impact of those strong, hawklike features. Undoubtedly some would call him handsome, yet there was nothing pretty about his face. He had an untamed look to him, feral. It made the breath catch in her throat.

He stopped several yards from her with a curt bow of his head. "My lady," he said.

She could not tell if the title was for her rank or if he was making a deeper statement. She was, indeed, his lady or about to be, and the thought set the blood roaring behind her ears. "My lord," she replied, dipping into a curtsy.

She could scarcely hear Eileen's whisper, "Hisst, sister. Ye needn't call him lord until the vows are spoke."

Then he was beside her, his warm hand enfolding her icy fingers, and her father and his were signing papers and clasping forearms in the traditional sign of alliance. Cormac said nothing further to her, and she didn't dare look up at him for fear the shaking that had started somewhere deep inside her would erupt to the surface.

She was dimly aware of Father Brendan's arrival and her bridegroom's impatient refusal of prenuptial sacraments. The priest waited while she murmured agreement. She cared little for the form. All that was important was that this man was to be her husband and she his wife, and they would lie together this very night in sacred consummation of that bond.

The vows were spoken in Latin and, as a gesture to the ancients of Tara, in the old language, as well. Then the thin-faced priest nodded for them to kneel to receive the final blessing and be pronounced wed.

"Hold!" Cormac said abruptly.

His harsh tone shocked her out of her daze, and she looked up at him in surprise. In the last reddish rays of the sun, he looked as if he, himself, might be one of those kings of old. Inexplicably, she shivered.

"I'd have you wait a moment for the final pronouncement," he said to the priest.

Claire looked from her sister, who gave a puzzled shrug, to her father, who stood at some distance from the bridal couple. Her father's face was troubled.

"Is there a problem, my son?" Father Brendan asked.

" 'Tis done, Cormac," said one of the other Riordan brothers. "Leave it be."

But Cormac shook his head. "I'll not be pronounced wed to the dying sun. We'll wait until it's sunk over the horizon."

Members of the two families looked at each other in uncomfortable silence, then began to murmur. A wedding ceremony at night was nearly unheard-of.

Claire pulled her hand from Cormac's and turned to face him. All traces of her earlier happiness were gone as she asked, "Would you tell me why you wish to delay, my lord?"

He looked down as if almost surprised to see her there, but after a moment, he answered, "I mislike traditions. A nighttime matrimony will be something different."

His words made little sense to her, but she saw no reason to contradict her new husband before they'd even signed the wedding contract. "As you will," she said, returning her hand to his and facing the priest once again.

For several moments, no one spoke as all watched the slow descent of the sun over the gentle mounds to the west. When the last sliver of light had disappeared, Cormac nodded at Father Brendan and said, "You may proceed."

Shifting nervously, the holy man raised his hand and gestured for the couple to kneel. Cormac withdrew his hand from hers and slipped his arm around her, supporting her as she arranged her dress to kneel on the ground. Once they were settled, he kept his hand fixed firmly on her waist. She could feel the heat of his body through her thin garments.

The priest spoke the blessing in a rush, and behind her she heard one of the Riordan brothers let out a long breath of relief.

Cormac looked down at her. " 'Tis done, milady, for better or worse." His eyes looked almost black in the darkening light.

"Aye, milord, though all new brides hope and dream 'twill be for better."

He didn't answer for a long moment, then said,

"Grooms have the same hopes and dreams."

She smiled. "Then we're already agreed after only moments wed. Surely 'tis a good sign."

He still didn't smile, but his expression seemed to soften, and a touch of warmth lit his eyes. Behind them the crowd moved restlessly. Cormac rose to his feet and offered his arm to assist her.

When they were standing, he dropped his hold on her while they waited awkwardly, facing Father Brendan, who appeared to be waiting as well. Finally Claire recognized the voice of the youngest Riordan, who said in a loud whisper, "You must kiss your bride, brother."

Claire's cheeks flushed. She turned her face to her groom. His expression was unreadable as he bent and touched his mouth to hers. She had the feeling that he'd meant the caress to be quick, but once their lips met, he lingered there, as though savoring a rare, new flavor. Her knees went weak.

Then it was over. As the breeze picked up around them, the ceremony was suddenly at an end, and the bride and groom were swept up in the congratulations of family and friends and carried off to the far side of the mound where the fires had been built up for the wedding feast.

The mood throughout the dinner had been festive, with the two families laughing together and joking as though there had never been a blood feud between them. No one seemed to notice that in the center of the revelry, the bride and groom sat stiffly, barely exchanging a word.

While most of the celebrants were sprawled on cloths that had been laid over the soft ground, Claire and Cormac were sitting side by side at a small table that had been set up for them at some distance from the rest.

Claire shook her head to refuse the piece of beef Cormac was offering her from the tip of his hunting knife. Over the past half hour her throat had become more constricted, until now she was sure that it would be quite impossible to swallow another bite. Something was wrong. In all the imaginings she had had of her wedding feast, she could never have pictured this—sitting next to a bridegroom who maintained a stony silence while around them their families celebrated a marriage that she was beginning to believe was a terrible mistake.

"I can't," she told him.

"You've scarcely eaten," Cormac replied.

"I don't care for anything more."

" 'Tis a chill night to go without food."

The slight concern in his voice encouraged her. She smiled. "Forgive my boldness, my lord, but a new bride hopes for other means of warmth on her wedding night."

One corner of his mouth tweaked up, and Claire felt a sudden rush. There it was—the crooked smile she remembered from all those years ago when a cocky young knight had been kind to a gawky child. Almost before she could be sure she'd glimpsed it, his expression had turned dark again, though his tone stayed gentle.

"You needn't call me lord. I'd have no such formality from a wife."

Claire forced her tightened shoulders to relax. Perhaps she was misreading her new husband's silence. Perhaps he was not as displeased with the match as she had begun to fear.

"Shall I call you Cormac, then? And what shall you call me? If I recall, when we first met, you called me princess."

"Princess?"

"Aye. It thrilled me. I thought you were the most gallant lad I'd ever met."

"How can you remember such a thing? You were but a lass."

Claire grinned. "An *impressionable* lass. I remember every detail of that meeting." At Cormac's skeptical glance she continued, "I remember that you wore a green cloak and a hat that was cocked to one side. You smiled at me and said, 'Good morrow, princess.' "

Cormac laughed. "I don't remember. It sounds more like something Niall would say."

"I even remember your horse. 'Twas not the monster you ride today, but a smaller dappled gray."

Memory flickered in his dark eyes. "Aye, that was my childhood mount, Cobbledy."

"Cobbledy?"

Now the smile was definitely there, transforming his stern features. "My father let me name her when I was only eight years old. I thought her coat resembled the cobblestoned streets of Dublin."

"Ah, I like that. No doubt you've chosen a more fearsome name for your big stallion." She nodded toward the west end of the complex where the Riordan horses were penned in a makeshift corral.

"He's called Taranis."

"The ancient god of thunder. A fearsome name, indeed." The warmth of the childhood memory past, Cormac's expression grew serious again. Claire gave him the smile she always used to tease her brothers and asked lightly, "Is Taranis's master fearsome as well?"

"So it's been said."

The brief moment of tenderness appeared to be over. Claire bit her lip in frustration. "I don't find you fearsome, Cormac. Nor do I believe that the youth who rode beside me on his 'cobbledy' horse that long-ago springtime has forgotten how to laugh."

He was silent for a long moment, then said, "Forgive

me, my lady. 'Tis a sorry match you've made, but there was no help for it. I'll beg your pardon for this—and for all the hurts you may suffer as a result of this day's deeds." He pushed back his stool and stood. "I'd best see to the Riordan relations now, and you'll be needing to do the same with the O'Donnells."

Claire watched, confused, as he made his way over to a group of Riordan clan revelers. Tears of hurt prickled in her eyes, but she refused to let them fall. She hadn't been mistaken, she told herself. There had been tenderness in Cormac Riordan's face when he'd looked at her as they talked of his old horse. She remembered the words he'd spoken as they knelt before the priest. *Grooms have the same hopes and dreams,* he'd said. And the kiss they'd shared had been wildly sweet.

Across the fire her sister was watching her with a worried expression. Claire gave her a smile of reassurance and rose from her seat to go join her.

Niall and Eamon had both had too much to drink. Under other circumstances, Cormac might have joined his brothers and made a night of it, but this night he had other plans. As soon as he and Claire were left alone in the bridal tent, he intended to take his leave and ride off alone.

It was the coward's way, perhaps, to leave his brothers and father to face the O'Donnells' questions. But if he stayed at Tara, refusing his wife's bed, he might be forced into a confrontation with his new in-laws. This way, only his wife would know that he hadn't consummated their marriage. He couldn't imagine that she would say anything about what had passed between them—no woman would willingly admit to such an insult.

"Cormac, take another mug of ale. We've a whole keg

left to down." Niall's words were slightly slurred as he pushed a tankard toward Cormac's chest.

"You and Eamon can drink my share tonight," he told his brother, waving away the mug.

"Nay, I'll not have the O'Donnells say that the oldest Riordan drinks like an old lady."

" 'Twill do no harm, Cormac," Eamon added. "In fact, it might help take that scowl from your face. You're looking fearsome, brother."

I don't find you fearsome, Claire had said, her light blue eyes dancing in the firelight. He scanned the crowd for her. She was kneeling beside her sister, their heads close together in earnest conversation. With their silken wedding robes draped around them, the two girls looked as graceful as swans.

Cormac felt a heaviness inside his chest, and an unwanted pulse of desire. Slowly, he reached for the stone mug in his brother's hand and lifted it to his lips. "I may have just one cup," he said, "to uphold the family name."

Claire had done her best to enjoy the evening and forget her new husband's coldness during the dinner. Soon it would be time for her to retire to the bridal tent. The O'Donnell lands bordered Tara, and her family home was near, but it had been decided that the newlyweds would have better privacy in a tent all to themselves. Tents had been set up for most of the Riordans as well, since Riordan Hall was two hours' ride away.

She looked around the gathering for Cormac. He was some distance away, standing in the joint embrace of his two brothers, who were laughing and lifting a large mug of ale to his lips. All three were grinning that same crooked smile.

Claire had been only ten the first time the oldest Riordan brother had smiled at her, but even then, she'd known that never in her life would a man affect her more than Cormac. Up to now, her wedding day had not been what she had hoped, but there was still time to make some of those long-ago fantasies come true. She and her husband had the wedding night ahead of them, and she was ready for all the wonders it might hold.

Two

Cormac lay back on the mound of cushions someone had arranged in the wedding tent. He'd intended to greet his bride on his feet and not venture anywhere near the carefully prepared bower, but his brothers had half carried him into the tent and had thrown him on the bed with rough slaps of affection and ribald jests.

It was little different from the typical horseplay they'd engaged in many times in the past. But tonight was not typical. It was his wedding night, and if he didn't get up, his bride would no doubt think she'd married a drunken sot.

His head was spinning. The pillowed bed felt comforting and warm. The last thing he wanted to do was seek out his big stallion and ride away into the black night, but his bride would be here soon. He had to move.

He boosted himself up on his elbows, his eyes shut to keep the room from circling around him. Lord, he was sick, as well as dizzy. He'd consumed more ale than he should have. With a grunt he let himself fall back on the cushions. Behind his closed eyelids, lights danced and colors spiraled. He felt as if he were floating while the colors slowly merged into a perfect sky blue, the color of Claire O'Donnell's silken wedding dress.

Suddenly, he opened his eyes and she was there.

"I was afraid you'd fallen asleep," she said. Her smile

was much more tentative than it had been at dinner. It gave him a surprising pang.

He scrunched his eyes into better focus, then swallowed hard. "Nay, I'm not sleeping, though I fear I had more ale than I'd intended."

Her smile became more genuine. "If so, I believe 'twas your brothers' intentions, not yours."

"Mayhap, but 'twas good-natured foolery. They meant no harm."

"Aye, it put me in mind of my own three brothers as I watched the three of you. They are ever jesting, but they love me dearly and I them."

Cormac did not want to be reminded that his bride had brothers who cherished her. Indeed, he did not want to think about her at all. He struggled to sit up, wincing as his head throbbed.

Claire dropped to her knees on the cushions beside him and placed a hand on his chest. "Nay, do not bother to rise. That is"—she stopped as a blush made its way up her cheeks—"if you're tired we can simply . . . lie. . . ."

She broke off, gesturing at the bed, her cheeks now thoroughly aflame. Cormac felt another unaccustomed twinge, centered somewhere in the middle of his chest.

"Don't be afraid, *chara,*" he said. Then he began to explain, "This marriage was decided long ago—"

She interrupted him. "I'm not afraid, my husband. Some may call your visage fierce, but I see the gentleness in you. I sensed it at dinner when you spoke of your childhood horse. I feel it in the way you hold my hand." She reached to take his hand in both of hers as if to prove her words.

Cormac pulled his hand out of her grasp and shook his head. "Claire, you know nothing of me or my family. For generations the O'Donnells and the Riordans have been enemies. Our ancestors killed each other in bloody massacres, which our fathers sought to end by this match between us. This wedding is a symbol. It has nothing to do with the two of us."

She moved her hands back to her lap. Her chin went up as she said stiffly, "Symbol or no, Cormac Riordan, you're my husband, and I intend to be a wife to you."

Her eyes were bright with hurt and there was a barely perceptible quiver to her bottom lip. Cormac reached his hand toward her and traced his fingers along her mouth, then cupped her cheek. Her skin was soft as sea foam. She smelled of crushed heather. Unable to resist the impulse, he leaned close and kissed her.

At first the kiss was light, but as she opened to him, he deepened it with a gentle urgency of lips and tongue. She made a small sound of pleasure at the back of her throat and wound her arms around his neck. Instant lust licked at his loins.

He could feel the hardening of her breasts against him, and when he drew back to look into her face, her eyes were wide and unfocused. He bent closer once again and ran kisses along her long, white neck to the hollow beneath her cheekbone, where he could feel the pounding of her pulse.

"I would be a wife to you, Cormac Riordan," she said again in a husky whisper.

With a groan he pressed her back against the pillows. He moved over her, lifting her arms over her head and allowing the entire length of their bodies to press intimately together. His hardness nestled into the soft place between her legs and his chest rubbed the firm nubbins of her breasts. She looked up at him with a smile that held both innocence and age-old promise. "Will you make me your wife now, husband?" she whispered.

With his drink-fogged brain, Cormac tried desperately

to remember his resolutions of earlier. Claire's lips were scant inches from his own, full and moist. "Aye," he growled, "you'll be my wife." Then he took her mouth again, the gentleness gone.

His rough kiss surprised Claire, but was not unpleasant. In fact, as she lay with her arms pinned by his hands to the cushions above her, she felt a delicious anticipation at the pit of her stomach. Her lips were swollen and tingly from the repeated movement of his mouth and the occasional rasp of his whiskers. She shifted beneath him, enjoying the unaccustomed feel of a man's hard body against her own.

Somehow she had known that it would be like this—instant fire. She'd known it even as a child, when she'd had little clear idea of what transpired between a man and a maid. She'd waited years for this night, and now that it was finally here, she would let no maidenly shyness deprive her of full enjoyment of every minute.

Cormac had begun to remove her overdress, and she moved to accommodate him, laughing a little breathlessly as they struggled with the voluminous folds. At last it was free, and he pulled it over her head, leaving her clad only in the sheer undertunic. "Shall I remove this as well?" she asked with a teasing smile.

But his eyes were fixed on the small black swan she'd labored to stitch on the fine silk. "What's this?" he asked abruptly, loosing his hold on her and sitting up.

Her smile faded. "Why, 'tis your swan. The Riordan badge . . ." She faltered as his expression grew dark. "I'd thought to please you," she ended, struggling to sit up.

Cormac sat in silence for a long moment, his expression unreadable. Finally he said, "This cannot be."

"I don't understand. . . ."

Cormac spoke harshly. "We can't do this. I'm not going to make love to you this night."

He sounded angry, and, for the first time, Claire felt a responding anger of her own. He'd pulled away from her when he'd seen the black swan. Did Cormac think that an O'Donnell was not good enough to wear the Riordan badge? Her voice was defensive as she said, "I'm sorry if the gown displeases you, but as we were about to remove it in any event . . ." She began to loosen the clasp.

His hand stopped her fingers. "Nay, leave it," he said. He stood and gave a brisk bow of his head. "We're not to continue, my lady. Forgive me, but this thing between us was not meant to be."

She sat back on her heels and looked up at him in disbelief. "We're married, milord. Husband and wife."

He shook his head. "Aye. The Riordans and the O'Donnells are legally joined, and, God willing, 'twill put an end to the feuding between our families. But 'tis as I said—you and I are a symbol, nothing more."

Claire clasped her hands tightly in her lap to keep them from shaking. "Do you find me unattractive?" she asked.

Cormac gave a snort of exasperation. "You've not seen your own reflection if you can ask such a question as that, madam. I'd be hard pressed to match your beauty in all the courts of Europe."

"Then what . . . ?" She would *not* cry.

Cormac merely shook his head. "I must leave you, milady, before my resolve weakens. Once again, I ask your forgiveness." Then he turned on his heel and walked out of the tent.

For a moment, Claire couldn't believe that he had actually gone. She sat in the middle of the cushions, stunned, clutching her arms against the sudden cold. But she was not about to give up so easily on the wedding night she'd dreamed of for years.

Jumping to her feet, she snatched Cormac's wedding cloak, which he'd left discarded on the floor, and wrapped it around her thin chemise. Then she ran to the door of the tent and looked out. She was going to find him and demand an explanation for his strange behavior. She didn't care if she had to walk straight into the Riordan tent and confront him in front of his brothers and father.

She stepped out into the quiet night and pulled the cloak around herself against the chill. The wedding party had ended and it seemed that everyone had retired to sleep. Cormac had simply vanished.

Suddenly, she heard the sound of a horse rearing. From the far side of a temple mound, she could barely make out the form of a big black stallion and rider, heading away from the camp at a fast gallop. The horseman was her bridegroom, and he was riding away from her into the night.

She reached back to grasp the edge of the tent flap for support. What had happened to make him leave? How could the wedding night she'd dreamt of have gone so terribly wrong? She'd known, of course, that this marriage had not been a love match, but somehow she'd thought that after she'd held the image of Cormac Riordan in her heart all those years, he would *have* to want her. It appeared that she'd been wrong.

The flush from her cheeks cooled as she stood staring into the darkness, listening for the sound of hooves, willing him to return. But all she heard was the night breeze sighing over the gentle mounds of Tara Hill. The sound was as chill and haunting as a voice from a grave.

Claire had not slept. She wasn't sure how long she had stood outside the wedding tent, staring into the night after Cormac's departure. Finally, she'd given herself a shake and gone back into the tent to retrieve her discarded overdress. She'd folded the Riordan wedding cape and left it in the middle of the unused bridal bed. Then she'd walked to the edge of the camp where the O'Donnell horses were staked and had consoled herself by stroking her mare, Vixen.

Once again, she didn't know how long she stood, rubbing Vixen's bristly muzzle, but streaks of light were licking the eastern sky when she finally sucked in a deep gulp of cool morning air and went to the tent where her father, three brothers, and Eileen had chosen to spend the night instead of returning the short distance to O'Donnell House.

Her anger had faded, to be replaced by a feeling almost of shame, though she was struggling to convince herself that she bore no responsibility for the evening's strange events. The reaction of her family helped.

She'd awakened them, and they watched her with sleep-dulled eyes as she told them without embellishment exactly what had occurred.

"The man's a bastard!" her youngest brother, Rory, hollered, jumping to his feet.

"'Twas a cursed idea to join an O'Donnell with a Riordan," added the middle brother, Seamus. Seamus scanned his sister's face with worried eyes. He and Claire had always been particularly close, and it seemed that he was sharing his sister's hurt.

Conn, the oldest, remained silent, but his face grew dark with anger.

Eileen and her father, Raghnall, regarded her with expressions that reflected only sympathy for what she must be feeling. Eileen ran lightly to her side and slipped an arm around her sister. "He's daft," she whispered for Claire's ears alone. "And blind in the bargain, if he didn't want you."

Raghnall was not a man to give consolation easily, but his face was tender as he asked, "How are you faring, daughter? Why didn't you come to us immediately?"

Claire shrugged. "The deed was done. There was no point in everyone losing a night's sleep."

"I'd have gone after the blackguard and hauled him back here," Rory said.

Rory, only sixteen, was already tall and strikingly handsome. He was his father's favorite, but Claire, though she loved him dearly, had always thought that he was a bit hotheaded. He had some of the "hard growing" left to do, as their nurse, Fiona, would say.

"We may do that yet," Raghnall said. "But we'll try to learn exactly what happened first. I intend to talk to Ultan Riordan."

"Talk, talk!" Rory was getting more agitated. " 'Twas talk between old men that got Claire into this situation in the first place. Now her honor's been besmirched, and all you can think to do is talk more?"

"Don't speak to your father in such a manner," Conn chided, though all of them knew that Rory could say anything he pleased with little fear of recrimination from his doting parent.

"Someday, son, you'll learn that talking is always better than fighting if it can accomplish the objective," Raghnall said.

"When the objective is avenging my sister's honor, nothing less than blood will serve."

"Rory's right, Father," Seamus agreed.

Claire listened to their words in a haze. It was as if they were talking about some other person, not her. She wished she hadn't come to the family tent. She wished she had taken Cormac's example and ridden Vixen into the dark night, away from this place.

Raghnall was shaking his head as he began dressing himself. "Help me, Conn," he said, struggling with a leather breastplate. There won't be blood if I can help it, but I'd go to the Riordans fully armed."

"No!" Claire exclaimed. "No one should be armed. I will not have this matter lead to fighting."

"Leave this to us, daughter," Raghnall said in a tone that brooked no argument.

Claire and Eileen clasped hands and watched from the edge of the tent as their brothers and father helped each other don the warrior garb they'd brought to the wedding for ceremonial purposes only.

As they started to leave, Claire made one last attempt to defuse the confrontation. "Let me talk to the Riordans first."

Her father only shook his head and said, "Leave this to us, daughter."

"Ye both knew of this idiotic notion?" Ultan Riordan's thundering bass voice always made his sons snap to respectful attention, even now that all three towered over their stocky father.

As usual, Eamon put himself forth as the peacemaker. "Father, remember that Cormac lost three mothers instead of one. Every woman who came into the household and began to show him tenderness ended up dying on him."

For a moment the weight of past griefs showed on Ultan's face, but he gave an impatient wave of his hand and continued, "Did I raise a trio of ninnies? How did ye think the O'Donnells would react to their daughter being insulted in such a way?"

"Cormac thought she would never confess the slight," Niall explained. "I must say, it surprises me that she complained to her family. Most women would suffer in silence."

"Claire O'Donnell is not most women, as I wish Cormac would have perceived before he did such a bloody fool thing."

They'd been awakened in their tent before dawn by one of the O'Donnell servants inquiring as to the whereabouts of the groom. The man had stammered and apologized for the early summons, but had been firm in relaying the message from Raghnall O'Donnell. The O'Donnells would have an answer by midday or any understanding of peace between the families would be over.

Ultan had stood in the middle of the tent, bootless and still sleepy, and listened to the man in dumbfounded silence. But the silence had not lasted. The minute the messenger had left, he'd turned to Eamon and Niall, loudly demanding an explanation of their brother's behavior. They'd been listening to his rantings for nearly a quarter of an hour, not daring to move.

"Where has the dunderhead taken himself off to?" Ultan bellowed, when both his sons remained quiet. He'd sat on his cot again to put on his boots and the rest of his clothes, but the lower position did nothing to soften his voice.

The brothers exchanged glances, then Eamon said, "I believe his plan was to spend the winter at Kells Castle, Father."

Ultan threw up his hands. "Wonderful! That way the entire country can know that the Riordans are afraid of the bridal bed. Does he intend to issue a proclamation on the subject as well?"

"I could ride after him," Eamon suggested.

"I'll go with you," Niall added. Both looked as if they would be happy to ride immediately if it would take them beyond the reach of their father's temper.

Ultan stood and walked over until he was just inches from his sons. "Aye, ye'll bloody well ride after him, and so will I. We'll bring the scoundrel back here in irons, if need be, and he'll beg pardon of the entire O'Donnell family or my name's not Ultan Sean Banyon Riordan."

Through the thin walls of the tent it was apparent that it had grown light as they talked. Niall looked down at his feet. "Should we get dressed now, Father?" he asked.

"Unless ye think to ride to Kells Castle barefoot!" Ultan roared. Then he stalked to the door of the tent and almost knocked the entire structure to the ground as he shoved his thick frame through the flap.

Ultan Riordan barreled out of his tent and practically into the arms of a contingent of angry O'Donnells, led by the head of the family.

"Where's your son?" Raghnall asked grimly.

Ultan waited until Niall and Eamon emerged from the tent to stand beside him, then spoke evenly. "I don't know."

"Are you aware that he left my daughter abandoned and unbedded on the day of her wedding?" Raghnall's voice was loud and angry.

Ultan looked behind the group of armed men to where the two O'Donnell sisters stood side by side. He addressed his words to his new daughter-in-law. "My lady, I swear this thing will be put to rights. My son may have had reasons for what he did—"

Rory elbowed past his father and planted himself in front of Ultan. "Your son's a vile coward, old man, who has insulted the honor of my sister, and if you're defending him, then that makes the rest of you as guilty as he." His gaze took in the two Riordan brothers, as well as Ultan. "Someone will pay for this treachery," he yelled, pulling a hunting knife from his belt.

"Don't be a fool, Rory!" Raghnall cried. He stepped forward to hold his son back.

Niall Riordan jumped in front of his father to shield him. "Only young cowards fight with old men, stripling," Niall taunted the young O'Donnell. "If you're out for blood, make your challenge to someone who's worthy."

"I'll fight you all, one by one, if you like," Rory snarled. From the back of the crowd, Claire could hear the note of exhilaration in her brother's voice. She shook off her daze and started pushing her way to the front of the group of men. But just as she broke through to reach the area where her father stood with her brothers, she gasped in horror, as the meeting spun out of control.

Rory broke the hold his father had on his shoulders and rushed toward Niall Riordan, just as Ultan Riordan stepped around his son to place himself between the two men. As Rory surged forward, his knife sank into Ultan Riordan's back, hilt deep.

Ultan stiffened, then toppled to one side like a great fallen oak.

Three

Cormac stretched his hands out toward the small fire. The chill of autumn had set in, but he had deliberately chosen to camp outside one more night instead of riding on ahead to Kells Castle, where the crowded great room would be warmer, if not as fresh.

After his nearly frantic ride the night of his wedding, he'd been traveling at a leisurely pace, in no hurry to reach people. Taranis was all the company he wanted in his current humor.

It had been seven full days since he'd left Tara Hill, yet he'd been unable to banish from his head the image of Claire's face as he'd turned to leave. When he closed his eyes at night, he saw her eyes, clear and blue and devastated.

It had been poorly done, he told himself for the thousandth time. He should have insisted that his father find another way to end this feud with the O'Donnells. He should have remained unwed, just as he'd always sworn he would.

Or perhaps, in spite of his father's orders, he should have told her the truth, confessed that the curse of the Riordan brides made it impossible for him to love her or any woman. Would she have scoffed at his superstition? Or would *she* have then been the one to flee from him?

In any event, it was too late now. The deed was done, and there was not a woman alive who would forget an insult such as the one he had paid her. He doubted he'd ever lay eyes on Claire O'Donnell again.

The wind had picked up, rustling the leaves of the poplars in the small grove he had chosen for his night's stay. Cormac hunched his shoulders against the breeze, too listless to search for more wood for the fire. No doubt they'd be sharing hinds of beef and drinking endless rounds of ale at Kells Castle this night.

He called a promise to Taranis, who was tethered to one of the trees. "One more night under the stars, old boy. Tomorrow you'll have a stable stall and hay aplenty. Tomorrow you and I will face the world again."

"You'll face it sooner than that, brother," said a grim voice at his back.

Cormac turned abruptly, his expression relaxing when he saw Eamon coming out of the trees, leading his horse.

"You're not the world I fear to face, Eamon," he said with a smile, jumping up and going to clasp his brother's forearms.

Eamon did not return his smile. "I'd thought to find you already at Kells."

"I've traveled slowly."

" 'Twas only by chance I saw your fire."

Cormac began to feel uneasy. His brother's manner was uncharacteristically somber. "I'm glad for the company. I've not talked to another soul in a sennight."

"I've not come to give you company, Cormac."

"Is aught amiss?"

Eamon finally met his gaze. "Aye. 'Tis father. We must return at once, and even then he may not be with us by the time we can make it back."

Cormac felt the blood rush to his head. "What is it? Not the wedding? Was it too much for him at his age?"

"A knife to the back is too much for most men. At any age."

"He was stabbed?"

Eamon nodded.

"Who did it?" Cormac asked with sudden foreboding.

"Rory."

A chill ran up Cormac's back. "Rory O'Donnell?"

"Aye, Rory O'Donnell." Eamon's tone was bitter. "Your wife's brother."

Christ almighty, Cormac swore silently. Swallowing hard, he asked Eamon, "How grave is it?"

" 'Tis as I said before, brother. It's bad. We must return at once."

"But surely—you've tended the wound?"

"Aye, of course. He's being given the best care—"

"The herbal woman from the village?" Cormac interrupted.

"Aye. We've done everything possible."

"But his condition is . . . ?"

Eamon's expression softened slightly and he put a hand on his brother's arm. "I fear he was already dying when I left to find you."

Cormac clenched his teeth, struggling for control. "What's been done to Rory?"

"Nothing yet, but everyone's out for his blood. If Father dies, I wouldn't give much for Rory's chances of living to an old age."

Cormac felt as if he would lose the dried meat he'd had for dinner. He looked up at Eamon, who waited tensely. "Let's ride," he said.

Even on his deathbed, Ultan Riordan looked more robust than anyone else in the room.

"Ah, finally ye come. Get yerself over here so I can see yer face," the old man barked as Cormac stepped into the master's bedroom at Riordan Hall. The spacious room was crowded with kinsmen and Riordan retainers, but Cormac had eyes only for his father.

He and Eamon had ridden day and night to get back, nearly killing Eamon's horse in the process. Taranis, as usual, had had no trouble holding up to the pace.

From across the room, Ultan looked almost normal—his complexion had the ruddy glow that seemed an outward reflection of all the inner strength of the man. But as he approached the bed, Cormac could see that his father's face was not ruddy, but scarlet. The whites of his eyes were red with fever, as well, and the edges of his mouth had begun to take on an ominous bluish-white tinge.

For the first time since he was a boy, Cormac reached for his father's hand. The old man's grip was still strong.

"Ye ever were the most troublesome of boys," Ultan said, scowling.

Cormac smiled sadly. "I'm my father's son."

"Aye, that ye are, boy, that ye are." He withdrew his hand from his son's. "And a brave one, to boot, but this was a piece of foolishness."

Cormac nodded. "Would it were I who had taken the O'Donnell's knife."

Ultan gave a weak snort. "Fathers die before sons, lad. 'Tis the law of nature. And my time's come."

Cormac wanted to take his hand again, but physical contact had never been the custom in the Riordan household, unless it was a wrestling match or some other contest of strength. He flexed his fingers and let his hand stay where it was by his side.

"We're not ready to lose you, Father. Stop talking nonsense and get yourself well."

"Nay, I've served my threescore years and more on this vale." There was a sudden twinkle in the bloodshot eyes. "And, don't forget, I've three lovely colleens awaiting me on the other side."

Cormac's throat closed. Through the brave words he had heard the ominous rattle of death coming from deep inside his father's chest. Cormac squeezed his hands into fists and forced himself to speak. "How do you intend to manage that, old man? Three of them at once?"

Ultan's grin was weak. "I reckon I'll let the good Lord figure that one out for me. He's the one who arranged things this way."

Cormac looked across the bed to where Eamon and Niall were standing. "Has the priest—?" he began.

Niall nodded.

Ultan waved his arm weakly. "They've already said their words over me. Now I just want to be with my three sons—my three brawny sons." He moved his head slightly to look at each of them in turn. Suddenly his voice became much weaker and the rattle intensified. "Thank ye for bringing him back," he said to Eamon.

Eamon nodded. "Aye, Father," he said.

Ultan looked at Cormac. "Take care of them, son— all of them. I leave it in yer hands now."

The old man's eyes closed, but his mouth stayed open as the rattle became a long gasp. Then his breathing ceased altogether. Cormac looked over to see his own anguish reflected in his brothers' eyes.

"They'll pay for this," Niall said, his voice breaking.

Cormac sank to his knees beside the bed and reached for his father's hand.

"The Riordan is dead." Claire's father made the pronouncement to the hushed dining hall at O'Donnell House.

At Claire's side, her sister whispered, "Lord save us."

Raghnall O'Donnell gave Eileen a brief glance, then

turned toward Rory, who sat at the end of the family bench staring straight ahead, his mouth set in defiance. "This is calamitous news, son. We'd best prepare for a fight. The Riordans will be wanting to stick your head, bloody and dripping, on the gates to Riordan Hall."

Eileen gave a little cough as if she were about to be sick. Claire put her hand on her sister's arm and said, "They're not savages, Father."

"Nay, but they're as close to it as you'll find in this part of the world," he answered her.

"And they are still our kin by marriage," she said.

Her father looked exasperated. "Do you think that kinship will be worth a pennywhistle when one of us has killed their father and leader?"

"Aye, it will. I don't believe Cormac Riordan is the kind of man who would make war on the family of his wife."

Claire couldn't believe that she was defending the man. She'd barely been able to speak his name in the twelve days since the wedding. But as furious as she was with Cormac and all his clan, she couldn't bear the thought of another violent feud erupting between the Riordans and her family.

"A man's not likely to feel much obligation to a wife he has never bedded," her father said bluntly.

Her face flamed. She knew that her father hadn't intended the words to hurt her, but they did. "Nevertheless," she said, holding her voice steady, "the vows were spoken, and Cormac Riordan is my husband by law and by God. I'll not have our families at war."

Her father glared at her, his light blue eyes a mirror of her own. She held his gaze without flinching. Finally he looked over at his son and said, "Rory, perhaps you should leave for a time—go join the O'Donnell cousins in the north."

"Aye, brother," Claire urged. " 'Twould be for the best."

Rory pounded the palm of his right hand on the table. " 'Twas for you I did it, Claire. To avenge your honor. Now you're trying to send me away?"

"Just for a time, Rory," she said. "They will be burying their leader at Riordan Hall, and the grieving will be fierce. It would be best if you were not in the territory."

Rory shook his head. "Nay, I'll not run away like a coward. If the Riordans want a fight, we'll give it to them."

To Claire's dismay, her two older brothers nodded agreement. Fortunately, her father had more sense than his hotheaded sons. "There will be no fighting if we can avoid it," he said. "I've already asked for a meeting with the Riordans to try to settle this matter peacefully."

Claire looked at her father in surprise. "You'll go to Riordan Hall?"

"I've asked for a neutral meeting at Tara Hill. Tomorrow at midday." His shoulders sagged, and suddenly her father looked old. "We owe the Riordans a blood price for the death, and I'm prepared to pay it. Better gold than the lives of my sons."

"Who—?" Claire faltered a moment, then began again. "Is the meeting to be with Eamon and Niall?"

Raghnall shrugged. "I'll meet with whoever can settle this, but 'tis said that the new head of the clan has come back. The duty should rightly fall to him."

"Cormac has returned?"

"Aye."

Her oldest brother, Conn, spoke for the first time. "I mislike the idea, Father. How can we be sure they'll not take their revenge the minute you arrive at the meeting?"

" 'Tis to be without weapons, on both sides."

"I'd not trust them," Rory said, and once again his brothers nodded agreement.

Conn added, "Rory killed their father. They could plan to do the same to us by killing you. An eye for an eye."

Claire pushed back the small bench she shared with Eileen and stood. "They won't be able to kill our father because he won't be going to the meeting," she said calmly. "I will."

Her brothers all looked at her as if she'd suddenly turned a different color. "Nay, daughter," her father said. "This is not a matter for females."

Claire was adamant. "I'm the one who was wed to Cormac Riordan, and I'll be the one to face him over this matter."

"You can't let her, Father," Conn protested. " 'Tis too dangerous for the lass."

But Raghnall O'Donnell was looking hard at his daughter's determined expression. He stepped close to her and asked her in a softer voice, "Are you sure you want to see him after the way he treated you?"

" 'Tis because of it that I *must* be the one to see him," she replied.

"And you trust him to do you no harm?"

"Aye." Claire didn't know how she could speak with such certainty, but somehow she was sure that Cormac would not hurt her.

Her father hesitated a long moment, then he nodded and said, "Then, aye. You may go. You'll take Conn as your second." All three of her brothers sprang to their feet in protest, but their father waved them off. "The new leader of the Riordans is still your sister's husband," he said firmly. " 'Tis her right to go to him."

·   ·   ·

"You've buried your father, today, Niall. Can you not leave the talk of killing until tomorrow?" Cormac had had no sleep in three days, and his voice was sharp.

"Not when you've agreed to meet with the vermin," Niall snapped back. "Poor father will be a-turning in his newly dug grave to think that his son is such a molly-coddle."

"Cormac's no mollycoddle, Niall, as well you know," Eamon argued. "But this meeting sets ill with me, as well, Cormac. The O'Donnells killed our father."

The mourners had left or sought out beds in the hall, and the servants were clearing the remains of the funeral feast out of the dining room, but the three brothers were reluctant to leave.

"The O'Donnells didn't kill him. Rory did."

" 'Tis all the same."

Cormac sighed and rubbed at his burning eyes. "Nay, 'tis not. Rory's scarcely more than a lad."

Niall's thick brows shot up. "Ah, then perhaps we should just take him some bloody sweetcakes and forget it ever happened."

Cormac shook his head. "Nay, but neither will I have us charging over to the O'Donnell lands and starting a war. If Raghnall O'Donnell wants to parlay, I'll listen to him."

"He'll want to pay you a blood price. For our father's *life.*" Eamon's tone was milder than Niall's, but equally firm. " 'Tis unthinkable."

Cormac stood and stretched his arms. "I need to sleep. I've said I'll listen to Raghnall O'Donnell on the morrow, and I shall. Then we shall see what's to be done."

"The O'Donnell himself is coming?" Niall asked, his tone suddenly enthusiastic.

"Aye, so 'twas proposed."

"Then, it's perfect. They killed our father. Now we'll

kill theirs. He'll be walking right into our hands."

Eamon looked doubtful. " 'Tis a truce parlay—" he began.

Cormac interrupted. "Aye, 'tis a truce parlay. And there will be no killing tomorrow by either side."

"They're murderers, Cormac. I can't believe you're ready to stroll over and break bread with them." Niall waved his hands in disgust, then paused as a thought struck him. "Is this because of the girl?" Niall asked.

Cormac winced. "Don't forget 'twas my insult to Claire O'Donnell that began this."

Niall stood. "I've heard it said before that a beautiful woman robs a man of his spine, but I'd not have believed it of my own brother."

The two brothers stood facing each other, eyes angry, until Eamon finally stood and placed a hand on each one's shoulder. "We'll be no good against the O'Donnells if we start to fight each other," he said. "Let it go for tonight, both of you."

Cormac nodded agreement, then his younger brother reluctantly did likewise. "Aye," Niall said. "First we need to sleep. Tomorrow will be time enough to settle with our enemies."

Unlike the day of her wedding, which had dawned bright and mild, the winds swirling around Tara Hill held a hint of winter. Claire drew her cloak more tightly around her, but continued to sit straight and proud on her horse. She wasn't going to have it said that the representative of the O'Donnell clan had ridden into the meeting cowed and humble.

Even if Rory had not actually meant to stab anyone, he had been impulsive and foolish in drawing his weapon on the Riordans. Claire agreed with her father that the O'Donnells owed the Riordans compensation, but she didn't intend to come pleading on her knees. Especially when the one she would be facing was Cormac Riordan. After all, she had her own grievance with the oldest son of the Riordan clan.

Conn rode beside her, and they were escorted by four of their men, as had been previously agreed. The four corresponding Riordan men were waiting outside the tent that had been set up for the meeting. With grim irony, Claire noted that it had been placed in the same spot where she had stood to watch Cormac ride away from her on their wedding night.

"They've arrived ahead of us," Conn said. "I don't like this, Claire. We could still turn around and go home."

She gave her brother a reassuring smile. "Now I'll sound like Rory, but I'm not about to let the Riordans see that we're afraid of them."

"It would be different if it were just us men. 'Twas a harebrained idea for you to come, sister."

Claire made no attempt to argue. She'd been gratified when her father had agreed to let her represent him at the meeting. His concession had surprised her, but it was not entirely out of character. Unlike most fathers, Raghnall O'Donnell had always viewed his two daughters as equals to his sons. She didn't intend to let him down. She would be calm and dignified, even when facing the last man on earth she had ever wanted to see again.

Two of the Riordan men held their horses as she and Conn dismounted. Father Brendan, whose attendance at the meeting was planned to ensure good behavior on both sides, was standing next to the tent. There was no sign of Cormac or his brothers.

The priest was regarding them with his mouth open in surprise. "Where's Raghnall?" he asked.

Claire nodded a polite thank-you at the man who held

her horse, then she turned to the cleric. "I am representing the O'Donnells today."

"But, my child . . ." Father Brendan stammered.

" 'Twas my marriage that started the hostility," she said calmly. "My family decided it proper that I be the one to come."

"So let's get on with it, Father," Conn snapped. "Where are the Riordans?"

Father Brendan tipped his head toward the door of the tent. "Inside." He hesitated and looked nervously at Claire. "Child, did you know that your hus—that Cormac Riordan has come back?"

Just hearing the name made Claire's pulse beat stronger, but all she said was "Aye."

"Come on, Claire, let's get this thing done." Conn started toward the door of the tent.

He was stopped by a burly Riordan man who put a hand on his shoulder and spun him around, growling, "We need to search you for weapons first."

Conn shook the man off. "Keep your paws off me, lout."

The O'Donnell men had not dismounted, but Claire could see that all four had tensed in their saddles on hearing Conn's angry tone.

"We have no weapons," Claire said. She looked at the priest. "I swear it, Father."

The man whom Conn had pushed away looked uncomfortable, but he persisted. " 'Tis my orders, milady. I must, er, I'm to see if you might be carrying a knife. Er, since one of yours did already knife one of ours."

Claire stiffened at the reminder of Rory's crime. She took a step back from the group and, grasping the edges of her cloak, flung it wide open, revealing her snug-fitting velvet riding dress underneath. "Very well," she said. "Search me."

The guard turned bright red. Both Father Brendan and Conn began to protest, but before anyone could move, the door of the tent opened and Cormac's deep voice said, "There's no need for a search. We'll accept the word of a lady."

Four

The remark was addressed to his guard, but Cormac's gaze was on Claire. She let her cloak drop back around her and said, "Thank you."

Their gazes held for a long moment, then Cormac stepped out of the tent and held up the heavy cloth door, clearing the way for her to enter.

He looked different than he had at the wedding—somehow older. His face was drawn and dark circles heightened the depth of his eyes. Claire's heart was still thumping erratically. She forced herself to take in a deep breath of air. This enemy of her people, who had none-theless ignited her girlish notions of romantic love, had become an enemy once again. The anger she'd kept tightly furled inside her since the day of the knife fight threatened to uncoil, but she willed herself to keep calm. Now was not the time for her personal grievances. Rory had killed this man's father, and she'd come to buy back peace for her family.

Taking care not to brush against him, she ducked under the raised flap. The middle Riordan brother, Eamon, was seated inside on a low stool. He rose to his feet when she entered, his eyes wide with surprise, and ac-knowledged her presence with a bow of his head.

"Milady," he said. "We had expected your father."

Cormac and Conn followed her inside. "The meeting

was to be between the heads of the clans," Cormac
added. Though he showed his emotions less than his
brother, it was obvious that he found Claire's presence
unsettling.

She turned to face him. "I have been authorized by
my father to represent my family," she said. "Conn will
vouch for it, if you have any doubt."

Cormac shook his head. "As I said, we accept the
word of a lady. I'm just surprised that Raghnall would
send—"

"A woman?" Claire interrupted. "Perhaps the
O'Donnells hold women in higher esteem than the Riordans do. 'Tis said your household is largely male."

" 'Tis a male household by circumstance, not by
choice, milady," Eamon said.

Claire didn't ask what he meant by the remark. She
was not here to discuss the Riordan household. She was
here to try to repair the damage done by her little
brother, and the sooner she accomplished it, the better.
Though the tent was not the one she had briefly shared
with Cormac on their wedding night, it was similar,
and she was entirely too aware of him standing not a
yard distant from her in the small enclosure.

Cormac cleared his throat. "If you act for your father,
so be it," he said, gesturing to the two sets of stools that
had been placed facing each other. "Please have a seat."

Claire took her place beside Conn. Since the Riordans
were the aggrieved party, she sat quietly, waiting for
them to open the discussion.

"Your father sent word that the boy acted on his own
and that he did not truly mean for the fight to turn
deadly," Cormac began.

Claire was surprised. She'd expected rage, but Cormac's tone was almost conciliatory, and his characteri-

zation of sixteen-year-old Rory as a "boy" was more than fair.

"Nay, he did not," Claire said. " 'Twas a terrible, impulsive deed for which the rest of the family is ashamed and sorry."

She could feel Conn bristle next to her, but she gave him a warning glance to remain silent.

Cormac seemed to notice her brother's disapproval. "What say you, O'Donnell?" he asked him. "Do you agree with your sister's assessment? Is the O'Donnell family ashamed that your kin brutally knifed an old man?"

Conn began to speak, but Claire clutched his arm and answered for him. "Rory says he had not set out to hurt anyone. The fight escalated. No one approves of his actions, and we're ready to pay compensation."

"I'd hear your brother's opinion," Cormac said.

Claire shook her head firmly. "My brother's here as observer, as is yours. The meeting was to be between two family heads."

Cormac gave her a long look, but Claire neither flinched nor looked away.

"Then let's make it between two," he said finally. "Eamon and your brother can wait outside."

"I'll not leave my sister alone with you again, cur," Conn said, jumping to his feet.

Without taking her gaze from Cormac, Claire said to her brother, "Do as he says, Conn. They have the right to state the terms of our meeting. 'Tis their father who was killed. I'll speak with him alone."

"Leave us, Eamon," Cormac said.

With some grumbling the two brothers left the tent, leaving Claire and Cormac facing each other, their eyes still locked.

"I do want this thing settled," Cormac said after a moment, his voice low.

Claire took a deep breath. "In truth, I'll admit that I'm surprised. Rory killed a Riordan. Your *father*. I'd expected to find you ready to mount an all-out assault."

"If it were up to my brothers, we would."

"But you are less bloodthirsty than they?"

"Not appreciably," he admitted, "but I am more guilty."

"Guilty?"

"Aye. If I hadn't left you that night, none of this would have happened. I'm as responsible for my father's death as anyone."

The conversation was not going as Claire had expected. Cormac Riordan had not struck her as the kind of man to feel remorse. He still hadn't apologized for his conduct, but he was admitting the wrong. "If so," she said, " 'tis a heavy burden for any man."

"Aye."

Even in the dim light of the tent, she could see lines of pain etched in his face. She steeled herself not to feel pity. This was the man who had shattered her childhood dreams, who had callously rejected her on the most important night of her life. She'd *not* feel sorry for him.

"We reap what we sow," she said, lifting her chin.

"Aye," he said again.

"My father has taught me to move on from past mistakes. 'Tis why he wanted this alliance between our families in the first place. He says 'tis foolish to let the sins of the past ruin the present."

"Your father is a wise man, milady."

"Aye, he is, and a good one, as well. He was sick about Rory's actions. We all were."

Cormac's brow lifted. "I sensed your brother did not share your remorse."

Claire shook her head impatiently. "Young men are full of pride and arrogance. Wisdom is a commodity of age."

Her words were more conciliatory than Cormac had expected . . . and wiser. She was evidently as intelligent as she was beautiful, he realized. He sat back, crossed his arms, and willed himself to concentrate on the meaning of the words and not on the person delivering them. It was not an easy task when every time he looked at her full lips, he was remembering how they had tasted. Her brother had killed his father, but he found his gaze slipping to her slender white neck while he recalled that he had placed kisses along its length.

"Don't you agree?" she asked. He hadn't the slightest idea of what had come before.

Perhaps Niall had been right. He was letting himself be unmanned by a beautiful woman. The thought made him straighten on his stool and speak more harshly than he had intended. " 'Tis time to talk terms, milady. What price are you intending to offer for my father's life?"

"One hundred crowns in gold." Her chin tipped up defiantly.

The O'Donnells were not as wealthy as some of the Irish barons. Cormac knew that it would mean no little sacrifice to pay the amount she had specified. Nevertheless, hearing the cold statement of the modest sum made the bile rise in his throat. As Niall had said, it was unthinkable to place a price on Ultan Riordan's life.

"We've no need of money," he replied. It was true. The Riordans were the richest clan in the Midlands. "We'll take the O'Donnell holdings nearest to Tara Hill."

Claire's jaw dropped. "Those are our richest lands," she protested.

"My father was greatly loved. It will take a great price to keep my kin from seeking revenge."

Her expression was a mixture of anger and despair that added to Cormac's discomfort. If Raghnall O'Donnell had come, it would be a different story, but this was impossible. He'd already wronged this woman. How could he sit across from her and demand to take away a part of her family's heritage?

"My father wants to pay in gold," she said finally. Her eyes were a little too bright as she looked up at him. "Perhaps we could raise two hundred crowns."

"We don't want gold," Cormac said again, his heart twisting. He'd told her the truth. He knew his family, and there was no way the Riordans would let the death of their leader pass for a mere two hundred crowns.

Claire stood. "I'd thought to settle this thing today, but I can't negotiate land. You'll have to deal with my father after all."

Cormac breathed a sigh of relief and stood as well. "Aye, that would be a better plan." He waited, but she did not turn to leave.

"I'll send one of my men to arrange it," he said after a moment.

Still she stood. She appeared to be studying him. He shifted from one foot to the other. "I think we are finished, my lady," he said after several uncomfortable moments.

"Why did you leave that night?" she blurted.

He'd been waiting for the question since he'd first seen her standing proudly in front of his guard with her cloak flung wide, but he had yet to decide what to say. In his long days on the road after the wedding, he'd begun to realize that the reasons he had fled were complex. The bride curse was only part of the answer.

He'd seen his father grieve three wives, and then proceed to raise his boys in a largely womanless house. He'd never been shy about bedding a comely wench, but he'd always been determined not to fall in love with any of them. How was he supposed to explain all of that to the woman who was legally his wife? Especially when she was standing in front of him, her eyes glistening and the tip of her nose turning pink.

He had delayed his answer for too long. Her expression changing from hurt to anger, she whirled around and stalked to the door of the tent. "Aye, Cormac Riordan," she said over her shoulder, " 'tis best after all if you decide this thing with my father. For I have no intention of ever setting eyes on you again."

Then she flung open the door of the tent and was gone.

"You did right, Cormac," Eamon said. "Our kinsmen would never have accepted such a humble sum, least of all Niall."

"I can keep Niall in line," Cormac replied. "But as to the others—aye, there could be trouble. I intend to meet with Raghnall on the morrow."

The two brothers were riding alone back to Riordan Hall. They'd sent the contingent of four men who'd been at the Tara meeting to O'Donnell House to arrange the subsequent meeting with Raghnall.

"I don't know why he didn't come in the first place," Eamon said. "I can't believe he sent a scrawny female to do a man's job."

Cormac gave a fleeting smile. "Are the eyes failing at your tender age, Eamon? Claire O'Donnell is hardly scrawny."

"Skinny, then." Eamon corrected with a shrug. "She has a pretty enough face, but I like my women with more curves."

Cormac had a sudden memory of his wedding night and how the tops of Claire's white breasts were revealed by her silken bodice—just above the black swan emblem she had sewn.

"I'd rather not discuss the matter," he told his brother sharply. "Claire's my wife, in case you've forgotten."

Eamon looked surprised. "Considering the circumstances, I thought you'd be the first one to want to forget that troublesome detail."

Cormac merely grunted, and the two continued on in silence. As they neared the road to Riordan Hall, the century-old castle the Riordans had lived in for four generations, Eamon smiled sadly and said, "Every time I turn in here, I expect Father to be bounding down the steps to pull me off my horse and twist me into one of his affectionate headlocks."

"Aye, and to rage at us for being gone so long." Cormac looked away from his brother, his eyes moist.

"'Tis best to get this thing settled quickly, brother. Now that the funeral's past, there are many who are crying for vengeance. It won't be easy to convince them to keep the peace, no matter what the O'Donnells agree to pay."

"I know. We'll settle it on the morrow, one way or another."

"Good," Eamon said, and they rode the rest of the way in silence.

"I can't believe you sat there quietly talking with the man, Claire," Eileen said with a sniff. "I would have marched right up and smacked his face."

"That would hardly have been a positive way to start the meeting, Eily. And I am still his wife."

The two sisters were snuggled against the morning chill in the bed they shared at O'Donnell House.

"Nay, you're not his wife," Eileen insisted. "Not in the eyes of God. Not until you . . . *you know.*"

Since childhood, the two sisters had freely shared their thoughts about the various qualities of the men who had visited O'Donnell House, but they rarely discussed those secret activities that went on between a man and a maid behind a bedroom door.

"Father Brendan married us. 'Tis legal."

"But you could get an annulment in an instant without having, er, cohabited."

Claire smiled at her sister's careful choice of words. "Aye. Father has told me the same thing. But first we must get this matter of the killing resolved."

"They are meeting today?"

"Aye, 'tis to be at midmorn, back at Tara Hill."

Eileen pointed to the narrow, recessed window that let a shaft of sunlight filter into their chamber. "We've slept half the morning away like two slugabeds. No doubt the meeting has already started."

"No doubt." Claire burrowed deeper into the covers.

"Aren't you curious to know what's happening there?"

Claire shook her head. "Nay. I just want it to be over, all of it. 'Twas a mistake from the beginning."

Eileen reached over to give her sister's shoulder a squeeze. "Claire, all those years you thought Cormac Riordan was like some kind of hero in a romantic minstrel ballad. You used to talk of him coming to sweep you up on his noble horse and ride off with you."

" 'Twas the foolish talk of a child, Eily, best forgotten. As I say, it's all over now, or it will be as soon as Father settles things."

"What if they can't come to terms? You say Cormac refused to even consider accepting gold. And Father will never agree to cede the Tara Hill lands."

Claire sighed. "I know."

A sudden pounding on the door made them both jump. Claire recognized the voice of her second oldest brother, Seamus. "Claire, Eily! Open the door!"

Eileen slipped out of bed and crossed over to unlatch the door. Their brother stood on the other side, his clothes disheveled. He was breathing hard, and with horror. Claire saw that there was fresh blood on his doublet. She sprang from the bed as Eileen exclaimed, "Seamus! What's happened to you? Have you been hurt?"

" 'Twas the Riordans," he gasped. "We met a group of them along the road and—" He broke off and looked apologetically at Claire. "I don't know how it started, Claire, honest. 'Twas that hothead Niall Riordan having words with Rory—"

Claire drew in a sharp breath. "Rory? Is he hurt?"

Seamus nodded. "He's got a nasty gash across the arm from Niall's sword."

Claire felt sick. "Was anyone else wounded? What about the Riordans?"

"Some of the village folk came out to try and stop us and the Riordans took off—escaped without a bloody scratch, the blackguards. But as soon as I get someone to tend Rory, we're going to ride out and find them again. Then they'll taste some O'Donnell steel."

"You'll do no such thing," Claire said. "How bad is it with Rory?"

Seamus shrugged. "He'll live, I reckon. 'Tis just the arm, but it needs dressing. I've put him in Father's chamber."

Claire hesitated for a long moment, letting the ramifications of yet another confrontation tumble around in her head. Finally, she took a deep, determined breath and turned to Eileen. "Can you see to Rory's arm?"

Her sister looked puzzled. "Aye, but no doubt he'd rather have you."

Claire reached for her dress, her face set in grim lines. "Nay, I have another mission."

"Are you going to fetch Father?" her sister asked.

"Aye, I'm going to Tara Hill." She glared at her brother. "And I don't want one single O'Donnell man leaving the grounds until I get back. Do you understand me, Seamus?"

Seamus nodded meekly. Since the death of their mother five years ago, the O'Donnell brothers had grown used to following their sister's orders.

Eileen looked at her with sudden suspicion. "What do you intend to do, Clairy?" she asked.

"I'll not have one more drop of blood shed over this disastrous wedding." Claire met her sister's gaze with her chin up. "I intend to put things to right."

It was easier sitting across from Raghnall O'Donnell than it had been his daughter even though their light blue eyes were disturbingly similar. But the meeting seemed to have reached an impasse.

Cormac knew that his kin would not except a small price for their leader's death. The coveted land north of Tara Hill would have been a good solution, but Raghnall refused to consider it.

Cormac had a great deal of respect for the leader of the O'Donnell clan. He seemed to be a fair man, strong without bluster, compassionate without weakness. He was, in fact, much like Cormac's own father. But Raghnall still lived to lead his people, while Ultan Riordan lay buried in the churchyard at Kilmessen. And for that, someone had to pay.

"Perhaps we could consider a different portion of land," Cormac said after a long silence.

Raghnall sat with his hands on his knees, palms up, as if to say that he was willing to be open, but his words were firm. "I cannot let go of O'Donnell land, lad. The family has lost it piece by piece through the years. 'Tis little enough that's left to us. Now if the bloody English have their way, they'll see us all run clear into the ocean. A man has to hold to what's his."

Cormac hadn't come to discuss politics. He leaned toward the older man. "Lord O'Donnell, you don't have enough gold to pay the price my kin demand."

The man's gaze did not waver. "Then God help us, lad, for it will mean war between us."

From outside the tent they could hear the sound of a commotion, and then the tent door lifted and Claire entered. Both men rose in surprise.

"What are you doing here, daughter?" Raghnall asked.

She looked first at her father, then at Cormac. "I've come to put an end to this meeting," she said.

"We haven't yet been able—" her father began.

She waved off his words and continued, "You will have your blood price, Cormac Riordan. One hundred crowns, as I originally offered."

Cormac frowned, "I've told you—"

Claire ignored him. "And you will have your bride as well."

This statement silenced both men.

"I believe you to be a man of honor, Lord Riordan," Claire continued. "A man who would not allow his kin to make war on the family of his lawfully wedded wife."

Cormac looked uncomfortable. "I'm not sure the wedding is any longer considered—"

Raghnall interrupted him. "You're nothing to this man, Claire. I've already told Father Brendan to begin the proceedings to wipe any trace of that cursed day from the holy record."

"Then, you'll have to tell him to stop those proceedings, Father. The wedding stands. Cormac Riordan is my husband, and I intend to be a wife to him."

Raghnall and Cormac exchanged confused glances.

"You can't mean—" her father began.

Claire gave a firm nod. "I'll see this feud ended, once and for all. I've already given orders to have my things packed and moved." She turned to Cormac and said, "For better or worse, my lord. As of this day, Riordan Hall has a new mistress."

Five

Riordan Hall was at least three times the size of the rambling wooden house Raghnall O'Donnell had built twenty years ago to house his growing family, but to Claire the big old castle seemed crowded. To begin with there was *rubbish* everywhere—broken pieces of pottery and discarded boots and pieces of disassembled furniture that looked as if it hadn't been used since the days of Henry Tudor.

The windows were draped with rich imported silks that were so crusted with grime it was impossible to distinguish either pattern or color.

Cats prowled the halls and walked in sleek procession along the stone balustrade on the second floor that over-looked the grand entrance hall. Or, Claire corrected her-self as she stood in the middle of the room making an assessment, a hall that *would* have been grand if it had been cleared of the piles of leather and armor that lay in heaps along the walls.

Following her surprise announcement at the Tara Hill parlay, Claire had not waited to listen to the arguments of her father and the Riordans. Instead, she'd stalked from the tent and had ridden directly home to collect her things, her maid, Lindsay, and two other O'Donnell ser-vants before heading to Riordan Hall.

When she arrived at the imposing stone keep, the

Riordan brothers were nowhere in sight. A motley collection of Riordan servants stood bobbing their heads gawking at her like a gaggle of geese.

By late afternoon she, along with the O'Donnell servants she had brought along and a few others she'd recruited from the Riordan household, had managed to clear a pathway from the front door to the top of the wide stone stairway. The assorted armor and leather pieces had been placed in a neat pile outside. It had been a good day's work, and she stood surveying the nearly empty hall with a smile of satisfaction, pushing a wisp of hair back under the kerchief she'd used to tie it up.

She was just thinking about seeking out the cook to see what plans had been made for dinner, when a deep male voice could be heard through the thick front door. "She's already mucking about with our things, Cormac!"

Claire gave a grim smile and waited as the door opened cautiously. Cormac was the first to enter, followed by Eamon, then Niall. All three stopped and stared, first at the clean hall, then at her.

"What have you done with our things?" Niall raged.

Cormac gave him a withering glance, then addressed Claire. "I'm sorry you arrived to find things in this condition. We weren't expecting visitors."

Claire answered dryly, "Nor have you evidently for the past twenty years."

"Welcome to Riordan Hall, my lady," Eamon said with a grin.

"Thank you." She rewarded the middle Riordan brother with a smile.

Niall frowned at his brother. "Peacemaking again, Eamon? Leave it to you to show a soft face to the sister of your father's murderer."

Claire's smile faded. "If it helps you, Niall, you can think of my coming as a kind of penance. Do you think 'tis by choice that I exchange the loving arms of my family for this cold and messy excuse for a home?" She gestured to the formal side salon, a room that appeared not to have been entered in years from the look of the thick dust that covered every part of it.

Niall looked unappeased, but Cormac told him roughly, "Find Molly and tell her that we'll have dinner tonight in the dining hall. All of us."

"The hall is a bit disordered—" Eamon began to protest.

"Then put it to order," Cormac barked. "We'll eat there in an hour. In the meantime, I'd speak with my wife—alone."

"What about our armor?" Niall asked.

" 'Tis unharmed," Claire explained. "I've simply put it outside the door for transport to the"—she paused— "well, to the barn or stables or wherever else might be more appropriate than your front hall."

"Leave it for the moment," Cormac said. "Tomorrow we'll put it in the armory shed where it belongs."

"You have an armory? Who would have believed it?" Claire murmured.

Niall and Eamon disappeared out the back hall door, apparently to carry out Cormac's orders about the dinner. He stood watching her, his face wary. "Why did you decide to come here?" he asked.

"I would think that the answer is obvious. So that your brothers will not kill mine, nor mine kill yours."

"Your father and I were working on a settlement. There are some bottomlands south of—"

She interrupted him. "While in the meantime, Niall and Rory slice at each other like butchers carving a roast."

Cormac sighed. "Is Rory badly hurt?"

She shook her head. "I think not—a gash on the arm."

"If 'tis the arm he uses for brandishing knives about, the disablement could be a blessing. His next opponent might be more prepared than my father was."

Claire put her hands on her hips. "As I've already told you, Cormac Riordan, I'm sorrier than I can say for my brother's rash act. But if you're going to throw it in my face every other minute, then this attempt at a truce will not work."

Cormac gave a reluctant smile. "Is that what this is? A truce?"

"Aye, and you should be grateful to me for it. 'Tis *my* pride that was stained the night of our wedding. And if I'm willing to swallow that hurt and come here for the sake of our reckless families, then you should be willing to meet me halfway."

He was silent a long moment, watching her, and Claire was suddenly aware once again of how big he was. It was impossible for her to believe that she had once lain briefly in those powerful arms and felt his mouth moving along the sensitive skin of her neck. She'd worked hard all afternoon without breaking a sweat, but now she could feel beads of moisture collecting along the edges of her hair.

"I'll meet you halfway, milady," he said finally. "As you say—for the sake of our families."

He'd said not a word about the two of them, nor had he given any apology for the way he had hurt her, but it would have to do. She had no other choice.

"Very well," she agreed. "I'll go see if your brothers are having any luck clearing the dining hall."

Once the Riordan staff had been prodded by the brothers and given some explanation for the unexpected turn of events, they acted admirably. Within an hour of the brothers' arrival, the big oak table in the dining hall had been scrubbed clean; benches had been found and put in their places; the worst of the debris that littered the room had been removed; and a passable meal had been produced and placed on the table in steaming hot platters.

"My lady," Cormac said, holding a chair for Claire at one end of the table.

Claire took a seat, then waited as Cormac walked to the other end of the long table to sit in the master's chair. Eamon and Niall sat in the middle across from each other. Four people around such a huge board looked a little silly, Claire thought. If others of the Riordan household were accustomed to eat with the brothers, they had chosen not to appear. She held back a sigh, remembering the overcrowded O'Donnell table back home, which was always the scene of so much laughter and revelry.

"Do none of your kin join you at supper?" she asked.

Cormac shook his head and muttered, "Not tonight."

"Beg pardon, milady," Eamon said gently, "but after what has occurred, 'twill take some doing to convince the Riordans to break bread with an O'Donnell. Ultan was well beloved."

Claire looked up in surprise. "Of course he was, no doubt by his sons above all, yet you are here."

Niall glowered. "Eamon and I are here because of our brother, and for no other reason—*my lady*."

Claire looked down the table at Cormac, but he said nothing. She turned back to Niall. "Well, then, we will just let people take their time getting to know me. I'll start by reminding you all that I'm a Riordan now, as well as an O'Donnell—and as such I'd appreciate it if you would call me by my Christian name. 'My lady' sounds too formal for a sister."

Niall and Eamon looked at Cormac, who shrugged. None of them spoke.

Claire pushed away her plate of food, her appetite gone. It was going to be hard enough living away from her family without suffering open hostility in her new home, but this was just the first evening. They all needed a chance to get used to each other.

"Come on," she urged, making her voice much lighter than her mood. " 'Tis an easy enough name. Give it a try. *Claire.*"

There was another long moment of silence, then Eamon smiled at her and said, "And 'tis a beautiful name as well, Claire. I've always wondered what it would be like to have a sister."

Claire felt a wave of warmth toward the friendly middle Riordan brother. She waited a moment for Niall to follow Eamon's example, but he stayed silent, as did Cormac.

One out of three. It was a beginning, she supposed, but she wished it had been Cormac who had been the first to say her name. After another moment of awkward silence, Claire pushed back her chair, forced a smile, and said, "If you'll excuse me, I'll just go thank the cook for providing us with a nice meal with such little warning."

She turned abruptly and left the room without looking back, careful not to let the Riordans see the tears glistening in her eyes.

Cormac had moved his things into the master bedchamber of Riordan Hall the very night of his father's funeral. He hadn't done it for himself, but for his brothers and the rest of the Riordan household. It seemed that no one wanted the spacious room at the end of the north wing to sit vacant, not even for a night. Cormac himself in no way felt himself ready to fill his father's role as chief of the Riordan family, but it appeared that everyone else was looking to him to fill the gap Ultan Riordan's death had left.

His new chamber still felt strange. For the three nights that he'd slept in his father's old bed, he'd had restless dreams. At night, the room seemed haunted by memories. It was only in the mornings, when the bright sun streamed through the large windows that faced east toward the hills, that he could dispel the notion that the shade of his father still lingered.

As he mounted the stone stairway and turned down the hall toward the north wing, Cormac wondered if this night he'd find more than a phantom waiting in his new room. He hadn't seen Claire since she'd left them at the dinner table. Earlier, he'd been tempted to ask one of the servants where the new mistress of Riordan Hall had put her things upon arrival, but he'd decided the question would have been considered odd. They were newly wed. He imagined that it would be assumed that they would share a room. He didn't know if his new bride shared that assumption, and if she did, he wasn't sure what he was going to do about it.

As he rounded that corner, he saw that the big oak door was closed. When he wasn't inside sleeping or dressing, Cormac left the door open, just as his father had, so the closed door meant that Claire, as he had feared, was probably inside. Every fiber of his body tensed.

He stopped a few feet from the door, considering what to do. He could turn around and go back to sleep in his old room in the south wing. He could pretend he wasn't sleepy and take Taranis out for a long midnight ride until there was no possible chance that Claire would be awake. Or he could go inside and finish what he and Claire had started the night of their wedding, forgetting everything he'd ever heard about ancient curses.

Damnation. The Riordans had always been known as the fiercest fighters in the Midlands. He was not about to turn hesitant and indecisive just because there was a woman in his bedroom. Sucking in a deep breath, he strode briskly to the door and, without knocking, opened it.

She was still awake, sitting on the bed, rather than in it, brushing her long black hair. What was worse, the glow from the lamp on the nightstand behind her silhouetted every one of her perfect curves through the thin material of her nightrail. Cormac was instantly aroused.

"Your steward brought my things here," she said, stopping her long strokes with the brush.

"I suppose 'twas the logical choice. It's my . . . it's the master bedchamber." He tore his gaze away from her and looked around the room. "I still see my father in this place."

"This was his room, then?"

"Aye."

"And your mother's, as well."

Cormac nodded and looked back at her. "Briefly. Then came Eamon's mother and then Niall's."

She looked startled. "Three different women?"

"Aye." Though his father was no longer around to urge his silence, Cormac was oddly reluctant to go into the story of the Riordan brides. " 'Tis the largest room in the house," he said. Then, gesturing to the nearly ceiling-high windows, he added, "With brilliant sun come morning."

Claire smiled. "Aye, it's lovely. O'Donnell House is much smaller. Eileen and I shared a room."

Cormac shifted uneasily. He couldn't expect to stand here all night making awkward conversation, but he didn't know what else to do. If he removed his doublet in preparation for bed, his wool hose would most certainly reveal the obvious state of the lower portion of his unruly body. If he lay beside her and felt those long, slender limbs against his as he had once before, he'd not guarantee that he'd be able to keep that body under control.

With a sigh, he admitted defeat. "I'll be sleeping back in my old room," he said.

She frowned and asked simply, "Why?"

"It will be easier. As you said, this arrangement is for the peace of our two families. It has nothing to do with the two of us."

She leaned over to put the brush on the nightstand. Cormac could see the swing of her unbound breasts. His neck grew hot. "It has everything to do with us," she argued. "We are husband and wife, and any hope of peace between the O'Donnells and the Riordans is based solely on that bond."

Her hair hung glossy and sleek all the way to the bed. He could picture her wrapped in it, her white body naked in the glow of the lamp.

"The bond is legal. The vows have been spoken, but it would be best if our marriage were one of name alone." She looked bewildered, and Cormac couldn't blame her. He himself could hardly credit his own words. He couldn't remember the last time a woman had so fired his blood. She sat ensconced in his own bed, her knees tucked under her and her head tilted in an unconscious and age-old pose of seduction. Yet he stood like a wooden soldier in the middle of the room without making a move.

Her expression slowly changed. "So, 'tis like your brother said at dinner. The Riordan minions won't break bread with an O'Donnell. And the head of the Riordans won't deign to sleep beside an O'Donnell wife."

Cormac could see the hurt in her blue eyes. He began

moving toward her, then thought better of it. Wouldn't it be easier for them both, he thought, if she were angry? Circumstances might force him to live side by side with her in the same house, but he had not forgotten his vow not to cause the tragic death of another Riordan bride. And if Claire were angry with him, it would be an excuse to see as little of her as possible.

He stiffened and made his voice deliberately cold. "You may put whatever interpretation you like, madam, but I think we would both be more comfortable in separate quarters."

She hugged her knees close to her chest. "As you will. I'll not beg any man to share my bed."

Cormac hesitated, then finally nodded and turned to leave. As he reached for the door latch, she added, "But nor will I live one minute longer than necessary where I am obviously not wanted. When this thing between our families is settled, I shall leave this cold place."

Cormac stopped to listen to her, but did not turn around. When she finished speaking, he quietly opened the big door and left the room.

Exhausted as she was, sleep would not come. Claire found herself going over and over the events of the day, from her early morning conversation with Eileen to her drastic decision to end the family feud and her cold reception by the Riordans. Her thoughts dwelt mostly on the last encounter of the evening—with Cormac in what she had supposed would be their shared chamber.

She was a novice in matters of mating, but she was virtually certain that the predatory gleam in Cormac's eyes had been nothing short of raw desire. He wanted her. She was sure of it. Yet he had rejected her—again.

As the dark minutes stretched to hours, she admitted to herself that she had rather deliberately taken pains to provoke his desire, all the while telling herself that she had come to Riordan Hall out of duty alone. Evidently some part of her was still clinging to the youthful fantasy that Cormac Riordan would prove to be that shining knight on a great horse who would sweep her away from her home and love her with a passion meant only for the ages.

Fine passion, she thought, with an audible snort. She flung back the bed coverings and got up, then padded over to the nearly dead fire, her bare feet cold against the flagstone floor. She threw a couple of small logs on the embers and seized a poker to stir the blaze back to life. The activity made her feel better.

"I'll not accept that the fault lies with me," she said aloud. If Cormac could walk away from their bridal bed, coldly and without explanation, then so be it.

She would put away her foolish childhood fantasies. She would do whatever it took to settle things between the O'Donnells and the Riordans, then she'd leave Riordan Hall and never look back.

One of the logs suddenly caught, and sent up a burst of flame. "Aye," she said, whacking the poker against the hard wood. "'Tis his loss, not mine, and I'll think on it no more."

Replacing the poker carefully on its hook, she walked back over to the big bed and scrambled up into it, burying herself in the soft down. Then she went instantly to sleep.

Anyone could see that despite the neglected-looking conditions, the Riordan estate was prosperous, Claire decided as she made her way along the path to the stables, which were a couple of hundred yards beyond the cluster of outbuildings that included the buttery and the kitchen. She had visited the latter the previous evening following her supper with the brothers. She'd talked with the head cook, a roly-poly woman named Molly, who had seemed unconcerned that the roof of her kitchen was cracked in three places.

Molly had introduced her to two bright young kitchen maids, a cooper who came once a week to use the Riordan forge, and Molly's husband, Rolf, the chief gardener.

It had been an informative evening. She'd learned that the domestic affairs of the Riordan estate had muddled along without much management and with varying degrees of efficiency for years. She'd also learned that not all Riordans were as hostile toward an O'Donnell as the Riordan brothers had warned at dinner.

Her visit had helped her regain her good spirits, but the bedroom encounter with Cormac had doused them again.

Today she had resolved not to let that particular subject enter her head. As long as she was mistress of Riordan—temporarily—she would do what she could to put things to right in a place that had obviously lacked a mistress's touch for far too long.

She gave Molly a wave as she passed by the kitchen on the way up the path toward the rambling wooden structure that housed the estate horses. On one side of the stable was a livestock barn and on the other a chicken house. The vegetable gardens lay beyond that.

Molly had told her that the official stable master was a distant cousin from Cork named Aidan Shaw, but that the real master of the Riordan horses was Niall.

"Since he was a wee one, he's taken more to the beasts than he does to humans," Molly had said with a cluck of her tongue. " 'Tis what comes of leaving a babe with no mum to care for him."

Sure enough, as she neared the wide-open double

doors of the stables, she could see the youngest Riordan brother kneeling in the straw next to a sleek brown foal. A burly man with a round face and soft features stood behind him. Cousin Aidan, Claire guessed, though only his chestnut hair declared his kinship.

Niall looked up briefly, scowled, then turned back to his study of the little foal's leg.

The stable master acknowledged her arrival with a tug on his cap and a small bow.

"Good morrow," she said, ignoring Niall's silence.

"Good morrow, milady," the stable master stammered as his face turned a mottled red. Was it a Riordan trait to be uncomfortable around women? she wondered. Growing up among the easy teasing of the O'Donnell household, especially her brothers, had not prepared her for causing consternation with a simple greeting.

"Aidan, is it not?" she asked the man with a smile. At his nod, she continued, "I've come to see your domain."

He bobbed his head several times. "You're very welcome, milady. Any time."

"Master Shaw is busy at the moment," Niall said, finally looking up at her.

"Good morrow to you, too, Niall," she said with a slight edge to her voice. "I've not come to cause problems. I can just wander around myself."

Aidan looked apologetic. "We have a foal in some trouble here," he explained.

Claire looked more closely at the foal, and now she could see that the tiny horse's leg was swollen around the hoof. Instantly forgetting her irritation with Niall, she walked over to the animal and knelt beside him. "What's the problem?"

"The hoof has split from the leg," Niall said curtly.

He held the hoof up for her to see. " 'Tis a bloody shame. His sire is Taranis."

"Cormac's horse?"

"Aye. The finest in the county." He let the foal's foot drop to the hay and stood, dusting off his hands. " 'Tis a bloody shame to lose him," he repeated.

Aidan nodded gravely. "D'ye want it done now?"

Claire looked up in alarm. "Surely you're not planning to put it down?"

"What else?" Niall asked. "It's done for." The horse master nodded agreement.

"But you must give him a fighting chance!" Claire jumped to her feet and faced the two men, hands on her hips. "The break could heal."

" 'Twas injured in the birthing, milady," Aidan explained gently. "Now it's got poisons sucked up into the blood. We'll just put the poor thing out of its misery."

"Nay, we will *not.*" She was close to shouting.

" 'Tis none of your affair, madam," Niall said stiffly.

Aidan turned away and shuffled over to a worktable where he picked up a curved knife. His face mournful, he turned back with the knife poised, his gaze on the young horse's sleek neck.

Claire stepped between him and the foal. "I order you not to harm this animal," she said.

Aidan stopped, surprised, then looked at Niall.

"Go ahead," the young man told him.

Claire turned and put her arms around the foal's neck. "I'll not let you touch him."

Niall gave a snort of exasperation. He looked at her for a long moment and appeared to be considering the consequences of laying violent hands on his brother's wife. Finally he said, "What would you have us do? Call a death watch to view the creature's agony?"

She looked up at him, eyes blazing. "I'd have you

treat his injury as it should have been treated from the time it happened."

"There's no treatment—" Aidan began.

Claire interrupted him. "Aye, but there is. With a salve of feverfew and marjoram, and proper bindings, this hoof will heal and seal itself together." Aidan and Niall exchanged a skeptical glance, but Claire continued, her voice insistent. "You must dress it twice daily and keep the area clean. The bindings must be very tight to promote the joining."

Both men were silent.

"At O'Donnell House we had a horse master with many of the ancient remedies, and I often helped him. I've seen this work," Claire said.

Finally Aidan shrugged. "Mayhap 'twould be worth trying. 'Tis a fine foal. Your brother would be mightily pleased if we saved it."

This last statement appeared to sway Niall. The anger drained from his expression as he looked down at his sister-in-law, still clinging to the foal's neck. "Very well, then," he said slowly. "Show us what to do."

Six

"*Do you not* get tired of salted meat?" Claire asked.

The round cook looked up from the long strip of beef she'd been rubbing. "We always salt the meat here at Riordan Hall, milady. Else it rots before we can eat it all."

"Of course, that's one way to preserve it, but there are other methods as well."

Molly sighed. "Beggin' yer pardon, milady, but here at Riordan we've never been much for fancy cooking ways. The men mostly just want their food hot—and plenty."

Claire was inspecting the shelves built along one entire wall of the roomy wooden kitchen. She picked up a crock, pulled off the cork, and sniffed. "Ah, vinegar," she said, wrinkling her nose at the pungent smell. "This will do nicely for one batch."

Molly had stopped working the grains of salt into the bloody slab on the table in front of her. "Vinegar, milady? 'Tis for the sallats."

"Aye, for sallats, but we can also preserve some of the meat this way—in vinegar and bay leaves. Do you have any?" She continued her study of the contents of Molly's larder and gave an exclamation of pleasure when she found a row of dusty pouches filled with dried herbs. "There should be some here."

" 'Twill alter the taste of the meat," Molly said with a little frown.

"Aye, that's what all these herbs are for. Don't you use them to make the dishes taste different?"

Molly shook her head. "Lord Riordan never paid much mind to the food. Though I do remember"—she stopped, straining for the memory—"when my mother was cook, the second Lady Riordan used to come around—or was it the third?"

"Well, this household has a mistress again, after all these long years, and if you're willing, Molly, you and I are going to start to produce some cooking that will have the Riordan men drooling on their bibs the minute they sit down at the table."

Molly giggled. " 'Tis true my Rolfie gets a bit cranky by the end of winter when all the vegetables are gone."

"Not this winter. We'll have them feasting all winter long." She pointed to a smaller slab of beef on the sideboard. "We won't salt that one, either. 'Tis veal—good and tender—and we'll just keep it that way under a thick coat of butter."

"And it won't rot, milady?"

"Nay." She smiled at the cook's round-eyed look. "Are you ready to start producing some masterpieces here, Molly?"

She nodded. "Aye, I've always wanted to try some new ways, but whenever I'd bring up the subject to Lord Ultan, he just wasn't interested."

"Men have never been good with the important things in life such as the food we eat," Claire said, pushing up the sleeves of her fine jersey dress and hoisting the smaller slab of meat onto the table. "They'd rather spend their time dashing around and whacking each other."

Molly's smile faded. "Have you heard how your brother's doing, milady?"

"I've not had word in three days. The wound should be healed by now, God willing."

Molly crossed herself. "God willing," she murmured.

They both were quiet for a moment, then Claire reached for a bowl and began to pour the vinegar. "Come on now, let's get this meat done, then I'll show you how to make a frumenty for supper today."

The dining table was full. The three Riordan brothers had been joined by assorted cousins, estate officers, and Riordan retainers. Claire had yet to get them all straight. She sat at one end, still the only female, but she was gratified to see that in the five days that she had been helping Molly with the cooking, the attendance at the midday meals had steadily grown. The good-natured raillery among the group made her feel more at home than she had the first couple days when she had presided over an almost empty table. She still was mostly excluded from the conversation, and when she asked a question, there was often a moment of awkward silence before she would receive a polite, but guarded answer. Nevertheless, it was a beginning.

"The foal is improving," Niall announced loudly to the gathering.

"Taranis's foal?" Eamon asked. "I thought 'twas done for days ago."

"As did I." Niall gave Claire a rueful grin. "And so it would have been if his neck hadn't been saved by a beautiful young woman."

Cormac looked up from his trencher in surprise. "What's this about?"

Niall turned to his brother. "It appears we have a new horse doctor at Riordan Hall. Your, er, wife has been treating the animal."

Claire had visited the stables that morning and had

been elated at the foal's progress. The colt's leg had been cool to the touch, and when she'd removed the bindings, it was apparent that the hoof was definitely healing.

"I thought the hoof was torn asunder," Cormac said, addressing his brother, not Claire.

"Aye, but she's been putting on a salve"—he paused and turned to her—"well, you tell them, sister."

Claire was not sure that everyone at the table noticed Niall's use of her title, but she was sure that Cormac did. His gaze went to her as she confirmed, "I've treated the foot and bound it. He's doing well. With time, he'll be good as new."

Eamon gave a low whistle. "If it lives, we're in your debt, Claire. That foal has the best lines in all of Ireland."

Several of the men at the table nodded agreement.

"So, what say you, Cormac?" Niall asked. "Do you have a name for Taranis's fine new son?"

Cormac was still looking down the long table at Claire. "I reckon 'tis for the animal's savior to name it," he said.

Everyone in the room was looking at her and Claire felt her cheeks grow hot. She had, in fact, found her own special name for the beautiful little colt as she had treated it over the past few days, but judging from the name Cormac had chosen for the sire, she wasn't at all sure her choice would be acceptable. He was watching her, waiting for her to speak, his dark eyes inscrutable. Suddenly she remembered how those eyes had softened when he had spoken of his childhood horse.

"The colt's sire is Taranis, the Thunderer, god of war," she said, making her voice loud enough to reach to the far end of the table. "I'd thought about calling the son Dian Cécht."

"God of healing," Eamon put in.

"Aye." Claire's chin went up a notch.

Cormac was quiet a moment, then said, "Very well. 'Twill be Dian." His gaze continued on her.

There was a long silence, then Eamon said loudly, "If no one is going to finish the gooseberry torte, I'll thank you to pass it this way. I swear, 'tis nothing short of ambrosia."

Cormac knew that it was utterly unwise for him to be heading down the hall of the north wing toward the master bedchamber. He could very well wait to speak to Claire in the morning, when she was bustling about the house in her usual whirlwind of activity, making it easy to remember that their relationship was strictly one of convenience. If he visited her in her chambers, he'd risk once again facing her in the soft glow of candlelight, her hair loose and flowing. She may even have already removed the practical, heavy linen dress that she'd taken to wearing for her household tasks and donned a sheer nightrail such as he had seen her wearing that first night in the hall. His throat dried up at the memory, but his feet continued on their path.

She had worked like a plowhorse all week, he told himself. A generation of debris had been removed from the house. The haphazard estate gardening efforts had been set up on a schedule with special crews assigned each task. Each noon meal brought new delights from the formerly mediocre Riordan kitchen. And through it all, Cormac had kept his distance, remembering his vow, remembering how nearly he'd come to breaking it on their wedding night after too much ale. All week long, he'd been careful to stay sober—and to stay away from her.

Fortunately, it hadn't proved too difficult, since Cor-

mac had been busy assuming his new duties as head of
the family. He'd paid several visits to outlying farms,
trying to assure the families under his protection that in
spite of Ultan Riordan's death, there would be no re-
sumption of the fighting that had plagued the land for
so many years. Each time he said the words, his resolve
hardened. He would keep the peace, and if that meant
living side by side with an O'Donnell wife, he'd do that
as well. He'd simply keep his distance—it wasn't that
difficult.

But now, on top of all else, she'd saved his new horse.
He couldn't go any longer without thanking her. It
would be churlish and ungrateful, unbefitting the head
of the Riordan family, he told himself, as he reached for
the brass door latch of her bedroom. He started to pull
the door open, then stopped. With no women in the
household, the Riordans had never had to worry about
matters such as privacy, but things were different now.
He pulled his hand away from the latch and knocked.

He couldn't hear anything behind the thick wood, but
in a few moments, the door opened. Claire looked out
at him in surprise. She was still dressed. Cormac discovered that he'd been holding in his breath.

"I hope 'tis not too late, milady," he said.

She took a step back into the room and gestured for
him to enter. "Of course not, but I'd prefer that you call
me by my name, especially in private."

He nodded. "I meant no offense. Indeed, I've come
to thank you. 'Tis wondrous what you've done here in
such a short time."

"I'm merely filling my place as mistress of your
household, Cormac. 'Tis part of the wifely duties."

He wondered if she realized that her words brought
to mind other wifely duties she had yet to perform, but
he brushed away the notion. At the beginning of this

arrangement, she had made it clear that it was no more to her liking than it was to his. She was here in order to keep the peace.

He cleared his throat. "The horse you saved was valuable. I'd like to give you something for your efforts. I'd give you the horse itself if it were a female."

Her dark brow arched. "I need no reward for fulfilling my duties. I'm happy little Dian will live to breed more strong mounts, and I hope to be able to ride him one day."

"He'll be another like Taranis, I'm afraid—good only for the strongest rider. I'll find you another more suitable."

"A swaybacked mare, long in the tooth?" she asked with a smile.

"A mare, aye."

Claire continued to look amused. "I'll forgive you your prejudices, Cormac, since you grew up without sisters. But someday you'll see me ride with Eileen and realize that we'd make a match for any two Riordan men. We regularly outride our brothers."

He frowned. "I've no doubt you're a fine rider, milady, but I'd put no sidesaddle on such as Taranis."

"Then I'd ride without one." She looked suddenly impish, and he could see a glimpse of the young girl who had challenged her brothers in their childhood matches.

"Perhaps when Dian grows, you can give it a try while he's still gentle." They were standing in the middle of the room. He'd intended to say his piece and then leave, but he found himself wishing he could stay to enjoy more of her company. His gaze flickered to the fireplace, where big pillows formed a cozy seating area.

Claire turned her head to follow his glance. "Would

you care to sit down for a spell? There's warm ale by the fire."

He hesitated only a moment, then nodded. They walked to the pillows and, without thinking, he reached for her hand to help her to a seat. Unlike his, her hand was cool.

"Ale?" she asked, lifting the pewter pitcher.

In spite of his determination to keep a clear head, his throat had been dry since he'd entered the room. "Aye," he said.

Claire filled two mugs, handing one to him. "This is nice," she said. "We've not had a chance to talk all week. You've been so busy."

"As have you."

"Aye, there's much to do with such a big change in a household, but it seems to be going smoothly."

"I believe that is due in large part to you, milady."

"Claire," she corrected.

"Claire." It was the first time he had said her name, and he could feel his voice grow soft and husky as the word left his mouth. "Claire," he repeated, more loudly.

She grew still, watching him, then smiled and said, "I like hearing you say it."

He took a big swallow of the warm ale, feeling its heat all the way down to his stomach. "Have you been finding what you need here?" he asked after a moment. "My people are cooperating?"

"Contrary to my fears after our first lonely supper, everyone has been kind and helpful. Even Niall seems to be getting used to me." She grinned, and there was the childhood imp again.

" 'Twas the horse that did it," Cormac agreed. "He's always cared for horses more than people."

"Yet he and your stable man were ready to kill the poor little thing."

Cormac laughed.

Her full mouth pursed with indignation. "I don't see how that's a matter for jest."

"Nay, I'm not laughing at the foal's dilemma. It's just that here at Riordan Hall we're not used to the female point of view. If a horse needs to be sacrificed, so be it, 'tis the law of nature. There's never been a lady around to mourn for the 'poor little thing.'"

"There's been no lady in residence since Niall's mother died?"

He shook his head.

"How old were you then?"

"Niall's mother died when I was eight. Eamon's died when I was five."

"You must scarce remember them."

Cormac stared into the fire. He couldn't remember his own mother, but he had acute memories and even more vivid dreams of his two sweet, gentle stepmothers. For a few short, happy months they had come into his life, cherished him, sung to him, given him the caresses he lacked from his stern father. Then they, each in turn, had died, and his short taste of tenderness had been once again pulled away from him. "I remember them," he said.

Claire seemed to sense that she had ventured into a painful subject. "It must have been hard to lose them. But surely there were other females who cared for you boys. Your father did not raise you by himself."

"Aye, but he did. I daresay you're the first female to enter this wing of Riordan Hall other than the occasional cleaning maid."

"Very occasional," Claire added with a grin.

Cormac looked around the chamber, which for the first time in memory was tidy and fresh-smelling. "Aye. I fear much was neglected here all those years. I'm beholden to you for all you've done putting things to rights. You've worked hard these past days."

There was unmistakable warmth in his tone, and Claire found it more heady than the ale she was sipping. All her resolutions to remain detached from her new husband seemed to have fled. It was impossible to sit by the fire in cozy intimacy with him without feeling the heightening of senses that Cormac Riordan always seemed to produce within her.

She was sure that her cheeks were growing pink, and only hoped that Cormac would think the color due to the ale or the heat of the fire. Forcing her voice to normalcy, she said, "As long as I'm here, I want to make myself useful. My father always says he bred his daughters to be strong, not simpering."

"He succeeded well."

Neither spoke. Claire jumped as a log broke in the fire, sending up a shower of sparks. She looked away from Cormac's dark gaze and sipped her mug of ale. The brew was unwatered, and the pungent drink seemed to help her racing pulse.

"Raghnall O'Donnell is a lucky man," Cormac said finally. "His daughters are not only strong, but beautiful as well." His voice was altered, the tone deep and husky.

It was happening again, Claire thought, dazed. This thing between them that neither one sought, yet neither one seemed to be able to control.

She raised her head. He was watching her with hooded eyes that sent an unmistakable message. The mug of ale slipped from her fingers.

In an instant, Cormac was on his knees beside her. He plucked the spilled cup from her lap and used the towel from under the pitcher to sop up the ale that had fallen into her skirts. "Oh, dear, how clumsy," she cried, her cheeks now flaming in earnest.

"Nay, shh," he comforted her. Gently he took each one of her hands and wiped her fingers. She let him tend to her like a child, since her limbs seemed unwilling to move of their own volition.

"I'm sorry," she murmured, as the worst of the mess was contained. "I should get some water and rags and—"

But Cormac still held one of her hands and shook his head. "It'll keep," he said shakily, "but this won't."

Then his lips were on hers, warmed by the ale and the fire, insistent and determined. She moaned a little and let her head fall back to give his mouth full access to hers. His tongue entered her, velvety heat that melted a liquid path through her midsection.

She fell back against the soft cushions and he followed her down, his mouth still working its rhythmic magic. In the twisting of their bodies she could feel his hard thigh against her leg. His hand brushed her side, and moved upward to cup her breast.

Then it was over. He pulled back, breathing hard. "Forgive me," he said in a strangled voice. He jumped to his feet and was gone before the moisture of his kisses had dried from her lips.

Claire watched in disbelief as the door closed softly behind his retreating form. Her dress was still soaked from the spilled liquor. Her lips stung from a final rasp of his whiskers.

"Of all the—" she began aloud. She sat up slowly, gathering her wet skirt with one hand. As the shock wore off, the anger began. She couldn't believe that he had done it to her again. The arrogant, insufferable man had once again left her smack in the middle of what appeared to be mutually enjoyable lovemaking. It was intolerable, she huffed, as she stripped off her wet clothes and pulled on her nightdress. Insulting and rude and boorish.

Yet as she grew calmer and climbed up into her big
bed, she began to realize that it was also exceedingly
odd. Granted, she was still a novice in matters of bedding, but she trusted her feminine instincts enough to
believe that Cormac Riordan had been as carried away
by their kisses as she. She could *swear* that it had been
desire she had seen in those hooded eyes. Yet in the
midst of their most ardent embrace, he had dashed off
like a kitchen boy caught stealing a pastry.

Something was not right. Cormac was a healthy male
with appetites to match any man's, if the local whisper-
ings about the three Riordans were true. And she no
longer thought that her family name was keeping him
from her. He'd been perfectly courteous to her all week,
and had even come here tonight to thank her.

There had to be some explanation for his behavior,
she decided as she burrowed into the soft bed. Whatever
it was, it might not be easy to discover. She couldn't
exactly go about asking his brothers or people of the
estate why Cormac seemed so reluctant to bed his own
wife. It wouldn't be easy, but somehow she would find
the answer.

" 'Tis late, Cormac. Are you not for bed?" Along with
everyone else in the hall, Eamon knew that his brother
slept in his old room, not in the master suite alongside
his new wife, but he had made no mention of the fact
to Cormac. He'd come in late from a visit to one of the
estate families and found Cormac in the dining hall, a
nearly empty jug of wine at his elbow.

"Are you playing the nursemaid, now, brother?" Cormac asked.

"No need to turn sour. 'Twas but a friendly question."

Cormac looked up at his brother, focusing his eyes

with some difficulty. "Forgive me. I'm a bit out of sorts tonight."

Eamon lifted the jug and peered inside. "So I see. I suspect 'twill be your head that is out of sorts on the morrow if you keep up this pace."

"Go to bed, Nanny Eamon. I've had my lessons for today."

Eamon stood looking down at his brother, a frown of concern on his face. "This thing is working out better than anyone could have expected, Cormac. Everyone likes her. Lord, she's transformed the place, and there's been no trouble between the families since she arrived. You should be happy—"

Cormac lifted his hand to stop the flow of his brother's words. "Aye, 'tis a blessed miracle. The woman's an angel come to bring peace and happiness to our gloomy home. She fairly rains happiness wherever she goes. Is that what you want me to say?" He blinked his reddened eyes. "All right, I've said it. Everyone's happy. Now go on to bed and leave me to get happily stewed."

Eamon shook his head. "Ah, Cormac, why don't you just go ahead and sleep with the maid? She's everything a man could want and more."

"Thank you, brother," Cormac replied dryly. "I need you to tell me that."

Eamon grinned. "Mayhap you do. Sometimes I look at her and think, my brother must have been struck blind."

Cormac glared at him. "We're brothers, Eamon, but I'll thank you not to look at my wife in that context or I'll have to knock some of your teeth loose."

Eamon shrugged. "You could try. Still, I say it's time for you to give up this notion of the curse. 'Tis nothing more than ancient superstition."

"Which is why we were raised with no mothers."

"I'll not stand and argue with you at this hour of the night. Come to bed."

Cormac shuffled to his feet. "I may as well. The wine seems to have lost its effect."

Eamon clapped a hand on his brother's shoulder to steady his somewhat wobbly stance. "You may as well admit it, Cormac. Curse or no curse, you're not going to hold out much longer. You have a willing, handsome woman sleeping in your bed, a woman who would fire the blood of any man, and that's more than a true Riordan has ever been able to resist."

Seven

Eamon looked around the Riordan stables and grinned at Niall. "Brother, I warrant these stalls haven't been so clean since blessed St. Patrick drove out the snakes."

The stable master, Aidan, walked by the two brothers carrying a load of harness on his shoulders. " 'Tis the lady's doing," he said with a gruff laugh. "The lady Claire be a regular visitor these days, and Master Niall always wants to put things just right when she comes around."

Niall looked embarrassed. " 'Twas time someone took things to hand here. Father simply hadn't paid enough attention to the place these past few years."

Eamon's expression grew more serious. "Aye, he should have appointed a warden long ago, or named one of us to the post instead of letting us go about fighting feuds that never led to any end."

It was a beautiful fall day and Eamon had agreed to accompany Cormac on his rounds among the tenants. All three Riordans were doing their best to make sure the Riordan legacy and holdings remained loyal and strong following Ultan's death, and as they did so, they each had come to realize that their father had become increasingly neglectful in the past few years. Age had taken a toll on the proud patriarch, yet he had refused to call his sons, who had been off on their own adventures, back to Riordan Hall to help him. Well, now they were back—all three. Their presence had injected new energy into the place, but what had brought more changes than anything was the fact that Riordan Hall now had a mistress for the first time in years.

"So Claire has been visiting the stables regularly?" Eamon asked.

Niall busied himself untying a stubborn knot from a rope hanging over one of the stalls. "Regular enough. She likes to check on Dian."

"Whose hoof is now mended," Eamon added.

"Aye."

"Does she ride?"

Niall shook his head. "She says she hasn't time, and anyway she sent the O'Donnell horses back to her family, so she doesn't have a mount."

"Surely Cormac has told her that she may ride any of the Riordan horses she chooses."

Niall shrugged. "In truth, I'm not sure what our brother has told her. He seems to be avoiding all contact with her. If I didn't know that my big brother has never feared anything or anyone in his life, I'd say he was afraid of her."

" 'Tis himself he's afraid of," Eamon muttered, then became quiet as he saw Claire coming toward them up the path from the kitchens. "Good morrow, sister," he called.

She smiled warmly and waved. She was wearing a bright dress the color of bluebells and looked fresh as a flower herself. Both brothers stood stock still as they watched her approach.

"Cormac's a bloody fool," Niall said under his breath.

Eamon nodded. His gaze, still on Claire, had turned thoughtful. "Aye. Perhaps he needs a little help from his younger, but wiser, brothers."

Niall looked puzzled. "What kind of help?"

"Just follow my lead," Eamon said under his breath as Claire took the last few steps to reach them.

"What a brilliant day!" she said, throwing out her arms. "Just look at the sun and the blue of that sky. How are my new brothers today?"

Niall's welcoming smile was uncharacteristically tender. "Eamon and I are busy looking at the blue of your bonny eyes, sister Claire."

Eamon was not to be outdone. "Aye, and a bonny smile that shines brighter than any sunlight."

Claire giggled happily at their sallies. She had come a long way with the two younger Riordan brothers in the days she had lived among them. They had now begun to greet her with genuine warmth and an open admiration that was unmistakable. She only wished their older brother had shared some of the transformation of attitude. She had scarce seen Cormac since the night he had kissed her in her room.

"You lads are wasting your charms on an old married lady," she said. " 'Tis the village colleens you need to be flattering with such nonsense."

Eamon nodded. "Alas, we're only too aware that our clod of a brother has first claim on you, sister. Which no doubt is why he told me to ask you if you would accompany him on his ride around the estate today."

Claire's jaw dropped. "He did?"

Eamon looked at Niall. "Aye," the younger brother confirmed. "Er, at breakfast."

Claire looked down at her dress, which wasn't normal riding attire. "I'm not really prepared—" she began.

" 'Tis not a strenuous ride," Eamon assured her. "Niall will put a sidesaddle on one of our gentler mares."

Eamon had mistaken her hesitation, but Claire didn't bother to correct him.

"That I shall," Niall said, dropping the rope and hurrying to the back of the stable where a lady's saddle had lain collecting dust for over twenty years. He pulled it off a shelf and looked at it with a grimace. "I'll just be a minute," he yelled to them in the front.

"I wonder why Cormac didn't mention this to me himself," Claire said. "I would have worn my riding clothes."

Eamon tipped his head as if considering the matter. "Cormac's a bit reserved at times, but I got the impression he was quite eager to show you around."

Eager? Claire had been almost sure that Cormac had been deliberately avoiding her, and she had spent the week steeling herself to forget those few tender moments by her fire. She shook her head, confused. She could refuse to go, ask to put off the expedition for another day, but if he had indeed told Eamon that he was eager to ride with her, perhaps it was his way of making amends for his neglect over the past week, a sort of apology. The least she could do was meet his gesture halfway.

"Lindsay and I were going to tackle the linen store closet today," she said, "but the job will keep. 'Tis too beautiful a day to spend it in a dusty closet, and I would like to see around the estate."

"It's settled, then," Niall said, coming out of the stable leading a pretty gray roan. "This one is a real lady. She won't give you any problems."

Claire smiled and reached for the mare's reins.

"Nay, I'll hold her while you mount," Niall said.

Eamon moved around and took her elbow. "And I'll help you up on her," he added. " 'Tis best done from this side."

Hiding her amusement at their unnecessary concern, Claire looked down the path toward the house. There was no sign of anyone approaching the stables. "Shouldn't I wait for Cormac?"

Niall pointed up to the hill just beyond the stable. "He's already been out this morning and is just coming now to meet me—er, to meet you. You can go ahead and ride on up to him."

Claire swiveled her head. Sure enough, at the crest of the hill was the unmistakable form of Cormac, mounted on Taranis. They cut a proud figure against the sky. She felt a surge of excitement, but she kept her voice level and turned her attention to the horse, giving her neck a pat. "What's her name?"

"Cinder," Niall told her.

Eamon cupped his hands near the stirrup. "I'll boost you up and Niall will hold her still until you get the feel of the saddle."

Claire gave them her impish grin and, ignoring Eamon's hands, boosted herself lightly up on the mare's back. "Thank you, boys," she cried. Then she pulled expertly on the reins to steer the horse's muzzle out of Niall's grip. "Cinder and I will do just fine."

She danced the horse safely out of range of the two men before she gently kicked her into a full gallop up the hill toward the approaching rider.

Eamon and Niall watched her ride away with expressions of bemusement. "We should have known she'd ride as well as she does everything else," Eamon said finally.

Niall nodded. "Aye, we already knew she has a way with caring for them. 'Tis only sensible that she rides like the devil as well."

They were quiet for a minute, admiring how easily she sat in the saddle, her back straight and her black hair streaming out from its bindings.

"What's Cormac going to say?" Niall asked. Their

brother and Taranis were already halfway down the hill, and the two riders were close to meeting.

Eamon laughed. "I'd give a penny or two to hear the exchange, but I fear we'll never know."

"If she tells him 'twas you who sent her, he'll have your hide."

"Mayhap. Or he may thank me. I reckon it depends on how enjoyable the ride turns out to be."

Niall's gaze went back up the hill where the two riders had now reached each other and were talking, though it was too far to hear their words. "He'd bloody well better make it enjoyable," he said grimly. "The lucky bastard doesn't seem to know what a prize he's got."

The grin died from Eamon's face. "Nay, brother, you're wrong. He knows it all too well."

Cormac slowed his pace as Claire rode toward him. He'd come back to meet Eamon, but he could see his brother still standing in front of the stables making no move to fetch his horse.

Cormac frowned. Since the night he'd foolishly gone to her room, he'd avoided his wife. He'd arisen before dawn every day and ridden himself into exhaustion to ward off the memory of the kisses they'd shared. But at night, before he drifted to sleep, the visions would come, and he'd relive the touch of her lips, the feel of her soft fingertips against his cheek. It was driving him to distraction.

"Good morrow," she called as their horses neared each other.

Her tone was cooler than it had been that night before the fire, but the mere sound of her voice was enough to start the treacherous lust licking at his loins. *Jesu,* he swore silently. Was this, too, part of the Druid curse?

He managed a smile. "Aye, 'tis a fair day, right

enough." He pulled his horse to a halt in front of hers and waited for her to explain her purpose in coming to meet him, but she merely smiled back and appeared to be waiting as well.

Finally, he said, "Was there something you needed, madam?"

She seemed confused. "Nay, I—I'm ready." She looked down at her dress. "Ah, my clothes. 'Tis no matter. I didn't know we were to go riding today, so I had no chance to dress appropriately, but I can ride in any attire."

Now it was Cormac's chance to look confused. "Go riding?"

"On your rounds, that is, to visit the tenants. Eamon gave me your message."

Cormac looked down toward the stable. Niall and Eamon were still there, looking up at them expectantly. "Eamon gave you the message, did he?"

Claire gave a brief, tentative smile. "Aye, and I'm pleased to accept. I've wanted to see around the estate, but I've been too busy at the hall."

Cormac was trying to control the rush of irritation, which was making him want to ride down to the stables and throttle his brother. But his ire softened as he looked back and saw the eagerness in Claire's blue eyes. It was true; she'd been with them over a fortnight, and for all of that time she'd been confined to the house and grounds, working harder than any of the servants. She deserved a break.

"Then I'm glad you could join me," he said gently, and was rewarded with a smile that this time was without reservation.

When Cormac had ignored her for a week following the night they had shared kisses, Claire had sworn that *this* time, she would not be so forgiving. His behavior was insufferable, inconsiderate, and insulting, and she intended to meet any further interaction with indifference. Which was why she regarded it as the height of absurdity that when Eamon had told her that Cormac wanted to take her riding, she had instantly abandoned her plans for the day and agreed. Then again, when had logic ever ruled her head concerning Cormac Riordan? she asked herself with an inner sigh.

In fact, the day had been much more pleasant than she had anticipated. She'd resolved immediately that if she was going to accept the invitation, it would be with good grace. She hadn't chided him for his neglect of her the past week. Neither one of them had mentioned the evening in her room. Instead, they'd found plenty to talk about as they rode around the vast Riordan holdings, an estate fully ten times the size of the O'Donnell lands.

She tried to keep her mind on learning the names of the different tenant families instead of on the way Cormac's thighs gripped Taranis's powerful flanks, guiding him perfectly through rough terrain with practically no need of his reins.

They'd visited five farms. Claire had mostly watched and listened as Cormac had greeted all the residents by name, even the children. At each household, he'd calmly dealt with any problems or complaints. A backed-up creek was preventing water from reaching one farm's vegetable gardens, and he'd agreed to send a crew from Riordan Hall to remedy the problem. He'd quietly, but forcefully, mediated a dispute between two woodcutters, both named Kelly. They claimed no relation to each other, though each family was related to the Riordans by marriage.

Loosely, it seemed, everyone was related to the Riordans one way or another, which made the family immense, and by the end of the day, Claire was beginning to have some sense of the responsibility Cormac had taken on when he became lord and chieftain of the family.

"How do you remember all the names?" she asked, as they turned their horses back up the valley toward Riordan Hall.

Cormac shrugged. "I've grown up among them all. They're family, and my father always said that there's nothing more important than blood."

Claire was silent. She was loyal to her family, as well. Her very presence at Riordan Hall was testament to that. But, as far as she was concerned, there were things more important than blood. Things such as peace and love.

"When I was a boy, I didn't always understand his meaning," Cormac continued. "But now I feel it with every breath I take. I'd give my life for any one of them," he ended, making a sweeping gesture that seemed to encompass the entire land they'd crossed.

"They do seem to look to you for help and guidance."

"As they should. 'Tis my duty."

She'd never seen him more at peace, she thought. It was obvious that the mantle of family patriarch suited him well. But, she couldn't help thinking, what about his duty to his wife? Where did she fit into this picture of family responsibility? And, sweet St. Anne, was he so cold that he had no memory of the kisses they had shared just a week ago? Was it just she alone who had felt the pull of those memories every time he had touched her today to assist her from her horse?

"You perform your duty well, Lord Riordan," she said finally. If he noticed a strain of irony underneath her words, he made no comment.

Cormac was ready for the long day to end. He'd done a good job of forcing himself to concentrate on matters of the estate, but now, as the sinking sun was beginning to turn the landscape golden, he found his eyes and his thoughts wandering. Claire on horseback was a wondrous sight. She rode as though born to the saddle, moving with the animal, never fighting it. Instead of looking like the precarious perch it became for some women, her sidesaddle seemed comfortable and secure. Cinder was a docile enough mount, but he'd never seen the little mare more under a rider's spell.

His tenants seemed equally charmed by her. At every farm, she'd had special words of warmth for the women, who usually hung in the background on his official visits. She'd embraced every child, no matter how grubby or unkempt. The men's glances had held unmistakable admiration, though they'd been uniformly respectful, as was only proper for the wife of their lord.

By the time they'd started back toward the hall, Cormac found that he could think of little else but those few moments when he'd held her in front of the fire, his hands on her breasts, his lips on hers. He tried to turn his thoughts back to the crop rotation ideas of Patrick Mitchell or John Kelly's wood dispute claim, but it was impossible. As she rode ahead of him on the suddenly narrowed path, all he could see was the cascade of glossy hair. All he could think of was how it had felt when he had run it through his fingers.

"You will join us, then?" she was asking.

He had no idea what had come before. "Join you?"

She looked a little exasperated. "For supper. You've not come to the dining hall all week and I believe your brothers have missed you."

His brothers. The well-meaning torturers who had sent Claire out to join him today. They would do well to stay out of his way for a spell. "Nay," he said. "I've too much work to linger over food."

They'd arrived back at the stables. There was no sign of either Riordan brother, but Aidan came out to take their horses. "Did ye have a good ride?" he asked.

Cormac looked down sharply to see if the horse master's question held overtones of derision. He wouldn't put it past his brothers to have shared their joke with others. But the burly horseman merely looked up at him with his usual guileless smile. "Aye," he answered curtly. " 'Twas a fine day."

He dismounted and saw that Claire had jumped from her horse, without waiting for his assistance this time. She smiled at Aidan as she handed him the reins, but her expression grew cloudy as she turned to him. "You have to eat," she said. "You'll be of no help to any of your people if you get sick."

"I'll grab a bite from Molly in the kitchen." He avoided her eyes. "Go on ahead. You'll be wanting to see to supper. I'll help Aidan with the horses."

Her voice was stiff when she said, "Do as you please, then. I'll not argue with you."

Cormac felt instant remorse. She'd been such pleasant company throughout the day, and he had rewarded her by turning cold when she had mentioned supper. Surely he could keep his impulses under control long enough to sit at the other end of the table from her in a room full of people.

He opened his mouth to tell her to expect him for supper after all, but before he could speak she said curtly, "Thank you for the ride." Then she spun around and started walking swiftly down toward the house.

By the time Claire reached the hall, she was fuming. Her heart, which had been softening all day as she'd watched Cormac with his tenants, felt as if a sudden freeze had come along and turned it to ice. He'd been

thoughtful on their ride, at times even charming. Yet as
they'd ridden the final stretch home, she could feel him
turning more distant. When they'd reached the stables,
it almost seemed as if he were embarrassed to be caught
riding with her by his stable man. Evidently among the
peasantry, he was unashamed to acknowledge her as his
wife, but at Riordan Hall it was a different story. Here,
she was no more than an embarrassment and a nuisance
he was doing his best to avoid.

Eamon was waiting for her in the front hall, and
looked eager to hear about the outcome of her day. His
smile faded as he saw her stormy expression.

"I take it the ride was not all you had expected,
Claire? Were the tenants not respectful to you?" he
asked.

"Nay, the ride was lovely, as were your people. 'Twas
your brother who was the problem."

Eamon scowled. "Now what's he done? If he's been
unkind to you, I swear, I'll give him a good thrashing."

Claire sighed. "He's not been unkind. It's simply—
he doesn't seem to want to have anything to do with
me."

Eamon appeared to be considering something for a
long moment. Finally he asked slowly, "Has Cormac
talked with you at all about, er, other Riordan marriages?"

Claire was hot and tired after her long ride. She didn't
want to think anymore about Riordan marriages—not
her own or anyone else's. The collar of her dress was
damp with sweat. Perhaps she would skip supper tonight
herself, she thought, and have a tub of water brought to
her room.

"Your brother has had very little to say to me about
marriage or any other subject, Eamon. Now, if you'll
excuse me, I think I'll retire to my chamber for the eve-

ning. Cormac won't be joining you at supper tonight, either."

"Oh, but you must be at supper, both of you."

"I've already left word with Molly about the fare. You don't need—"

Eamon was shaking his head vehemently. "We've visitors. It would be an affront if the lord and lady of the hall were not present to dine with them."

"Visitors? Were they expected?" If Cormac had known that Riordan Hall was to receive visitors and had not told her, it would be one more sign of his insensitivity.

"Nay, 'twas a surprise, but now that they're here, we have to entertain them."

Something in Eamon's expression told her he wasn't entirely pleased about the new arrivals. "Who are they?" she asked.

"Sean Riordan and his brother Dermot of Ulster."

"More kinsmen?"

"Aye, but they've come as escort."

Claire was seeing her hopes for a bath and a relaxed evening disappearing. "An escort to whom?"

Eamon's mouth twisted. "They're escorting a General Bixleigh, the English emissary from Queen Elizabeth, come to review Her Majesty's dominions in Ireland."

Eight

The queen's emissary, General Reginald Bixleigh, was a sallow man, as tall as the three Riordans, but more slender. He had hair sprouting from his chin and cheeks in unlikely places. Claire supposed the beard was the latest in London fashions, but to her it merely looked ridiculous.

Sean Riordan, who was introduced to Claire as head of the Ulster Riordans of the north, appeared to be friends with Bixleigh, or at least seemed solicitous of the English general's every need. Cormac, Eamon, and Niall were more reserved with their visitor, but respectful. All the men at the table were obviously fascinated by the man's tales of naval maneuvers along the Flemish coast, before he'd been sent to deal with "the Irish problem."

Encouraged by their father, Claire and Eileen had always been active participants of the political discussions at the O'Donnell household, but she had never been able to fully define her feelings about English rule. On one hand, she knew that her father and brothers were passionately against the idea of anyone ruling Ireland but the Irish themselves. But she herself couldn't help a secret admiration for the fiery young woman who had assumed the throne of England when she was not much older than Claire herself and was building a nation that was becoming the marvel and envy of all Europe.

When there had been visitors to the dinner table at O'Donnell House, Claire had listened avidly to the tales of Elizabeth's magnificent court, where handsome suitors vied for her attention and wrote plays and sonnets in her honor.

Claire had always been less interested in the military exploits, and unfortunately these seemed to be General Bixleigh's specialty. He had now droned on for over two hours. As she looked around the big dining table, however, it was obvious that the men's interest had yet to lag.

Bixleigh had been accompanied by his adjutant, a lieutenant named Grenville. The young soldier had made some attempts to include Claire in the conversation, but had usually been drowned out by the general.

Finally, it seemed as if the general himself remembered that there was a lady at the table. "We are ignoring our hostess," Bixleigh said, turning to her after a particularly gruesome description of a ship ramming that left dozens of oarsmen drowning at their posts. He was sitting at the position of honor on her right. His chin whiskers bobbled when he smiled, reminding Claire of the twitching tail of a bunny.

"Not at all," she assured him graciously. "I'm sure everyone is enjoying your stories." She looked down to the other end of the table where Cormac had remained silent through most of the evening. His expression was noncommittal and it was too far to see his eyes, so she had no idea what he was thinking about the general's exploits.

"Nay, 'tis a crime to ignore such a beauty," Bixleigh said softly. His words had begun to slur from the quantity of ale he'd drunk. He leaned toward her and put a hand around her arm. She could feel a subtle pressure of his fingers rubbing against the side of her breast. His smile had turned to a leer, and Claire felt the bile rise in her throat. She pushed back her chair and stood, pulling away from the general's grasp.

"Very interesting stories," she repeated, flustered and out of breath. "But you'll forgive me. I rise early these days and must take my leave."

"Not without your husband following at your tail, I warrant," he said with a nasty laugh. Bixleigh looked from Claire to Cormac at the other end of the table. "Surely 'tis too close to the wedding night to let up on the rutting just yet, eh, Riordan?"

Claire could feel the gaze of every man in the room except Lieutenant Grenville, who had lowered his eyes with an expression of acute discomfort. Her face flamed scarlet. At the far end of the table, Cormac jumped to his feet and looked as if he were about to jump down their guest's throat. Eamon and Sean Riordan, who had been sitting on either side of him, stood as well and each put a steadying hand on Cormac's shoulder.

Her sense of propriety battling with her humiliation, Claire bobbed her head and mumbled, "Good evening, gentlemen," before leaving the room with as much dignity as she could muster.

Her ears still burning from Bixleigh's coarse description and her breast tingling from the pressure of his fingers, she could hardly remember ascending the stairs to her room and turning toward the north wing. By the time she reached the door to her chamber, Cormac had caught up to her.

"I'm sorry," he said. "The man was sotted."

"Aye." She pulled open the door and started to go in without looking at him, but he stopped her with a hand on her shoulder.

"There was not a man in the hall who didn't want to break Bixleigh's neck over that remark."

She turned around to look at him with a faint smile. "Are you telling me that the Riordans would be willing to defend the honor of an O'Donnell?"

"To a man," he replied firmly.

"Well, 'tis not necessary. I'm not that fragile. The man was drunk and that's an end to it."

His eyes were scanning her face as if looking for signs of damage. " 'Twould not be the end of it if he were anyone but Elizabeth's pet lackey," he said finally.

"There would be problems if anything happened to him."

"Aye."

Cormac looked more distressed than she herself felt. Of course, she imagined that a loving husband would take his wife in his arms to comfort her after such an insult. But Cormac had more than once established beyond all doubt that they had a marriage in name only. She took a step back. Raghnall O'Donnell's daughter had never been one to need coddling. The general had disgusted and scared her, but the brief incident was not worth causing further trouble.

"Then I suggest you get back to the dining hall before someone decides to take a poke at General Bixleigh's bearded little chin," she said.

Cormac hesitated. "Are you sure you're all right?" he asked.

"Aye."

He waited another moment, studying her, then gave a little bow. "In that case, I'll bid you good night."

She nodded stiffly and watched as he turned and walked away from her down the corridor.

•   •   •

Claire was relieved to see that there was no sign of the boorish general when she came down to breakfast the next morning. She had slept late, and it appeared that everyone else had already eaten. Though she hadn't eaten much at dinner, she wasn't really hungry. She picked up a piece of fruit from the table and munched absentmindedly. With English troops due to arrive, she needed to talk with Molly about the food supplies.

"I beg your pardon, Lady Riordan," said a quiet voice from the far end of the hall.

It was the general's aide, Lieutenant Grenville. She smiled at the young man who had tried his best to be nice to her the previous evening. "Good morrow, Lieutenant," she said. "Did you find your accommodations satisfactory?"

The man nodded, walking toward her. "Aye, thank you, milady. But I wanted to offer an apology."

"Apology?"

He stopped a short distance from her and said, "I believe the general was"—he appeared to be searching for the words—"offensive last night, and I wanted to tell you that such is not the custom of the officers of Her Majesty's army."

Claire was surprised. She didn't believe that many junior officers would take the time to apologize for the actions of their commander. "Thank you, Lieutenant," she said. "I'll keep that in mind. I must say I was disappointed."

Grenville hesitated, then said, "General Bixleigh is not always quite . . . *normal*. It's something that's been bothering me for some time, but I'm not sure what I intend to do about it."

The young man looked as if he were in genuine conflict, and Claire felt sorry for him. "I appreciate your telling me, and please be assured that I don't think all Englishmen are like the general."

He seemed satisfied with her answer. "That's kind of you, milady," he said.

"Do you have family back in England, Lieutenant?" she asked.

The strained look left his face and he smiled with genuine warmth. "Aye, milady. I have a new wife waiting for me as soon as this tour is over. She's the prettiest girl in Bath," he added with shy pride.

Claire smiled. "She's a lucky girl as well, to have such a handsome husband coming back to her."

Lieutenant Grenville blushed and looked down at his shoes. "Thank you, milady," he said. "And thank you again for being understanding about the general. Now, er, if you'll excuse me . . ." He straightened to attention, gave a little bow, and walked away.

"The man's a conceited wagtail and a fool," Niall said as he and Cormac rode back to Riordan Hall the next day after riding into Kilmessen to meet with the village armorer. Claire's cleaning efforts had inspired Cormac to put the estate's armaments in order.

"He's full of himself, that's clear enough, but I'm not sure that he's a fool." Cormac's answer was thoughtful. After Bixleigh's behavior toward Claire the previous evening, Cormac would have liked nothing better than to smash the man's face in, but he realized that such an action could have repercussions for the Riordan holdings. "He wields a lot of power, Niall."

"Aye, English power over Irish subjects."

Cormac smiled. "Now you're sounding like the O'Neill himself. I'd not taken you for a rebel, brother."

"I daresay there are many men in Ireland who haven't

yet spoken but who silently cheer on Shane O'Neill in his rebellion against the foreign queen."

"And you'd be one of them?" Cormac stopped his horse and turned to ask his brother the question directly. It was not a trivial matter. Niall had always been a bit of a hothead, and if his words were heard by some people, they might be viewed as treasonous. Even here at Tara, the seat of Ireland's past glories, treason against Elizabeth would be punishable by death.

Niall pulled his horse to a stop beside his brother. They were less than a league from home, but he knew well enough not to bring such talk into Riordan Hall when they were being visited by an English general. That morning, a number of Bixleigh's troops had arrived and were now camped around the hall itself, eating the estate's food and drinking its ale.

"I've no quarrel with the English if they allow us to exist here in peace," Niall said finally.

Cormac nodded approval. "I'm glad to hear it. Bixleigh's irritating, but Sean Riordan seems to think he'll be a fair commander."

"Cousin Sean doesn't necessarily speak for us southern Riordans."

"Nay, but he is kin. You know what Father would have said about that."

"I believe Father would have thrown Bixleigh out of Riordan Hall, English troops and all."

Cormac sighed. "You're wrong. Father would never do anything that would endanger the well-being of his people, and throwing Elizabeth's emissary out on his ear would do just that. Christ, Niall, 'twas my wife he insulted. Don't you think I'd have had the man's head if I hadn't known the consequences?"

Niall was unconvinced. "I've never known you in the past to be afraid of consequences, brother."

"In the past I didn't have the welfare of an entire estate depending on me," Cormac replied angrily. "Nay, brother, you'll have to keep your temper in check this time. We all need to try to get along with General Bixleigh."

Niall clicked to urge his horse forward. "Then let's hope he doesn't linger long. Until he's gone, you can look for me at the stables."

Cormac let him go without arguing. It was probably just as well if Niall stayed out of Bixleigh's way. Then he wouldn't have to worry about his youngest brother's hotheaded ways causing problems.

Even so, Cormac would be glad when Bixleigh and the Riordan cousins left. Niall was not the only Riordan with a temper. In fact, Cormac thought with a grim set to his mouth, if the English general put another hand on Claire, Cormac might just skewer the man himself and damn the consequences.

Claire herself seemed to have recovered from the previous evening's embarrassment. Bixleigh once again dominated the conversation, but he made no further move to touch her. The meal was a marvel, far beyond anything Cormac had ever thought to see at the Riordan table. He made a note to himself to thank Claire, as well as Molly the cook.

"Her Majesty is a benevolent sovereign," Bixleigh was saying. "Except for the very worst of them, such as this Shane O'Neill and his ilk, she's prepared to give pardons to all who will lay down their arms and pledge fealty."

Sean Riordan looked uncomfortable. "General, didn't you say that *all* the rebels would be granted pardon if we could get them to lay down their arms?"

Bixleigh took a long drink of ale. "I believe I said *most.*"

There was a moment of silence around the table. Sean's brother, Dermot, observed gloomily, "If we can't reach an accord soon, 'twill be too late. The moment an English soldier kills an Irishman, there will be no turning back from all-out war."

Bixleigh looked over at Claire. "What's your opinion, Lady Riordan? Do you not think Ireland to be better served as part of the empire of our Gloriana?"

"I believe Her Majesty is a remarkable woman," Claire answered mildly.

"That she is." Bixleigh gave his grinning leer. "A strapping woman as well. You should see her strutting around the court dogged by all those fawning jackanapes. Any one of them would give a fortune in gold to be allowed entry to the queen's 'chamber,' so to speak, but she keeps them at bay like a pack of howling wolves."

Claire was doing her best to hide her distaste at the Englishman. The Riordans appeared to accept this man, and she could not be so rude as to refuse hospitality to a guest in their house. But she found the general's crudeness insufferable. He'd paid little attention to her, but when he had turned his gaze on her, it had been to ogle the low cut of her gown. She hoped the man's visit would be short.

If it hadn't been for the decency of the English lieutenant, her opinion of the English would have been quite shattered. Grenville's warmth helped to make up for the general's bad manners.

The Riordan cousins who had brought the Englishman here also seemed to be thoroughly decent fellows. Claire liked them both immediately.

Sean reminded her a little of an older version of Cormac, though he was calmer and seemed more content. The younger brother, Dermot, was a charmer who had the crooked Riordan grin and knew how to put it to advantage.

"Perhaps the lady Riordan would rather hear something of court fashion, General," Dermot suggested now, giving her a wink of understanding.

Fashion had never been of much interest to Claire, but the subject seemed safer than Bixleigh's lecherous innuendoes, so she nodded.

Bixleigh was only too happy to show off his knowledge of the subject. "Well, now, 'tis her collars that are causing all the talk these days. Huge ruffs. Have all the ladies walking around like stiff-necked geese." He barked out a laugh. "Come to think of it, some of them would be plump and juicy if served up on the right platter. I wouldn't mind stuffin' a number of them meself."

At the far end of the table, Cormac stood, calling an abrupt end to the evening. "I'll escort you to your chambers, milady," he said to Claire.

She stood up gratefully. "Good evening, gentlemen," she said with a nod of her head. Cormac was beside her in an instant, taking her hand to lead her out of the room.

"How much longer do you think the general will be with us?" she whispered as they left the hall together.

"Lord knows," Cormac whispered back. "But another evening or two of this will have me sending for Shane O'Neill myself."

Claire nodded. "I'd heard the English were beasts, but I hadn't believed it up to now."

"Nay, they're not all beasts. I've been to London, and I've met many decent men there."

"Then Elizabeth has picked a poor example to represent them." They'd reached the top of the long stairs, and Claire stopped. "There's no need for you to accompany me. I can see myself to my room."

Cormac appeared to hesitate, but finally he nodded his head and made a little bow. "Sleep well, milady," he said. Then he turned and clattered down the long stairs.

After three solid days of work, Claire and Lindsay had nearly finished sorting through the linen storage closet. Claire had shaken her head more than once over the fine embroidered lawn shirts and underclothes, the lace chemises and collars, that were in tatters from wont of proper airing.

She held up a beautiful little christening dress, full of moth holes. "Look at this, Lindsay. What a shame."

The little redhead nodded. "See there, mum, it has initials sewn along the hem."

They read together *C.B.P.R.* "Cormac Brendan Patrick Riordan," Claire translated.

" 'Twas Lord Riordan's, then, mum?"

"Aye." Claire held the dress up to the light. It was hard to imagine her rugged husband, or indeed any of the Riordan brothers, in such a tiny form. She ran her hand over the finely stitched initials. Had they been sewn by Cormac's mother, the young woman whose life had been so tragically short?

She looked into the chest at the other carefully folded baby garments. Many of the others were also covered with laboriously stitched designs. A sad collection, Claire thought to herself. Once these young mothers had loved and planned and had dreams much like Claire herself. None of them had lived to carry them out. Though the day was warm, she shivered.

"They're eaten through, every one of them," Lindsay said, pulling out several more small outfits. "We should take them out to Molly for rags."

Claire winced. "Nay, I—" she paused. "I'll discard the linens, but these dresses we'll put in the sun for a spell and then wrap them up for keeping. Perhaps someday a new little Riordan will want to see the dress his father wore, or at least what the moths have left of it."

Lindsay dropped her hands to her lap. "Why, mum, could it be true? Are ye in *that way?*"

Claire was caught off guard by Lindsay's interpretation of her remark, since she had assumed that everyone in the household knew that Cormac had yet to sleep in her bed. "Nay, Lindsay," she clarified. "There's no baby on the way, but surely someday one of the Riordans will have a child, and these clothes can be passed on as part of their heritage."

She didn't add that she'd become increasingly convinced that she herself would never be the mother of any future Riordan progeny. In the several days that had passed since Bixleigh and his English troops had left, she'd hardly caught a glimpse of Cormac. He always seemed to have business at the far end of the estate that kept him away until long after everyone else had retired each evening.

Lindsay's freckled cheeks had turned a pretty pink. "Ah, well, 'tis sorry I am if I was too personal, mum. It would be a blessed thing if you and Lord Cormac were to have a wee 'un. The whole castle talks of it."

Claire smiled. The one thing that kept her from complete despair at the state of her marriage was the fact that she seemed to have been able to capture the love of the people at Riordan Hall. Cormac's brothers were now always friendly and affectionate and seemed genuinely pleased to have her living with them. Their cousin Dermot, who had stayed behind when his brother Sean left with Bixleigh, flirted with her outrageously. It was only her husband who remained aloof.

"They told me I'd find you up to your ears in work, as usual, sister."

Claire looked up to see Eileen standing in the low doorway of the closet. She jumped up with a cry and ran to embrace her. "Eily! How wonderful to see you!"

The two sisters clung to each other for several moments, but whereas Claire was all smiles, Eileen's expression was reserved. Finally, Claire pulled back and asked, "What's wrong? Why have you come?"

Eileen stepped into the closet and glanced at Lindsay, who had stood and was waiting with her head bowed respectfully. "Of course you remember Lindsay," Claire said.

"Pleased to see ye again, mum," Lindsay said with a little curtsy.

Eileen smiled at the girl briefly, then turned to Claire, her mind obviously on her mission. " 'Tis Rory."

Claire clasped at her throat. "He's not—"

"Nay, he lives. But his wound still festers, long after it should have healed. Father says we should take his arm before he loses his life, but Rory won't hear of it. And he says that you're the only one knows how to cure him."

Claire bit her lip. There was no question about what she would do. Rory was her baby brother—of course she must go to him. But she wanted to be sure her leaving would not be interpreted as abandoning the purpose that had brought her here. The peace between the families must hold, even if she herself had returned to O'Donnell House. What would Cormac think about her leaving? she wondered fleetingly.

Lindsay seemed to be reading her thoughts. "He'll understand, mum. 'Tis natural that ye must go when yer kin needs ye."

"We should leave immediately, Claire," Eileen urged.

"When I left, Rory's fever was rising again and he was starting to rave."

There was no help for it. With a sudden burst of energy, Claire clapped her hands together and said to Lindsay, "Just push all the rest of these things to the back of the closet and leave them until I return. But first, fetch Molly so we can discuss what they'll eat while I'm gone. And send someone to the stables to bring Cinder around. I won't pack much—"

Eileen reached out to pull her sister into another embrace. "I'm so glad you're coming home," she whispered.

Claire looked down at the rumpled pile of baby clothes. "Aye," she said with a deep breath. " 'Twill be good to be home."

"What do you mean, she's gone?" Cormac had arrived home late to find Eamon, Niall, and Dermot still in the dining hall, more than a little drunk.

Niall flung his hand in the air. "Gone! Your bird has flown, brother, and, if you ask me, 'tis exactly what you deserve."

"Shut up, Niall," Eamon admonished, then turned to Cormac. "Her sister came for her. It seems that her brother's wound has not healed. He may lose his arm, if not his life."

"If my aim had been what it should have, the little weasel would be bothering no one but the earthworms," Niall muttered.

"You should be hoping that Claire's powders can do for him what they did for your horse, Niall," Eamon snapped. "If the boy dies, there'll be more blood spilled between our families."

"When did she leave?" Cormac's voice sounded strained.

"This afternoon. She asked me to explain the circumstances." Eamon looked uncomfortable. "She said that since she's never sure at what hour you'll appear, she couldn't afford to wait to speak to you herself."

"I told you, Cormac, the woman's too bloody good for you." Niall's words were definitely slurred. "Hell, shee'sh too good for the whole bloody lot of us."

Cormac ignored him. "Did she say when she would be back?"

Eamon shook his head. "I reckon 'twill be when the boy's healed."

Cormac walked over to the table and served himself a mug of ale, then drank it halfway down. "But she said she *would* be back when he's healed?"

Eamon answered slowly, "Er . . . nay, she didn't really talk about coming back."

"Didn't you ask her?" Cormac roared.

Eamon and Niall exchanged a glance. Finally Eamon answered quietly, "Nay, brother, I didn't ask her."

Dermot had been listening quietly to the brothers' exchange. "She'll be back," he said.

Cormac turned on him and growled, "How do you know?"

Dermot smiled, undisturbed by his surliness. "Because the woman's in love with you. Though—no offense, cousin—God knows why."

Cormac merely scowled at him.

Dermot shrugged and said, "If you ask me, you're more than half in love with her, too. You're just not ready to admit it."

Cormac put the mug of ale to his lips again and tipped back his head to drain the draft to the last drop.

Rory looked better than he had in the three days since she'd arrived, and Claire had decided to take a few moments away from the sickroom to walk in the O'Donnell garden. She'd missed her flowers. The Riordan Hall gardens were limited to vegetables and the few flowering herbs needed for cooking and medicine. At O'Donnell House an entire section of the grounds was devoted to sheer beauty alone. Her mother had planned the original garden, and she and Eileen had tended it since their mother's death.

She particularly liked the roses, which were still blossoming in profusion, in spite of the lateness of the season. Their sweet scent filled the small arbor, where they twined up a white lattice.

"I thought I'd find you here, daughter." Lost in her musings, she jumped at the sound of her father's voice. She hadn't seen him come, but Raghnall O'Donnell stood at the far end of the arbor, watching her.

"Rory's doing well," she told him with a smile as he walked through the flowers toward her. She offered her cheek for a kiss.

"Aye, I've just been to his room. He was complaining about his supper, while at the same time teasing Bridget so that the poor lass was one big blush." Bridget was a young serving girl whose expression turned moony every time Rory was around. "I reckoned that he was better," Raghnall added dryly.

Claire laughed. "Aye, he'll be back to normal in no time. The arm only needed a good cleaning out and an herbal poultice. It should have been done long ago."

"We were lacking a nurse," her father pointed out. "Ah, Clairy, we do miss you something fierce. Are you sure you're doing the right thing, exiling yourself from your family? Are the Riordans treating you well in their fancy home? Is your husband good to you?"

Claire had learned her lesson after her disastrous wedding night. This time, she'd not confessed to anyone, not even Eileen, that Cormac had yet to make her his wife in more than name alone. "They treat me fine, Father."

They moved slowly to the center of the arbor where a small wrought-iron bench sat among a bed of bright marigolds. Raghnall took her hand and drew her to a seat beside him, then he lowered his head to catch her gaze. "I'd like to know that you're being paid the honor due a daughter of mine."

His light blue eyes studied her gravely, as though able to see the thoughts behind her words. She'd never been able to keep much from her father, but this was one secret she was determined to guard. "There was a bit of unpleasantness with an English officer who came to stay last week," she admitted, hoping to distract his attention from the subject of Cormac.

Raghnall frowned. "English?"

"Aye, the queen's emissary—a General Bixleigh."

"Another Satan's spawn, no doubt, sent to hold our necks to the ground with his foreign boot."

Claire was surprised at her father's vehemence. Raghnall was usually a man of peace, whenever possible. "I was not impressed by the man," she told him.

"I should think not. What kind of unpleasantness did you mean?"

Claire shrugged. "Nothing much. He was just a rude sort of fellow."

"Why in the devil did the Riordans have him in their home? They're loyal Irishmen. What's a queen's man doing in their home?"

In addition to sharp, Raghnall's tone was now suspicious. All at once Claire realized that Bixleigh was more than a disagreeable supper companion. He represented power and evidently, as far as her father was concerned, the enemy.

"I believe the Riordans were merely giving him and his men shelter for a time. They only stayed for three days."

She decided that she wouldn't mention that Bixleigh had been accompanied by Riordan kin, since her father seemed indignant enough at the idea of the family providing the Englishmen with food and lodging.

"Ultan Riordan would have thrown the man out," Raghnall said. "I'm surprised his sons did not do likewise."

Claire was sorry she had ever mentioned the matter. "Well, he's gone now, and there's an end to it."

Raghnall was running his fingers over the soft petals of a dark orange marigold, but at Claire's words, he closed his fist around the blossom, crushing it. "Nay, daughter, 'tis not the end. I fear 'tis only the beginning."

Claire felt a shiver of alarm. "What do you mean? Bixleigh and his men have gone, heading north somewhere. He shouldn't bother us again."

Raghnall shook his head. "North is exactly where your brothers have headed."

"Seamus and Conn?"

Raghnall looked grave. "Aye. I didn't want to bother you with the matter while you were involved with nursing Rory, but Conn and Seamus have taken a number of the men and have gone to Ulster to join forces with the rebel leader, Shane O'Neill."

Nine

"Go on ahead, then!" Claire snapped at her brother. "Go on and let some English sword do what the blood poisons couldn't. I've washed my hands of you."

Rory had been up from his sickbed for two days. Though he was still weak, he had insisted on going out to the stable to work on his armor and weapons. Claire had found him there, cleaning one of the new shooting sticks. "Would you have us wait until the foreign witch sends troops to bed down in every home in Ireland?" her brother asked.

In spite of her anger, Claire could not contain her curiosity about the new weapon. Heedless of her silk skirt, she plopped down in the hay beside her brother. " 'Tis called a musket?"

"Aye. The English soldiers have them now, so we're forced to arm ourselves as well."

Claire leaned cautiously closer to peer at the odd looking weapon. "Is it very powerful?"

Her brother's eyes flashed. "Aye. You fill it with gunpowder and it can blow a man's head clear off his shoulders, helmet and all."

His graphic words restored her anger. "Is that why you're so eager that you intend to ride away when you're still weak as a mewling pup? So some English soldier can blow your head off?"

"Nay, 'tis so I can go and blow *his* head off." As usual, it was difficult resisting her brother's grin, but Claire's heart was heavy as she left the stable and walked back to the house. If the talk she had heard during General Bixleigh's visit were true, before long there would be a confrontation between the English troops and the rebels. Cormac's cousins were supporting the English. If it came to war, would Cormac join them? *There's nothing more important than blood,* he'd told her.

Her marriage may have kept her family and Cormac's from fighting each other at Tara, but if the English started a civil war, she couldn't think of anything she could do to keep the families from meeting each other on the field of battle. Two of her brothers were already with the O'Neill, and now Rory was soon to join them. He'd paid no attention to her pleas to stay home so that her father would have at least one son safe by his side.

It was almost sundown. She'd always loved this time of day. The reddish gold rays splashed over the gravel path that wound through the gorse bushes up to the front door of O'Donnell House. Through the wavy panes of the big front windows she could see her father at his nightly ritual, warming a poker in the fire to steam his mug of ale. Her heart swelled. Why was it that men had to ride off to fight and be killed when all they should need in life could be found in the simple pleasures of home and family?

As she had so often throughout her life when she was feeling the need for comfort, she sought out her sister. Eileen was in the solar, attacking an embroidery hoop with uncharacteristic vehemence. "I've had to rip it out three times," she explained as Claire pulled a stool up next to her chair. "What's so infernally virtuous about tiny stitches, anyway?"

Her words reminded Claire of the embroidered baby

clothes she'd left in the closet at Riordan Hall. Had the Riordan wives fumed like Eileen when their stitches had not turned out as they should?

"Come back to it tomorrow, Eily. I promise you it will magically right itself. That's the way it is with sewing."

Eileen sighed and threw the hoop, needle and all, into a basket on the floor. "Aye, and 'tis almost time for supper. Did you have any luck convincing Rory?"

"What do you think?"

"I think if Conn and Seamus are off on an adventure, he's not about to sit home and twiddle his thumbs."

"Of course not." The two sisters exchanged a look of shared understanding.

"There's nothing we can do about it," Eileen said. "You always think you can do something to make things better, Clairy, but this time I don't see how. At least it will keep them from fighting the Riordans." Her expression brightened as a thought struck her. "You won't have to go back."

The same thought had occurred to Claire. If her brothers were all safely engaged fighting the English in the north, what was the need for her to continue her sham marriage? The idea left her feeling curiously bereft. "They'll be waiting for me," she said weakly.

"Let them wait until doomsday, Claire. What do you care? You only went to keep the peace among the Riordan brothers and your own. With Conn and Seamus and Rory safely away, there's no reason for you to be there." Claire was silent, and Eileen, who had always been able to read her sister's thoughts as surely as though they'd been spoken aloud, looked suddenly thunderstruck. "Unless you *want* to go back," she added.

Still Claire said nothing.

Eileen clapped her hands. "It's true, isn't it? You want

to go back. Oh, Clairy, don't tell me that you've fallen in love with the man after what he did to you."

Claire stiffened. "Don't talk nonsense. The marriage is one of convenience. Why, Cormac Riordan hardly acknowledges that I exist."

Eileen's blue eyes were troubled. "But you wish he would acknowledge it," she declared softly.

To Claire's chagrin, tears stung her eyes. She blinked hard. "I simply think that this thing isn't yet over between the Riordans and the O'Donnells. In fact, all the trouble with the English might make it all worse. The English general stayed at Riordan Hall when he was here. And now our kin are off siding with the rebels."

Eileen was shaking her head. "Nay, Clairy. Remember 'tis your sister you're speaking to now. This thing has gone beyond sacrificing yourself for the family. I can see it in your eyes, lovey, and in the wringing of your hands." She pointed to Claire's lap, where her hands were gripped tightly together. "You've fallen for the man. Or for some man." Her mouth opened in horror. " 'Tis himself you've fallen for, isn't it? Not one of the brothers."

Claire smiled faintly. "Aye, 'tis himself."

Eileen let out a breath. "Well, then, I don't see the problem. I still say that you're a muddlehead for letting yourself fall for a man who insulted you, but since when has love ever been logical? The lucky thing is—he's already your husband, Clairy. 'Tis all legal and binding."

Claire bit her lip. She still hadn't talked to Eileen about the exact state of her marriage. "Legal doesn't make it right—or happy."

"Nay, 'tis the people who do that, not the laws or the church." Since the death of their mother, the O'Donnells had looked to Claire for advice and support, but in matters of the heart, it had always seemed to Claire that

Eileen was more like the older sister. Something had made her wise beyond her years.

"Aye," Claire agreed. " 'Tis the people who make it so, and if the people are unwilling, all the laws in the world won't make it happen."

Eileen slipped out of her chair and slid to her knees in front of her sister, prying Claire's clasped hands apart to hold them in her own. "Our father raised us to carry ourselves proud, Claire. Are you sure you want to be in a place where you're not wanted?"

Now there were tears in earnest, but Claire ignored them as she answered, "I learned all about the O'Donnell pride, Eily. But Father never taught us how to make the pride overrule the heart."

Eileen sat in silence for a long moment, still holding her sister's hands. Finally she said, "That may be because in a contest between love and pride, love will be the victor every time."

Claire's nose had started to drip. She pulled her hands away from Eileen's and wiped her nose and eyes with her sleeve. "Eily, Cormac has never taken me to his bed."

Eileen's eyes widened. "Never? Even now that you live under his roof?"

Claire nodded. "I sleep alone in the big master bed-chamber while each night Cormac retires to his own room on the other side of the hall."

"What ails the man?" Eileen asked with a puff of indignation.

Claire shook her head sadly. "I reckon 'tis that he doesn't want me."

Eileen rocked back on her folded legs and regarded her sister with a firm expression. "I don't believe it. 'Tis simply not possible that any man with even half the brains of Cormac Riordan would not want you. Have you asked him why?"

Her blunt words made Claire laugh in spite of the tears. "What would you have me say? Lord Riordan, my sister thinks you are a fool not to want me?"

"Aye. Something of the sort." She lowered her voice. "Mayhap the man has—you know—some kind of *problem*. Something that could affect his, um, *abilities.*"

Claire laughed again, and the tears stopped. "I'm relatively certain Cormac Riordan is as healthy as any man—in *all* areas." A vivid memory of their kisses in front of the fire flashed through her mind, making her cheeks grow pink. "Aye, he's healthy enough."

Eileen's eyes sparkled with amusement. "Ah, sister, I won't be indelicate enough to ask you to tell me how you can be certain of such a matter in a man whom you profess to have scarcely seen. But I'm suspecting that there is more to this story than you are confessing."

"Perhaps," Claire admitted. "But don't you see, Eily? That just makes his indifference all the worse."

"Yet in spite of this indifference, you want him?"

Claire nodded miserably.

"Well, then, go after him. That's what you'd do if you were one of the maids down in Kilmessen. Down there a girl sets her cap for a man and before long she has him following her around like a puppy dog and picking daisies for her hair."

Claire shook her head. "I don't know how they do it."

"I don't either," Eileen agreed with a shrug. "But they do."

"I'm not sure Cormac Riordan is the type for such games."

"According to Nancy Hardy, all men are." Nancy was the daughter of the owner of the only tavern in Kilmessen. Her easy ways and cheerfully blatant sensuality had always been a source of fascination to the O'Donnell sisters. "And she should know, she's sampled enough of them."

"But we've never been able to figure out how she does it."

Eileen jumped suddenly to her feet and reached out to Claire. "So let's go ask her!" she cried.

Claire let herself be pulled up from the stool. "I don't think—" she began.

Eileen shook her head. "Clairy, if you want to ensnare your husband, you've got to learn the things women have known since the time of the ancients—things Father was never able to teach us. I wouldn't mind a few lessons on the subject myself."

Eileen's eyes were dancing, and Claire caught some of her sister's infectious mood. The truth was, she herself was curious about the secrets of women like Nancy Hardy who seemed to attract men so naturally and with such zest. The days spent with Cormac at Riordan Hall had only increased her curiosity.

"Very well," she said, suddenly decisive. What could it hurt? "Tomorrow we might find ourselves some errands to do in the vicinity of the Hardys' tavern."

Cormac had discovered that he wasn't the only one who was missing Claire. In fact, it was almost as if a spell had come over the entire hall, putting them all in a kind of trance. Work was being neglected. Meals were once again haphazard or nonexistent. He'd been out to the kitchens several times to discuss the matter with Molly, and she'd only sniffed and said that she was waiting for her ladyship to plan out the menus.

The gardening crew, which Claire had prodded into a system of hoeing and weeding and reaping that had doubled the estate production, had now fallen back into their old hit-and-miss ways, missing some days entirely.

Aidan and Niall had gotten into a tremendous row out at the stables and Aidan had threatened to leave Riordan altogether and return to his family down in Cork.

Lindsay, Claire's maid who had stayed behind when her mistress went back to O'Donnell House, walked about with a woeful face and perpetually reddened eyes.

"Hellfire, Eamon, things seemed to manage well enough before she ever came here, didn't they?" Cormac asked his brother as the two sat side by side on the settle in front of the great room fireplace.

"I reckon." Eamon's tone was noncommittal.

"We've a house full of servants who should be more than capable of filling the shoes of one woman."

"Aye. If they're willing, and if they know what they're supposed to do. 'Twas Claire giving the orders that had things hopping around here so all-of-a-sudden."

Cormac put his elbows on his knees and leaned toward the fire. Claire had been gone nine days, and instead of getting used to her absence, people seemed to be getting more out of sorts each day. "I suppose you'll tell me that you miss her as well," he grumbled.

"She was a sight more pleasant company than you've been this past week," Eamon confirmed.

"She's taking care of her brother. 'Tis a family thing." Cormac knew his voice sounded defensive. He also knew that Eamon, along with most everyone else at Riordan Hall, was blaming Claire's absence on Cormac himself.

"Aye," Eamon said mildly.

"But you think I should go ask her to come back."

Eamon turned his head to look at his brother. "Back to what? To a household of strangers and a cold bed at night?"

Cormac glared back at him. "We're no longer strangers. As to the bed—do you want to lose her completely in a few short months? Now that we all really know her—her laugh and her spirit and how she orders around those big men up at the garden and then wrinkles up her nose and smiles so that they love every order she gives? Can you imagine losing her?"

Eamon sat up straight on the bench. "Jesu, Cormac, Dermot was right. You've fallen in love with the lass," he said, his eyes wide.

Cormac shook his head. "I'm just telling you how difficult it would be for all of us if the Riordan curse claimed another victim."

Eamon was regarding his brother with amazement. "I never thought I'd see the day. My big brother—besotted."

Cormac stood impatiently and walked over to throw wood on the fire. "Don't talk nonsense. I'm trying to figure what to do. Obviously, people here want her back."

"*People* do," Eamon repeated. His expression had changed to one of merriment and his dark eyes teased, but Cormac remained serious.

"Aye, people . . . everyone."

"So what are you going to do about it?" Eamon asked.

"I could send word that it's time for her to come home."

Eamon made a face of disgust at the suggestion.

"Or . . . I suppose I could go fetch her myself."

Eamon shambled to his feet and went over to give Cormac a hard slap on the shoulder. "Aye, brother. You could do that very thing."

The Hardy Tavern was a cozy place. Unlike the busy coach stop inns on the main highways, it was designed for the local folks. No one ever came to Kilmessen unless they were lost. Eileen and Claire had been inside the tavern once or twice with their brothers, when they'd been to town and needed refreshment on a particularly hot day, but the visits had been rare. They had never before come without an escort.

As usual, the taproom was full of men. Claire recognized most of them from the village, but that didn't keep her from feeling uncomfortable at all those pairs of male eyes watching her.

Nancy greeted them with her usual broad smile. "This is a surprise, ladies," she said. "What can I serve ye today?"

Claire looked around the room, where the conversation had almost totally ceased. Suddenly the idea they had had the previous evening at O'Donnell House seemed ridiculous. She looked at Eileen. "Perhaps we'd better forget about this," she whispered to Eileen.

But her sister shook her head and smiled back at Nancy. She leaned toward the fulsome barmaid and said in a conspiratorial whisper, "We've not come for refreshments, Nancy. We've come for advice."

Nancy tossed her head, setting her blond ringlets bouncing. "Lord love me, ladies. Advice from Nancy? I've not heard that request before."

Eileen looked around. Most of the men in the room seemed to be listening. She turned back to Nancy. " 'Tis advice of a rather, um, delicate nature."

Nancy's eyes widened and she gave a gap-toothed smile. "Now don't that sound juicy?" She giggled. "Just wait a minute and I'll be right with ye."

Eileen and Claire stood self-consciously while Nancy stripped off her apron and fetched a young lad from the keg room to take over her post. Then she motioned to the two sisters to follow her up a narrow stairway that led to the Hardy living quarters on the second floor. The stairs opened on a well-furnished room that looked little different from the parlor at O'Donnell House. Evidently the tavern business did very well for the Hardy family.

Nancy motioned to a wide settle across the room. "Have a seat, ladies, and I'll fetch us something to wet our gullets."

Claire and Eileen sat stiffly on the high-backed settle, feeling unavoidably prim in the face of Nancy's free and easy demeanor. She handed them each a mug of cider, and Claire tried to make her "thank you" sound relaxed.

After she'd served a drink for herself, Nancy ignored the other benches and boosted herself to sit on the thick table in the center of the room, her feet propped on a low bench. "Now, ladies," she said with a grin, "tell me about this delicate matter of yers."

It took several minutes before either one of the sisters could get up the courage to get to the heart of what they had come to learn, but once the subject was broached, Nancy's matter-of-fact manner made it as easy as talking about the making of cheese.

"Scents are good," she told them. "Ye can make sweetwaters out of lavender or roses or lemongrass. For some reason the creatures seem to like a sweet smell." She accompanied the words with a sly wink.

Claire found herself paying close attention, but it was Eileen who had the most direct questions. "Where, er, does one put these scents exactly?" she asked.

"Well, everywhere. Rub it on yer arms, yer neck, yer bubbies." Both sisters blushed, but Nancy continued on blithely, "Wash yer hair with it. Hair drives 'em wild, don't ye know?"

Claire and Eileen did *not* know, but neither one pointed out their lack of knowledge.

"There's a talc recipe I can give ye. That makes ye smell pretty *and* makes yer skin nice and soft. Makes 'em want to run their fingers *all* over ye."

Claire was beginning to feel warm.

Unconcerned with the effect she was having on her audience, Nancy continued, "Let me see what else." She tapped a finger to her temple, looking thoughtful. "There's oysters, of course."

Claire looked at Eileen, who shrugged, as ignorant as her sister.

"Which is more how ye eat 'em than anything else," Nancy continued, "since I'm not sure that I believe the other."

"Er . . . how you eat them?" Eileen asked.

"Aye, don't ask me why. They like to watch you eat. Nothing like slowly sucking an oyster into your mouth. Or, say, a nice chicken leg. You eat it slow and lingery, swirling your tongue a bit, then kind of moisten your lips with ale and lick them. There's a technique to it," she said breezily. "It has 'em swelling their hose in no time." Nancy let her legs fall open under her billowy skirt and made a lewd gesture.

Eileen and Claire looked at each other, eyes wide, then turned back to their teacher. "What else?" Eileen asked. Her voice was a little strained.

"The clothes are the most important. You've got to tantalize. Show a little, but not too much. Just a bit of shoulder here, a length of ankle there." She hiked up her skirt to look down at her legs. "Ankles are ugly things, when you think about it, but they seem to intrigue the blokes."

Eileen and Claire self-consciously looked down at their feet.

" 'Tis good to wear fabrics soft to the touch," Nancy continued. She rubbed her hands sensuously over her own bodice. "If you're all whaleboned up and encased in stiff linen, you may as well be wearing a suit of armor. You want silky and flowing, like satin or velvet. And petticoats." Nancy jumped off the table and gave an exaggerated sway of her hips. "There's nothing more intriguing to a man than the swish of hidden petticoats."

By the time Claire and Eileen left their generous mentor with a final, self-conscious thank-you, they both felt as if they'd spent the afternoon drinking their father's store of whiskey. As they walked slowly along the grassy shortcut from the village to O'Donnell House, Eileen was more talkative than her sister.

"We probably need to take into account the kind of men Nancy encounters," she said. "And what they might expect of a woman like her. If we're talking about gentlemen and *ladies,* things might not be so"—she struggled for the word—"so *shameless.*"

Though she'd been more quiet, Claire had been less shocked than her sister by Nancy's suggestions. Of course, she reminded herself, Eileen had never lain in a man's arms as she had with Cormac. Claire suspected that things that might have seemed shameless in theory somehow became less so when one was in the actual situation. Still, in all her youthful fantasies of love and romance, she'd never considered that the whole thing might be reduced to some kind of a calculated campaign.

"So are you?" Eileen asked, a little impatient.

"Am I what?"

"I asked if you are quite sure that you want to have a husband if it means parading around half-naked and dousing yourself with lotions and powders? Doesn't it all seem a bit absurd?"

Claire smiled. "That's just it, Eily. Love is absurd. Or at least, I have yet to make much sense out of the phenomenon."

"So you really want to go back there—to Riordan Hall?"

Claire hesitated a moment, then nodded. "If I don't go back, I'll always wonder . . ." Her voice trailed off.

Eileen kicked at a little stone that lay in the path, and said grumpily, "If you ask me, a man who would need scents and playacting in order to show some interest would not be worth having, but if you must go back, then you must. And so will I."

"You?"

"Aye. I'm going with you. If you're truly determined to have Cormac, I think I'd better go check out what manner of man he is. And I want to be sure those Riordans are treating my big sister the way they should."

O'Donnell House lay just down the hill. Claire's flower garden was bursting with fall colors and the arbor roses were in full bloom. It would be hard to leave her home again for drafty Riordan Hall. Eileen's presence would be a welcome touch of home, though she wondered how the Riordans would take to having two females living among them.

"With Rory leaving to join Conn and Seamus, 'twould leave Father by himself," she argued.

"He has Fiona and Mrs. Pratt in the kitchen, and you know the house is always full of O'Donnell kin. I'll make it a short visit—just to be sure you're all right. Father will want me to go."

Claire gave her sister a sideways glance. "You'll have to promise not to laugh if I suddenly take to wearing scents."

Eileen giggled. "I'll be the soul of discretion."

As discretion had never been one of Eileen's strengths, Claire had her doubts, but she nodded. It would feel less lonely going back with her sister along. "For a visit, then," she agreed.

"And who knows? Cormac's brothers are brawny fellows. I just may be wearing some of those scents myself."

Claire rolled her eyes. "You'll do nothing of the sort. I'll not have them thinking my sister some kind of a hoyden."

" 'Tis ever the way," Eileen complained with a pout. "The older sister is the one with all the amusement." She gave Claire a little push, then started running down the path. "Shall we make it a race?" she called over her shoulder.

Claire picked up her skirts and scrambled after her. " 'Tis not a fair contest!" she yelled. "You started first."

They'd run the same race countless times as girls. After an afternoon thinking about such an adult matter as lovemaking, it felt good to tear heedlessly along the lane like youngsters. With her head start, Eileen was several yards ahead. She looked back over her shoulder and grinned defiantly. "There are some things the baby sister will always do better," she yelled.

Claire laughed and shook her head, then increased her pace. The wind tore at her clothes and ripped a ribbon from her hair, but she kept running, slowly gaining on Eileen. They were nearly side by side as they reached the gate that led to the stone walk up to the front door. With a sudden burst of energy, Claire darted past her sister, through the gate, and up the path. She half stumbled the last few feet, then collapsed against the big front door, shouting, "I won!"

Eileen came up behind her and fell on Claire's back, laughing hard. "You pushed me," she panted.

"Nay, I never touched you. 'Twas a fair win."

"At the gate," Eileen argued.

A deep voice from the direction of the garden said, "I believe your sister has the right of it, Mistress Eileen. 'Twas a fair win."

Both sisters turned at once to see Cormac emerging from the end of the rounded arbor. "My apologies, sister," he said. "I would judge Lady Riordan to be the victor."

Claire's face flamed. She patted futilely at her hair, which had tumbled out of its pins, then blurted, "What are you doing here?"

Eileen had straightened up, the laughter dying from her face, but her greeting was more gracious. "Welcome to O'Donnell House, Lord Riordan," she said.

Cormac walked over to the two sisters, giving Claire time to catch her breath and offer a more gracious welcome herself. "Aye, you are certainly welcome, milord," she said. "But I'm curious about the purpose of your visit."

"We had word at Riordan Hall that your brother's arm is now healing," he said.

She nodded. "Aye." He was even more strikingly handsome than she had remembered. It had only been a few days since she'd left, yet the sight of him was making her jaw feel suddenly disabled.

"I'm glad to hear it," he said.

There was a moment of silence. Finally Claire managed to ask, "Did you come to see about Rory?"

The sun glinted off his dark eyes. "Nay," he said. "I came to ask you to come home."

Ten

Eileen's presence at the big Riordan Hall table finished the transformation that had begun when Claire herself had first arrived. In addition to the improved fare, which had resumed as soon as Claire returned and started working with Molly again, the atmosphere was lighter. The men seemed more willing to laugh and leave their talk of war and the growing tensions with England to after-dinner discussion in the parlor. Each night there was a jockeying of positions to see which of the Riordan kin would sit next to one of the pretty O'Donnell sisters.

Dermot, who still appeared to be in no hurry about joining his brother with Bixleigh in the north, usually managed to have the place of honor with one or the other. His attentions were equally divided between Eileen and Claire, and, for that matter, he usually had a charming word or two for any other female, servant or otherwise, who made an appearance. Even Molly was not ignored. On more than one occasion, he had the old cook blushing like a young girl.

"I don't think we really need those lessons Nancy gave us," Eileen said, laughing, as the two sisters climbed the stairs after supper on her third night at Riordan Hall. Her cheeks were flushed from wine and the barrage of compliments she'd received from the handsome Riordan men.

Claire smiled. "I've no doubt you could have the pick of the lot, Eily, if you were of a mind. Cousin Dermot seems to cast a fine eye on you with regularity."

"When he's not casting it on you or one of the serving girls," she agreed.

Claire laughed. "Well, there's Eamon and Niall."

"Nay. They're handsome boys, those Riordans, but a touch too rough for my liking. And I think you've already got the best one. He doesn't have as much to say, but he certainly is a brawny lad."

Claire didn't answer. Though Cormac himself had come to fetch her back to Riordan Hall, nothing had changed in their marriage since her return. He still left her each night with a polite "good evening" and went to sleep in his old room in the opposite wing. Nancy's advice may not be needed to attract the interest of the other Riordan males, but Claire was beginning to think that resorting to feminine wiles was the only way she was going to get Cormac's attention.

She said good night to Eileen, who had been given a room next to Claire's, and wandered slowly to her bedchamber, trying to remember the things Nancy had told them. Eating? She ruled that out. She couldn't see how watching her eat could possibly attract Cormac, with her at one end of the table and him at the other in a crowded room full of his kinsmen.

Clothing? She looked down at her stiff linen dress, the bodice properly laced over a heavy corset. She had softer gowns, velvets and satins. Raghnall O'Donnell had never stinted when it came to clothing his daughters. But she'd put the frocks aside when she'd discovered the amount of work to be done around Riordan Hall.

She reached her chamber and walked over to the wardrobe chest. Her favorite dress was a watered blue silk with an inset of green brocade in the skirt and the bodice. The neck was cut daringly low with a gauzy collar that just hinted at modesty. It was definitely too fine to wear cleaning or helping in the kitchens or tending animals in the stable. But perhaps she'd give it a try for supper tomorrow night.

She ran her fingers over the smooth material and remembered how Nancy had looked as she had smoothed her hands over her own dress. *They like things soft to the touch*, the tavern maid had said. And scents.

Slowly she walked over to the little dressing table and picked up a jar that Eileen had proudly presented her with earlier that day.

"I've made the talc, Claire. Just smell. Isn't it luscious?"

Nancy had told them that the talc was used by the finest ladies in the court of Queen Elizabeth herself. Claire had had her doubts about how a tavern wench in Kilmessen could possibly know such a thing, but Eileen had carefully taken down the recipe—orris root, marjoram, rose petals, cloves, calamus root. Claire fingered the jar thoughtfully.

She wasn't ready to give up on her marriage yet. If fine silk and orris root powder were what it took to arouse Cormac's interest, then so be it. Tomorrow would be the test.

She put the powder carefully back on the table, slipped on her nightrail, and climbed up into bed. Her resolve was tinged with irritation. It didn't seem fair that she had to go to such lengths for something that should be natural and easy between a husband and wife.

She stared into the darkness for a long time, considering. Finally she came to a decision. If after all this, Cormac was still indifferent, she was going to pack her things and leave Riordan Hall for good.

• • •

"I thought we'd have chicken for supper tonight," Claire said loudly.

Eileen's head went up.

The two sisters were helping Molly in the kitchens.

"Chicken, mum?" Molly asked, surprised. "We been cooking the brisket all morning."

"Aye, but I've, um, a hankering for fresh chicken."

Eileen choked on a piece of rhubarb she'd been sucking. "I had no idea you were so fond of chicken, sister," she said with a grin when she'd recovered from the coughing.

Claire ignored her and walked over to the drying rack, where two fat capons were hanging. "These should do," she said, plucking one off its hook.

Molly continued to look confused. "And the brisket?"

"We'll serve both, like they do in the fancy London houses. I've heard that in Elizabeth's court there may be a dozen meat dishes at one sitting."

"Are we expecting visitors tonight?" Molly asked.

"Nay, 'tis simply . . . Well, now that we've improved the quality of the fare here at Riordan Hall, I think 'tis time we worked on the variety."

Eileen had popped the rhubarb back in her mouth. Behind Molly's back she licked it with an exaggerated swirl of her tongue. "I think chicken would be delightful," she said with another impish grin.

Claire made a face at her sister, then grabbed the stalk of rhubarb from between her lips and threw it into the basket of parings that was to go out to the pigs. "In that case, don't spoil your appetite," she said.

The evening started out with some promise. Claire could see Cormac's eyes brighten as she came into the dining hall in her silk dress. She thought she noticed him straightening up and listening when she swished the voluminous petticoats she'd donned for the occasion.

She was afraid, however, that she may have overdone the talc. The room seemed to reek of the stuff wherever she went. Every time she moved her arms, she'd get a fresh whiff of powder, and it would make her burst out an unladylike and decidedly unromantic sneeze.

It was Dermot, not Cormac, who commented on her finery. "You look especially lovely tonight, cousin," he'd said. Then he walked to the end of the table to seat her while Cormac watched, unmoving.

Eileen gave a pretty pout. "Fie on you, Dermot. Claire has a husband to see to her needs, whereas I stand here alone like a neglected spinster at a ball."

Dermot grinned and pulled out Claire's chair, then scurried around the table to where Eileen was waiting impatiently, tapping her foot. "Ah, it's always been my trouble," he said. "The world is too full of beautiful women. What's one to do?"

Claire smiled at the banter, but secretly she, too, was hoping that Cormac would reward the pains she had taken with her appearance by paying her some notice. Instead, he stood watching her from the far end of the table, an odd look on his face.

She sighed and picked up a fork to signal the others to begin eating.

In addition to the more personal suggestions, Nancy had offered advice on conversation. "Get them to talk about past exploits," she'd said, "which is an easy enough job, when all is said and done, since most of them are more than eager to bend your ear about their own bravery."

After the usual mealtime pleasantries had been observed, Claire picked up a chicken leg and asked loudly, "Is it true what they say, my lord husband, that you yourself once caught the attention of the great English queen?"

The buzz of conversation died as everyone waited for Cormac's answer. "I went to London, aye, to try to stop the skirmishes. The queen had called for negotiations over the the troubles in the northwest."

Claire looked up in surprise. She knew only vaguely of the strife that had raged in the northern part of the country ever since the Parliament had passed the Acts of Supremacy. Her father and brothers had always held that Ireland wanted no part of England, or its church. She assumed that the Riordans, who were Catholic just like most families in the Midlands, would feel the same.

"You went to negotiate?" she asked.

"Aye. For all the good it did, since the conflict rages to this day. Still, it was worth the experience to see the queen."

"My brother caught the queen's eye, all right," Niall added. "She even gave him a gift."

Cormac scowled at him. "The queen said she appreciated my efforts to keep the peace between our lands. She gave me a dagger with a carved swan in honor of the Riordan crest."

Claire had seen Cormac's unusual swan dagger, but had assumed that it was a family heirloom. She gnawed grumpily at her chicken leg. Perhaps bringing up the subject of another woman, even a queen, had not been a good idea.

"Do you think such efforts would be successful now that Shane O'Neill has organized in the north?" Eileen asked.

"In my mind, it's never too late to talk about peace," Cormac answered. "But 'twill be hard to settle the grievances without bloodshed."

As usual when the subject of war came up, every man

at the table seemed to have an opinion to contribute. Claire finished her chicken and threw the bone down on her plate. If Cormac had been intrigued watching her eat the greasy piece of fowl, there was no sign of it. He seemed as immersed as the others in the discussion of what exactly would happen when Bixleigh and Shane O'Neill met head-on.

She picked up a goblet of the wine she had chosen especially for the meal and cleared her throat loudly. When everyone turned to look at her, she said, "Here's a toast to good company and"—she searched her mind for something that would please her husband—"and to the black swan of the Riordans."

The words were met with total silence. One would think she had toasted the devil himself, Claire thought. Then Eileen raised her glass and repeated, "To the black swan!"

One by one the men at the table followed suit until everyone but Cormac had taken a drink. Eamon, sitting at Cormac's right, reached to put a goblet in his brother's hand. " 'Tis your wife's toast," he muttered.

Cormac seemed dazed, but lifted the glass and took a long swallow. The rest of the table looked relieved, and immediately began striking up individual conversations.

Claire sat bewildered. Except for the gleam in Cormac's eye at the beginning of the evening, nothing had gone as she had hoped. He wasn't one bit more interested in her, for all her efforts. In fact, it appeared that he was taking care to avoid looking at her.

Tired and more disappointed than she cared to admit, she pushed back her chair and rose. "Excuse me, gentlemen," she said. "I'm going to retire."

Eileen followed her and insisted on joining her in her chamber. "I won't have you moping by yourself,

Clairy," she said firmly. "I'm sleeping with you tonight."

"It's not necessary. I never really believed in all that nonsense Nancy told us anyway." But her dull voice betrayed the high hopes that had been dashed.

Eileen jumped up on the bed, crossed her arms, and fixed her sister with a stern look. "What kind of craven talk is that? Is this my stalwart, never-give-up sister? Is this the daughter of Raghnall O'Donnell?"

"Well, at least now you see the way of it. Cormac Riordan has no more interest in me than in the new foal in the stables. And I'd better stop thinking otherwise."

"You haven't given it a fighting chance. Nancy had lots of other ideas—"

Claire interrupted her with an upheld hand. "I believe Nancy's tricks only work when the gentleman is so inclined in the first place."

Eileen flung herself back on the bed and sighed. "Ah, Clairy, 'tis a shame 'twas not Dermot you married. He's as bonny as Cormac and of much better humor. And I do believe he's sweet on you." She sat bolt upright. "That's it! What did Nancy say 'twas the very best way to get a man's attention?"

Claire was already shaking her head. "Jealousy. But Cormac's cousin would never dream of doing anything improper with his kinsman's wife."

Eileen pulled Claire down on the bed beside her. "His cousin doesn't have to do anything improper. It only needs to look as if he *wants* to. That would be enough to set Cormac steaming."

Claire gave a sad smile at Eileen's relentless scheming. "Nay, I would hope that I would be better than such nasty games. Anyway, I've decided that this love business is not as wonderful as they sing in the ballads. I'm not sure I even want the man anymore. You and I should just make our plans to return home."

Eileen was quiet as the two got undressed and climbed together beneath the coverlet, as they had for so many years as girls. It was comforting to have Eileen with her. It helped her put off thinking about the evening's disappointments.

Tomorrow she'd make plans to leave, she decided as she began drifting off to sleep.

"Clairy, are you asleep?" Eileen whispered.

"Aye." Claire's voice was thick with sleep.

"All right then, good night. But I thought I should tell you that as I left the dining hall I heard Cormac tell Dermot that in the future, he'd take charge of seating his wife at the table."

"Cormac said that?"

"Aye, and he sounded chaffed."

If Molly had served a platter of iron nails for pudding, Cormac would have cheerfully chewed the entire lot. He wasn't sure how many more evenings he'd be able to sit watching from the opposite end of the table while his brothers and cousins and Riordan retainers vied for her attention, their eyes scanning the milky white expanse above her low-cut gowns.

Tonight the gown had been particularly low, and he hadn't failed to notice how Dermot's gaze had gone to it immediately, and how his cousin had then jumped up to go to her side and guide her to her chair, his hand at her elbow. It was high time Dermot went back up north where he belonged, he fumed.

Cormac paced the length of his room, wondering if he should go out for one of the nighttime rides on Taranis that he had begun taking in order not to lie awake thinking about her in the big bed at the other end of the house. Somehow, he felt that tonight a ride wouldn't be enough to banish the image. The restlessness that had been building since he'd fetched Claire back from O'Donnell House had become nearly intolerable. He thought about her constantly, from his first waking moment each morning.

He stopped his pacing long enough to lay a hand on the leather knife sheath sitting on his bedside table. The sheath held his swan dagger, and from long habit he kept it beside him wherever he slept.

His fingers traced the familiar hilt of gleaming bronze that curved at the top into the graceful form of a swan, enameled in black. The damned swan of mourning. Ever present to remind him that his family was accursed. The Riordans killed the women they loved. He looked down and realized that he'd curled his fingers so tightly around the knife that his knuckles had gone white.

He unclenched his hand and forced himself to take a deep breath. She'd looked spectacular. Her dress had been of a wondrous, sheeny blue fabric that had shimmered when she walked, as though she were some kind of faerie princess. She'd had her glossy black hair piled high on her head, adorned by a circlet of gold that matched the gold chain around her slender neck. He could feel his pulse increasing at the memory as he stretched his cramped fingers.

He'd also noticed, however, that she'd sneezed several times. He hoped she wasn't coming down with a cold. It was almost winter. The nights had grown chilly. Had the servants built her chamber fire high enough to last the entire night? he wondered.

It wouldn't hurt to check, he decided, turning slowly toward his door. When he reached the hall, he hesitated a moment longer, then he shrugged and headed off in the direction of the north wing.

•   •   •

For a few moments, Claire thought the knock was part of her dream. She could hear Eileen's breathing, deep and even, next to her in the bed. The knock sounded again, and this time she was sure it was real.

Groggily she got up and reached for the shawl at the foot of the bed to cover herself. By the time she got to the door, she was awake enough to wonder who would be knocking at this hour and guessing the answer even as she asked the question.

"Oh, you've . . . er, were you asleep?" Cormac asked.

Claire blinked her eyes at the light of his candle lamp. "I'd just gone to bed."

He looked embarrassed. "Forgive me. I just came to see that your fire was fully stocked."

"My fire?"

"I wanted to be sure you were warm enough. You seemed to be, um, sneezing at supper. I feared you may be coming down with the catarrh."

Now it was Claire's turn to be embarrassed and also a little irritated. After all her effort, all he had noticed was that she'd been *sneezing?* "At this point, my health is just fine, milord, but if I want to keep it so, I doubt I should be standing here in the drafty hall half-dressed."

He glanced quickly down at her nightrail. "Of course, forgive me once again—"

Cormac broke off his apology. A movement from the room behind her had caught his eye. The room was dark except for the light of the fire, but he could distinctly see a shadow moving . . . in Claire's bed! Suspicion boiled into his brain like scalding metal. For a moment, the face of his cousin Dermot flashed through his mind.

"You're not alone," he said stiffly.

Her expression changed to one of disbelief. She took a step back. Cormac relaxed and let the unexpected rage drain from him. It had taken him only seconds to realize that his horrible suspicion had been absurd. Even if Claire were the kind of woman who would agree to such perfidy under her husband's nose, no kin of his would ever commit such an outrage, no matter how smitten.

He shook his head. "I'm sorry. I was just startled by seeing someone in your room."

" 'Tis my sister, Eileen. She's asleep, or she was before you arrived to cause a commotion. Now if you'll excuse me . . ."

She began to close the door. It was evident that she had seen his suspicion, and she was justifiably angry. Cormac held the door open with the palm of his hand. "Wait, I'm sorry. Truly. I was interested in your welfare and nothing more. Please extend my apologies to your sister if I woke her."

"I shall. Now may I go back to bed?"

"Aye, but on the condition that you ride with me tomorrow morning."

His invitation caught Claire off guard. After dinner she had resolved to spend the morning packing her things for a return to O'Donnell House. Now she inexplicably found herself saying, "Very well."

"Good," he said. "I'll meet you at the stables at midmorning."

Before she could change her mind, he had turned and stalked off down the hall. Slowly, she closed the door and walked back to the bed. The floor was icy against her bare feet, and a draft cooled her legs. Sliding between the covers, she curled up, trying to get warm again.

"What did he want?" Eileen's whisper came from the other side of the bed.

"He said he came to inquire about the fire."

Her sister sat up. "To inquire about the fire? What kind of an excuse is that?"

"He thought I'd taken cold because of all my sneezing at dinner."

Eileen giggled. "Nancy never told us exactly how much of her talc we should use. But, Clairy, a man doesn't come to a woman's room at this hour to ask about the fire."

"He also wanted to know who was in my bed," Claire added dryly.

"Why, surely he didn't think—" Eileen broke off her sentence and turned to pound excitedly on her sister's hunched back. "He's jealous, Clairy! It must be. He's jealous of that handsome cousin of his."

Claire, still chilled, drew herself into a tighter ball. But as she thought about the look on Cormac's face when he'd seen Eileen's shadow in her bed, she decided that her sister might be right. "It did appear that way," she admitted.

Eileen pounded her again. "Of course he is! You see, Nancy's advice is working."

Claire gave a big sigh. "All it proves is that he doesn't want anyone else to have me. It doesn't prove that he wants me for himself."

Eileen plopped back down against the pillows and groaned. "Well, you have to give it a chance."

"He asked me to go riding in the morning."

"That settles it. He's interested in you, Clairy. Perhaps he's just one of those men Nancy was talking about who take a longer time of it."

Claire wouldn't admit it to her sister, but she was beginning to have the same hope. The look on Cormac's face when he'd thought someone might be in her room was nothing short of furious. At least it had proved to her that he wasn't totally indifferent. Still, if

Cormac wanted this marriage to work, too, it was time for him to put forth a little effort himself. She'd done her part.

"I suppose I'll go riding with him tomorrow," she told her sister grumpily, "but I am *not* going to put on any more of that infernal powder."

Eleven

This time Claire was properly attired for her ride. Her fur-trimmed riding habit was comfortable and practical, but she knew that the close cut was also flattering. The look in Cormac's eyes as she walked up to the stables showed that he appreciated it as well.

"I wasn't sure you'd really come," he said, smiling. "You were a bit groggy last night when I asked you. I thought you might not remember the conversation."

He looked rather fine himself today in a fitted brown jerkin over a crisp white shirt. "I wasn't *that* sleepy," she replied with a smile.

"Did I wake up your sister?"

"Aye, but we had just gone to bed when you came. It was no matter."

He frowned. "I suppose she thinks it odd that we don't share a room."

Surprised, Claire answered slowly, " 'Tis more normal for a husband and wife to sleep together."

Cormac's expression had clouded. "Aye." He hesitated a moment, then nodded toward the stables. "I believe Aidan has our horses ready," he said.

Claire felt a little dazed as she followed him inside the stable. She had wondered if Cormac ever gave a thought to how their odd marriage looked to other people, but she hadn't really expected him to bring it up. It may have been a good opportunity to discuss the matter, but instead, he seemed to dismiss the subject as though it had been a comment about the weather.

"Good day, milady," Aidan said.

Claire gave herself a little shake. It was a beautiful fall day, and she was going to spend the morning riding across the green hills. She'd put aside other considerations for the moment.

"Good morning, Aidan." She smiled at the horse master, who was holding the bridle of Cinder, the gentle mare she'd ridden previously. She gave the mare a pat, but her gaze drifted to a sleek black horse in the stall behind. If she was going to lose herself in a ride, she would like a more challenging mount.

"What about that one?" she asked.

Cormac answered, "That's Taranis's brother. Cinder's a better choice for a lady."

"I'm sure she is. However, I'd like to try one with a bit more fire."

Aidan said gently, "You'd find more than fire with that one. He runs like the devil's caught his tail, but he's unpredictable, and he don't take to most—"

He broke off as Claire had already ducked under the stall gate and was stroking the big gelding. The animal tossed its head and snorted, but then seemed to turn its muzzle into Claire's hand.

"He won't let most people near him," Aidan said, surprised.

"I'll ride this one today, if I may," Claire said without turning around.

Aidan looked at Cormac, who hesitated a moment, then said, "I don't think he's ever worn a sidesaddle."

"I'd prefer a regular saddle, to tell you the truth." She turned around; her eyes were shining. "He's wonderful."

Once again, Aidan looked over at Cormac, waiting.

Cormac shrugged and said, "Saddle him up."

The big horse gave Claire no trouble as she and Cormac got on their horses and headed out the stable doors. Claire laughed, exhilarated by the joy of being on a such a worthy mount. "What's his name?" she shouted as she gave the horse its head to follow Taranis out of the stable yard.

Cormac looked back at her, doubt written on his face. "They call him Lucifer."

"Lucifer, like the devil?"

"Aye, like the devil."

Claire threw back her head and laughed as the two big horses turned up the road and started to run.

Eileen's thoughts were on her sister as she picked at the nearly cold porridge. She had arrived to breakfast late. Claire had arisen early to dress for her ride, but Eileen had snuggled into the covers and gone back to sleep. When she'd awoken, Claire was gone. Eileen could see telltale signs that her sister had taken pains with her appearance. The box of hairpins was scattered across the dressing table, and one of the bottles of sweetwater they'd brought from Nancy's was open.

"Faith, you'll be breakfasting until St. Swithin's Day at the rate you're goin', Mistress Eileen."

Eileen put her head up at the sound of her name. Dermot Riordan was standing at the entrance to the dining hall, leaning on the door frame and smiling his crooked smile.

She looked into the bowl at her place. "I don't think I'll finish it," she said. "I arrived so shamelessly late that it's turned a bit lumpy."

Dermot walked into the room. "Nay, 'twas lumpy from the start. I do believe Molly likes it that way." He pulled out a chair next to hers and sat on it backwards, crossing his arms over the back. "So ye're shameless, are ye?"

Eileen laughed. "Nay, you mistook my meaning, sir. I daresay I've a great deal of shame for being such a slugabed this morning, but the chamber was so frigid, I didn't want to get up."

"Aye, the mornings are getting chilly. Hot porridge helps, but of course"—he gave a teasing nod at her bowl—"ice cold porridge does no good at all."

She pushed the plate away. "No matter, since 'tis almost time for the noon meal."

"Your sister was up before the sparrows," he observed.

Eileen's eyebrow arched. "If I were you, I'd be careful about keeping such close watch on my sister. Aren't you worried that Cormac will be angry?"

His bewilderment appeared to be genuine. "Why would he be angry?"

"I should think that would be obvious."

"Not to me," he said.

"You've been flirting with his wife. Doesn't that raise the ire of most men?"

Dermot laughed. "Me? Flirt with my cousin's wife? Mistress, you are dreaming. I've but done my best to make the lady feel comfortable here. Some of my southern kinsmen can be a dour lot, and I understand many were resentful when she first arrived after Ultan's death."

"You do not, er, fancy her?"

"Do I fancy my own hide?" he asked. "For I'd surely lose it if I so much as *thought* about anything improper with Cormac's wife. Anyway, I'd never think it. 'Tis not the way with us Riordans."

Eileen wished she had never broached the subject. "Pardon me," she stammered. "I just thought . . . you were so attentive, and I heard Cormac at the dinner table last night . . ."

"Ah, Cormac's just peevish these days. I suppose I would be, too, if I had a wife who looked like Claire and I couldn't lay a hand on her."

Eileen forgot her embarrassment and went very still. She had a feeling that Dermot's offhand statement had been an important clue to the mystery of her sister's unhappy marriage. "And why would that be?" she asked carefully. "Why wouldn't he be able to lay a hand on her?"

Dermot looked surprised. "Why, because of the Riordan curse, of course. Not many of us still believe the old tales, but Cormac does. He's sworn not to touch her. I'd have thought you would have known all about it, being her sister."

Eileen shook her head. "Nay."

"I warrant women don't talk about these matters as freely as men do," he said.

Eileen didn't bother to correct him, but she knew very well that if Claire knew anything about a Riordan curse, she would have told her. "What is this curse exactly?" she asked.

Dermot had begun to look uncomfortable. "Mayhap I should not be speaking of it," he said. " 'Tis between Cormac and his wife."

Eileen smiled at him and laid her hand on his sleeve in a manner that she reckoned Nancy would admire. " 'Tis between Cormac and Claire, surely, but I can't imagine it would hurt for you to tell me about it, just so I won't feel like such an outsider."

Dermot turned around, as if looking to see that no one was within earshot. " 'Tis an ancient Druid curse," he said, his voice dropping several notches. "From the days before time. In retribution for the Riordans leading a raid that killed many of the rival clans' women, they were accursed."

"Accursed how?"

Now Dermot looked decidedly uncomfortable, evidently realizing too late the import of the information he was giving her. "The curse says that Riordan brides will die within a year and a day of their wedding."

Eileen felt a shiver of disquiet. "But surely, such a thing couldn't be. If it were true, there wouldn't be any Riordans left."

Dermot shook his head. " 'Tis as I say, most of us disbelieve it. But the elders say that more than a fair share of Riordan brides have died young."

"Didn't the mothers of Cormac, Eamon, and Niall all die young?"

Dermot's normally cheerful face was solemn. "Aye, that they did."

"Within a year and a day of their weddings?" Eileen asked, the shiver becoming a wave of cold.

"Aye," Dermot said.

This time she was a proper match for him, Claire thought as they thundered across a wide lea, skirted a small pond, and headed for the hills beyond. Lucifer was a magnificent horse, perhaps the finest she'd ever ridden, and far from causing problems, the animal seemed in perfect harmony with the rhythm of her own body. She imagined the two big stallions made a proud picture silhouetted on the horizon as they crested a hill.

Cormac pulled Taranis to a halt. At Claire's slight pull of the reins, Lucifer stopped smoothly next to his sibling.

Cormac gave a low whistle of admiration. " 'Twas not an idle boast, milady. I've seen few horsemen to match your skill."

Claire laughed, though she felt a twinge of disappointment at his formal tone and manner of address. " 'Tis the horse that's magnificent," she said. "A fine match for yours."

"Aye, which is to be expected. They're twins."

"Twins?" Her eyes widened. Twin births were rare, and it was even rarer that both horses came out robust and healthy. "The dam is a strong lady, then. I'd like to see her."

She could see him stiffen. "Her name was Mara. She was strong enough to bear two fine sons, but not strong enough to survive the birthing."

Claire leaned down to stroke Lucifer's neck. The horse was scarcely breathing hard after its run. "Ah, poor thing. At least she made her contribution to the world—two fine sons. And now Taranis has sired Dian. So, in a way, Mara lives on."

Cormac had seemed exhilarated and happy on their mad race across the countryside. He'd laughed as he shouted directions back to her and pointed out landmarks. Now it was as if a cloud had moved in front of the sun, darkening his humor. She didn't understand him, and for the hundredth time she asked herself why she continued to want a man who was so hard to reach.

"I've brought our midday meal," he said, his voice brightening.

To Claire's surprise, he pointed to a bulging saddlebag. The sun had passed its midday height and for the past several minutes she'd been worrying about being late back to Riordan Hall.

"I didn't leave word with Molly."

"Ah, but I did. You're my captive for the day, milady, and no one will miss you until sundown." He grinned, and once again she glimpsed the carefree Cormac of their wild ride.

Her heart lightening along with his mood, she followed his example and jumped off Lucifer. They took a few minutes to wipe the sweat from their horses' coats, then walked a dozen yards to a stream. The ribbon of water meandered past a grove of trees, then gathered speed as it started down the hill.

"Where are we exactly?" she asked him. She'd been unable to keep up with the twists and turns of the ride.

"We're just south of Tara. See?" He pointed down the hill, and in the distance she could see the distinctive stone ruins of the ancient city. "My brothers and I always loved to ride here when we were young. After we eat, I'll show you something we found up here."

Though some of the O'Donnell land bordered the north end of Tara, Claire seldom rode in the area. The place had always seemed haunted and gloomy to her. The local legends said that women and children were buried in the gentle mounds beyond the central ruins. They'd been left defenseless by their men and killed by a rival tribe.

Cormac was unrolling a blanket from his saddle and spreading it out on the grassy hill. "My brothers and Eileen and I stayed away from this place," she said. "Isn't it supposed to be haunted?"

There was a flicker of something in his dark eyes, but he smiled as he said, "Don't worry, I'll protect you from any phantoms that may happen along today."

He offered his hand to help her down to the blanket and she sank down gratefully. She hadn't ridden astride, especially on such a big horse, for a long time, and her legs were a little unsteady. Then again, she realized, as Cormac handed her a cup of ale, her hands were unsteady, too. Perhaps it had nothing to do with the ride.

The ale helped, as did the bread and cheese and cold chicken Cormac had brought. She began feeling better as they ate and drank. From the top of the hill, they could see a great deal of the surrounding countryside. Cormac pointed out to her the different features of the old capital city that could still be seen and the grassy areas that legend said covered other sacred areas. Claire relaxed, realizing that they were talking more easily than they ever had before, including the time she'd first met him when she'd been only ten.

But she didn't feel ten anymore. He leaned toward her frequently, brushing her arm. He put his hand at the back of her neck to turn her head in the proper direction to find another landmark. He offered her a bite of a sweet-cake, and, when she nodded, put it right into her mouth, his fingers sliding along her lips.

The oddest thing was watching him eat a chicken leg. She found something fascinating about the movement of his mouth and his tongue as he devoured the piece of meat, the grease making his lips glisten. It was just as Nancy had described. Then she caught herself. Nancy had described nothing of the kind. She'd said it was the *man* who was supposed to have these feelings.

"Are you warm?" Cormac asked.

The question startled her. "Nay . . . er . . . that is . . ." She realized that she'd been holding her cool mug of ale against her cheek. "The sun is a bit warm," she admitted weakly.

Cormac threw the chicken bone over his shoulder. It sailed out of sight into a clump of trees. "Have you had enough to eat?" he asked.

Claire had no idea what she'd eaten. She nodded.

"Then, come. Let's explore." He jumped up and extended his hand.

This was silly, Claire told herself firmly. Cormac had brought her to his childhood playground, and he was treating her with courtesy and nothing more. He may as well be here with one of his brothers. She reached out and willed her arm not to tingle as his hand enfolded hers. When she was standing, he continued to hold her hand as he led her along the crest of the hill toward the grove of trees.

Perhaps he wouldn't be holding hands with one of his brothers, she admitted, as the tingles began in spite of her resolve.

"We'd never heard anyone speak of this place." he was telling her, "so my brothers and I considered it our own special find."

She could hear the enthusiasm in his voice, and it helped her to concentrate on his explanation, rather than on their clasped hands.

"Is it a ruin?" she asked.

"Aye, partly. You'll see in a moment—just through these trees."

The wall of trees looked so thick, at first Claire didn't see how they would get through it, but as she followed Cormac she realized that there was a break just large enough for a person to walk through. Cormac went ahead, but continued to hold her hand behind him. With the trees towering on either side, the narrow opening was dark, especially after the bright sun of the hillside. She clenched Cormac's hand and let him lead her through the trees in a zigzag pattern. Just as darkness seemed to close in behind her, she could see the opening out the other side.

"Here it is," Cormac said, his voice a little hushed.

They emerged from the circle of trees and she moved up beside him as they both stood surveying the site. In the center of the grove of trees was a clearing, dominated by a small, mirror-smooth pond. On the far side of the water was a crumbling wall and what looked like the remains of a tiny house or perhaps an ancient shrine.

"What is this place?" she asked.

He dropped her hand finally, and moved toward the edge of the pool, then knelt beside it. "I'm not sure, really. We've always called it Cliodhna's Glen."

"Cliodhna? The faerie spirit?"

"Aye, one of the mythical race, the Tuatha De Danann. I can't remember how we learned the name." He looked puzzled for a moment, trying to remember. "Anyway, that's what we call it. We used to think we could talk to the ancients here." He turned around to look at her and smiled.

"Did they answer you?"

"Sometimes it seemed as if they did. At least in the fanciful mind of a child."

Claire walked up beside him and looked in the pond. "It's so clear."

Cormac stirred his finger in the water, making a ripple in the glassy surface. "Aye. I remember it always felt so"—he appeared to be searching for the right word—"peaceful to me."

She looked across the little lake to the ruins. "Can we look closer?" she asked.

He stood up and nodded. "There's not much to see— just old stone, but it makes a pretty sight."

They moved through reedy grass along the edge of the pond to the far side. "We'd use it as a fort when we were lads," Cormac told her as they approached the crumbling structure. "It seems much smaller now."

The wall had no particular markings, nothing to show its age. It looked much like crumbling walls on a farm anywhere. But Claire was interested in the small stone structure behind it. It was too little to be a house or even a workshed, yet it had been carefully built at one time, probably centuries ago.

"What do you suppose this was?" she asked.

"We never were sure. Perhaps something to do with worship or perhaps just a little storehouse for keeping food or kegs of ale. We'll probably never know."

"It's empty?" she asked, ducking under the arched opening to peer inside.

"Aye."

It was hard to see in the dark interior, but Claire could barely make out a form carved into the wall opposite the little doorway. "There's a shape there!" she exclaimed.

Cormac looked confused. "A shape? Nay. It must be the way the light is filtering into the building. If we had a torch you could see better, but it's just old stone."

Claire rubbed at her eyes, then strained to see again through the darkness. " 'Tis a woman."

Cormac put his head beside hers and peered through the doorway. "I don't understand. There's nothing . . ." He stopped as he, too, saw the form on the wall.

Claire got down on her hands and knees and inched her way through the opening, trying to get a better look. With her body blocking part of the light from the small opening, it was hard to see, but the carving on the wall was definitely the form of a young woman in the style of the old statues from ancient Greece or Rome.

Cormac was trying to squeeze in next to her. "God's teeth!" he said.

"You've never noticed her before?" Claire asked.

He shook his head, looking dazed. "Nay, I could swear . . ." He reached out a long arm and traced the pattern on the wall. In places it had crumbled away.

Obviously the carving was as old as the structure itself. "We never saw it."

Claire gave a gleeful laugh. "Then 'tis my own special discovery. What fun!" she cried. "Perhaps 'tis Cliodhna herself."

"You'd think we would have seen it," Cormac said, still looking bewildered.

"I warrant young boys playing don't pay much attention to those things. You may have even seen it and forgotten about it." As she turned her head to offer her explanation, she realized that within the confines of the tiny room, they were pressed against one another like lovers. She could see from a sudden darkening of Cormac's eyes that he had made the same realization.

"Nay, I would have remembered," he said after a moment, and started backing out of the tight quarters. "In fact it would have made the place that much more magical, since we had a household almost without ladies."

There was not enough room to turn around, so Claire backed out, as well, feeling a little undignified. "And here all the time you had a lady watching over you and you didn't even know about it," she said lightly as she cleared the doorway, dusted off her hands, and stood up.

He nodded slowly. "Apparently, but I still have trouble believing that we never saw it. It's odd. . . ." He stared into the water. "Sometimes when I came here I used to think I could talk to my mother or to Rhea—that was Niall's mother. She's the one I remember most."

Claire got a sudden pang as she thought of how lonesome it must have sometimes seemed for the Riordan boys to have no woman to love them. She looked around the beautiful little clearing. "Thank you for bringing me here," she said.

He seemed to be throwing off painful memories as he gave himself a little shake, then smiled at her and said, "My pleasure, *chara.*"

Chara—dearest. He'd first called her that the night of their wedding. It had sounded sweet to her ears then, but the ensuing events had made her forget the endearment. Now, it seemed natural to hear him say it, though perhaps it was just the spell of this place.

She looked around. "It's a magical place," she said. "Mayhap 'twas magic that made the lady of the stone appear."

Cormac ducked his head and peeked into the little building. "She's still there, plain to be seen. Yet you're right, 'tis like magic. For I'd swear there was no woman here for all the years we Riordans have been coming." He straightened and reached for her hand again. "It feels odd to have a *real* woman here, as well," he added.

She took his hand easily, getting more used to the feel of him. "Faith, Cormac, did you Riordan lads never bring a sweetheart up on this hill?"

He shook his head. "Nay, you're the first I've ever brought to Cliodhna's Glen."

She cocked her head. " 'Tis hard to believe."

Grinning, he admitted, "I'll not say I've lived like a saint, but my liaisons were lighthearted—meant for mutual pleasure and nothing more. I've never thought to bring any of them here."

Hand in hand they began to walk around the edge of the pond. "I had no serious rivals, then, while you waited to marry me?"

He glanced down at her. "I can't imagine one who could rival you, Claire O'Donnell."

Once again, his remark was loverlike, and she found it even more stimulating than the touch of his hand. They'd reached the other side of the pond where the path led back through the trees, out of the circle. She was curiously reluctant to leave.

" 'Tis lovely, your Cliodhna's Glen," she said, her voice barely a whisper.

"Not as lovely as you," he answered. Then he drew her into his arms and lowered his mouth to hers.

Twelve

Never in his life had anything seemed so inevitable. He didn't know where this would lead or what consequences may follow, but at that moment in this place, he simply had to kiss her.

Her slender body molded against him. Her mouth turned to melted honey. Her hands crept around his neck as she gave a sigh of surrender in the back of her throat.

Again he kissed her, his hands pressed at the small of her back. Then she went up on her toes, clinging to him, her hair tumbling down, her smooth cheek pressed against his. "Ah, Cormac," she whispered, her voice shaky.

While his mind tried to chant the litany of reasons he could not have this woman, his body continued its onslaught. His loins ached with wanting. His manhood swelled against her soft thighs with urgent pulses. *You will take her,* came the throbbing message.

He looked into her face to see her eyes, dazed and widened, her cheeks flushed, and her mouth already blurred from his kisses. Then she smiled at him in invitation, and he gave up resisting this thing he had wanted for too long.

He took a step back, scooped her up in his arms, and walked swiftly over to a mossy bank at the foot of the trees. "You should have a silken bower with soft sheets, *chara,"* he said, placing her tenderly in the soft green bed, "but I can't wait any more."

"Nor can I," she agreed, holding up her arms to him.

He lowered himself so that their bodies could connect once again, and she welcomed him with a sinuous little wiggle that made his blood race.

Her lips were half-open, and he kissed them again, this time opening her mouth deep with his tongue. He could feel the instantaneous hardening of her breasts underneath him. He moved a hand to one perfect globe and caressed her through the soft jersey of her riding dress. The nipple stiffened into his palm as Claire closed her eyes and gasped in pleasure.

After several moments, he switched his attention to the other breast. "Shall I rid you of these clothes, sweetheart?" he whispered.

Her eyes fluttered open and for the first time she looked a little nervous. "I'm not sure what I'm supposed to do," she murmured.

For a moment, with the reminder of her virgin state, the reasoning Cormac threatened to surface and put an end to the sensations shimmering through him, but then she pressed her own hand on top of his where it lay on her breast and whispered, "Teach me."

He rolled to one side and pulled her up, his hands nervously working the lacings of her bodice. She was lightly dressed, but it seemed endless moments before he'd shed his own clothes and helped her strip off her dress and corset. He used their clothes to make a little nest for them so she wouldn't have to lie on the cool ground, then, tenderly, he pulled off her chemise to reveal her naked white skin.

Remarkably, she didn't seem the least bit shy as he took his time admiring her, running his hands the length of her legs and kissing the tips of her breasts. "You're so beautiful," he told her. "Delicate and beautiful—like a freshly blossomed lily."

Claire was performing her own examination. Growing up among brothers, she'd seen naked men, but the men had never been Cormac, the object of her fantasy for so many years. And the men had never been exhibiting such blatant sexual desire. In fact, she hoped her eyes weren't revealing the extent of her amazement as she looked down at his male organ. After several moments of lying quiet while he caressed her, she began returning his touches, leading inevitably to touching him *there*. It was so much larger than she had imagined. And harder. And warmer to the touch. Her stomach was doing flip-flops.

He gasped when she touched him, but it was a gasp of surprised delight, and his hand immediately covered hers, showing her how to enhance his pleasure. Then he was touching her, too, in her secret place, his fingers gently prodding until a totally unexpected sensation spiraled through her.

"That's how it works, sweetheart," he said in her ear. "It came fast—you were made for loving."

For a brief time, her arms and legs were limp with weakness, but as he gently suckled her breasts and continued his slow strokes, the sensation began anew, only this time, before it could overtake her, he poised himself over her and carefully joined their bodies. For a moment, the fullness seemed unbearable, but as she relaxed, she began to savor the feel of his body moving inside hers. Once again the tension started to build. Their movements quickened. She clung to him, then shuddered at another spiraling explosion, stronger than the first.

She was aware that he had withdrawn quickly. He turned to one side and spilled himself on the grass. She found it vaguely disappointing, and her overheated body began to cool. It wasn't the way she had expected the encounter to end, but it had been too miraculous to quibble over the details, especially since he turned back to her immediately and took her in his arms, nuzzling her neck with little kisses.

"Are you all right?" he asked. "You felt no pain?"

She shook her head. She'd been warned to expect it, but if there had been pain, it had been lost in the discovery of the pleasure. "It was everything I could have imagined," she said.

It was true. This is what she had hoped for—what she had *expected* on her wedding night. This is what she had dreamed of as soon as she'd begun to understand what passed between a man and a woman.

He tucked her head into the curve of his shoulder and dropped a light kiss on her forehead. "I'm glad," he said.

She waited a moment, then asked, "Did you enjoy it, too?"

She could feel his chuckle rumbling under her ear. "Aye, *chara.* I enjoyed it."

They were silent for another stretch, but Claire had more questions. She lifted her head from his chest and leaned on an elbow. "I thought perhaps you weren't that fond of lovemaking since you've not wanted it for all this time."

"Not wanted it? *Chara,* I think I would have turned into a bonfire if I'd waited another hour."

She frowned. If he'd wanted her that much, why had he made them both wait so long? Perhaps he was just starting to want her. Perhaps it had been one of Nancy's tricks that had swayed him, after all. Had it been the silky dress or the slow eating? She hoped it hadn't been the talc, since she was determined not to go through that misery again.

She put her head back on his shoulder with a sigh of

contentment. It didn't really matter what had made it happen. The important thing was that now they were truly husband and wife. Their bodies had joined here in this special place of Cliodhna's Glen. She fancied their spirits had as well.

"I'm glad it was here," she said dreamily.

He seemed to understand her thoughts perfectly. "Aye, so am I."

She yawned. "I'm sorry. I seem to be sleepy suddenly, but I can't think why."

He laughed. "Go ahead and sleep, princess," he told her, using the name he had called her so long ago. "No one will disturb us here."

"Just for a minute," she murmured, and her eyes drifted closed.

The trees cast long twilight shadows by the time she awoke, still in her mossy nest. Cormac was gone, and she was covered by the blanket they had used for their lunch back on the hilltop. She sat bolt upright and looked around, then relaxed when she spotted Cormac at the other side of the pond, looking at the ruin again.

She grinned sleepily as he raised his head and saw that she was awake. She pulled the blanket up to her neck. It had grown chilly.

"I thought we'd have to camp here for the night," he said, teasing, walking back toward her around the pond.

She stretched and yawned. "I'm sorry. I don't know what came over me. I rarely sleep during the day."

He dropped down beside her and lightly kissed her cheek. "I fear I wore you out." He was smiling, but there was remorse in his voice that seemed to go beyond teasing.

"You did nothing of the sort," she answered firmly.

"If anything, I've had my most relaxed day in weeks. It's been lovely."

"You're not—um, you're feeling all right?"

He was just being solicitous, she decided. After all, she was inexperienced, and it was kind and sweet of her lover to be concerned for her welfare. She hurried to reassure him. "I feel just fine, Cormac Riordan, and if I weren't worried that they would send out a search party looking for us, I'd shed this blanket and invite you to give me another lesson."

The idea seemed to make him nervous. He jumped to his feet and said, "Tempting as the offer may be, I think you're right about the search party. I'm sure they didn't expect we'd be out this late."

His lack of response to her half-invitation was puzzling, as was the distance he seemed to keep from her as they made their way home. After an afternoon of such intimacy, she imagined that lovers should be more connected. She'd expected laughter and sweet words, perhaps some touches and another kiss or two. Instead, he rode beside her discussing the landscape and the estate and the occupants of the farms they passed, as though he were giving a tour to a curate new to the neighborhood.

At least the barrier had been crossed. They were now lovers, and she had to believe that from now on things would be different between them. Cormac would move into her big bedchamber, and she would have him to herself every night. With time he would learn to share his feelings and thoughts with her as well as his body.

Though she'd been joking about the search party, she could see from Eileen's face that her sister had begun to worry over their late arrival. She met Claire and Cormac in the grand hall as they came in together. Cormac had not held her hand during the brief walk from the stables.

"There you are!" her sister cried. " 'Tis almost time for supper."

"We rode all the way to Tara," Claire explained. "Cormac was showing me a place he and his brothers went to as a child." Suddenly she noticed that Eileen's expression looked strained. "Is anything wrong?"

"Nay, that is"—she glanced at Cormac, then back to Claire—"I need to talk with you."

"I need to check with Eamon," Cormac said quickly. "I'll take my leave so you ladies may talk in private."

This was not the way Claire wanted their momentous afternoon to end, but with Eileen obviously upset about something, she had no other choice but to nod at Cormac and let him turn and walk away. "What is it?" she asked Eileen.

Her sister shook her head. "Not here. Let's go up to your room where we won't be heard. There's something important I need to tell you."

Claire sat facing her sister on her bed, shaking her head in disbelief. "Are you trying to tell me that Cormac's been acting this way all these weeks because of some fool notion about an old curse?"

Eileen's face was tight with worry. "What if 'tis not a fool notion, Claire? Dermot said that many of the Riordans believe it to be true. Riordan brides *have* died young through the centuries—usually while giving birth."

Claire gave a bounce of sheer frustration. " 'Tis the young who give birth, Eily—young *brides,* if things are done properly. And everyone knows that death is simply one of the risks we females accept in order to bring life to our babies."

"But within a year and a day, Clairy, doesn't it seem—"

"Faith, Eily, you've seen the Riordan men. You yourself call them 'a brawny lot.' I warrant most of them would not leave a wife barren past her first moon cycle."

Eileen gave a weak smile. "Aye, 'tis hard to picture one of their women going long without a swollen belly."

"Well, there you have it. This curse business is just so much nonsense. Riordan wives have died? So have O'Donnell wives. So have the wives of every family in Ireland who want to survive to a new generation. 'Tis a woman's lot."

Eileen looked as if she were feeling better after hearing her sister so totally discount the news she'd been waiting all day to tell after her morning conversation with Dermot Riordan. "Then you're not worried?" she asked.

"Nay." Claire sat on the edge of the bed, her mind whirling as the implications of Eileen's revelation set in. It was true, she wasn't worried about the curse, but what had her feeling unsettled was finding out that Cormac had kept this secret from her for all this time. He'd not made love to her because he'd been afraid of a *curse?* She could hardly fathom it.

"So his escape on our wedding night . . ." she mused.

Eileen nodded. "Because of the curse, I reckon."

The more Claire thought about it, the angrier she became. The least he could have done was tell her his reasons. She may not have agreed with them, but she could have tried to have some understanding. Instead, he'd kept her in the dark, and his father was dead as a result.

What must that feel like to a man such as Cormac? she wondered, then steeled herself not to feel a whit of pity for him. She was the wronged party here. She was the one who'd been insulted and ignored for weeks without a word of explanation.

"At least now that you know, you can understand why he stays away from you," Eileen said, after Claire had been silent for several moments.

With a sudden flush, Claire had a vivid picture of their lovemaking in the clearing that afternoon when Cormac had decidedly *not* stayed away from her. What had changed his mind? she wondered. "Aye," she said. "It explains a lot of things."

Eileen looked relieved that the story was out and her sister did not seem to be affected. "Good, then," she said, jumping up. "I couldn't eat a bite this noon. Let's go to supper."

Claire looked up at her sister. "You go. I think I'll just stay in my room tonight."

Eileen's face fell. "But you are all right, Claire? Truly?"

Claire stood and gave her sister an embrace. "Aye, I'm fine. Just tired after a long day out of doors."

Still Eileen hesitated. "Should I send you up a tray of supper?"

"Nay, I'm not hungry. But thank you, Eily. And thank you for telling me all this."

Eileen studied her sister's face for a long moment, then, apparently satisfied, nodded and left the room.

She'd undressed and lain down in her bed, but sleep was impossible, especially after the long nap she'd had in the afternoon. Since Eileen had left, Claire's feelings had gone from anger to sorrow and back to anger again. The matter was complicated. If it was true that Cormac had refused to make love to her because he thought it would endanger her life, then in a way, his acts had been noble. If he'd only confided in her at the beginning, perhaps even before the wedding, they would all have avoided so much anguish. Why hadn't he?

And what had changed his mind about lovemaking today? Had it been Nancy's tricks after all that had made him give up the battle with his conscience?

Finally, she stood up, stretched, and peered out the window. The night sky was solid black. It was late, but she'd lain long enough in useless speculation. Her head would continue to ache until she'd had a chance to confront Cormac himself with her questions. He was her husband, she reminded herself. She had every right to go talk with him.

She thought for a moment about lacing herself back into her clothes, then decided that a robe would be enough cover. The halls would be empty this time of night. There was little risk of encountering anyone.

Holding a rush to the fire, she lit her candle lamp, then left the room, closing the door noiselessly behind her. She'd never visited Cormac in his room, but she knew which one it was from supervising the cleaning. At the far end of the south wing, it was as far away as possible from hers, so she had ample time to change her mind as she made her way through the dark corridors. But each time she had the urge to turn around and scurry back to her own warm bed, she'd think about the weeks of misunderstandings she had been through and her resolve would harden.

It seemed like an hour before she finally reached the end of the long south hall and stood in front of the door to Cormac's room. She'd not seen a soul or a light, other than the few that were left burning all night. Evidently everyone was already in bed.

She knocked softly and waited.

Silence.

After a moment, she tried again, a little louder, and whispered, "Cormac?"

Still there was no sound from the other side of the door. Perhaps he was already in a sound sleep, she thought, giving herself one last chance to turn and run.

Instead, she cautiously turned the latch and opened the door. "Are you awake?" she asked softly.

A fire was burning in the grate, giving enough light to show that Cormac's bed was empty, still fully made up. She glanced around the room, but it took only a moment to see that it was as empty as the bed. Cormac was not here.

"It's late, Dermot, and I've had a long day. You'll have to finish this pitcher by yourself."

"Nay, hold a minute, cousin," Dermot said, putting a restraining hand on Cormac's forearm. "I have something I need to tell you."

Reluctantly, Cormac resumed his chair. "What is it?" he asked.

Cormac had been disappointed and a little hurt when Eileen had come down to supper saying that her sister had already retired for the night. His head was still muddled about what had taken place that afternoon at Cliodhna's Glen, and he'd wanted to talk to Claire about it further. Then again, perhaps he didn't, he thought ruefully.

In any event, he'd agreed to stay on drinking with his brothers and his cousin long after the servants had finished cleaning up and the others of the household had gone to their beds. Finally, Niall and Eamon had risen to make their way unsteadily to their own rooms, and only he and Dermot were left.

Dermot had been unusually reserved all evening.

"What did you need to talk with me about?" Cormac asked again.

Dermot took another big gulp of ale. "Ah, cousin, I think you're going to be angry with me. I may have flapped my mouth one time too many today."

"What do you mean?" Dermot was known for his fast-talking, but Cormac couldn't see how his cousin's loose tongue would be of concern to him.

" 'Twas to the sister—Eileen."

That got Cormac's attention. He pushed aside his mug and straightened up. "You were talking to Eileen? About what?"

"Well, about . . . things. You and the lass's sister and . . . you know, things."

Cormac had a sick suspicion that he could guess the nature of Dermot's conversation. "Things such as the Riordan curse," he confirmed.

Dermot gave a miserable nod.

"What did you tell her?"

"I told her I didn't believe the thing personally, Cormac. Honestly, I did. But I suppose I told her that you were set on not providing the curse with another victim."

It did no good to be angry with him. Dermot was so naturally open with everyone, he was the last person to ever trust with a secret. And the Riordan curse had not exactly been a secret. Except from the O'Donnells. Once again, Cormac questioned the wisdom of his father for having made the agreement that started this chain of events.

Damnation. After today, Cormac doubted he would be able to stay away from Claire if there were a dozen curses predicting the couple's doom. And he should have told her that this afternoon, before they'd ever left Cliodhna's Glen. Instead, he'd let his guilt overtake him and he'd hardly spoken to her on the way home. Now it may be too late. If she'd already heard about the curse from her sister, that was undoubtedly why she didn't come to supper. Perhaps she'd already packed her things and left for O'Donnell House.

"Cormac?" Dermot was asking.

"What?" he snapped.

His harsh tone made Dermot look even more dejected. "You're angry with me."

"Aye, but 'twouldn't be the first time, Dermot. You're my kin. I'll forgive you by morning."

Dermot didn't look comforted. "Tell me what I can do to make it up to you. Let me talk to Claire."

"Thank you kindly, cousin," Cormac said, rising from the table, "but nay. It appears you've done enough talking. I'll handle this myself from here."

And he would, he thought grimly. He just wasn't yet sure how. He set his shoulders and headed toward the north wing.

Thirteen

Claire's disappointment over finding Cormac's room empty made her admit to herself just how much she wanted to clear things up with him. Just a few hours ago, she'd been supremely happy, lying in his arms and thinking that all the misunderstandings between them would be over now that they had become lovers. Since that moment, things had started to go wrong. First he'd been distant on the ride home. Then had come Eileen's disclosure about the Riordan curse. Now it appeared he had run away once again. Where could he be at this hour? Riding the hills on Taranis as she had seen him do on previous evenings?

Gloomy and chilled from her walk in the halls, she pushed open the door to her room.

"I didn't know you were in the habit of sleepwalking, princess."

His deep voice in the darkness, coming from her bed, lifted her gloom in an instant.

"Cormac!" she cried. Then, remembering her earlier pique with him, she asked in a more controlled tone, "What are you doing here?"

He sat up, swinging his legs over the edge of the bed. "I came to talk with you, but you were evidently out for a visit. 'Twas not with my flirtatious cousin, since I've been with him up to a few minutes ago."

There was no accusation in his tone, and, unlike the other night when he'd actually seen someone in her bed, she had the feeling he was not truly worried that she was coming from some kind of assignation. Still, she explained, "As a matter of fact, I'm coming from your room. I wanted to talk with you, too."

"You went to my room?" He sounded pleased. His gaze scanned her robe and slippers. "Dressed like that?"

For the life of her, Claire could not decide whether she was annoyed with him or pleased to see him. " 'Tis far more dressing than I had in your company a few hours ago, if you recall, sir."

Now he was definitely pleased. He stood and started walking toward her at a deliberate pace. "Oh, I recall *very* well, princess." The pupils of his eyes had widened, and his voice had already roughened with unmistakable desire, but Claire fought to keep herself under control. She had sought him out for answers, not for lovemaking that would leave her more befuddled.

"What did you come to talk with me about?" she asked, pulling her robe tightly around her like some kind of shield.

For a moment, he looked uncertain, then he seemed to regain his memory. "Oh. Aye. 'Twas about a discussion I had tonight with my cousin."

She'd already guessed that Dermot would have told Cormac about his conversation with Eileen. But Cormac evidently didn't know for sure what Eileen had told her, and she decided that, after all these weeks of silence, he deserved to have to stumble a little.

"A discussion about what?" she asked.

Moving close to her, he said, "Perhaps it wasn't that important. I warrant we could find more agreeable things to discuss." He reached out a finger and stroked the edge of her jaw.

"It wouldn't possibly have been a discussion about the infamous Riordan curse, would it?"

Cormac's smile faded as he took a step back.

"So your sister did tell you."

"Aye."

For a moment he didn't speak. Then he shook his head. "I should have told you myself."

"Aye, you should have. Why didn't you?"

It was the most urgent of the many questions that had been torturing her all evening.

Cormac took in a long breath. "Should we sit by the fire?" he asked.

She nodded agreement and followed him over to the cushions, carefully avoiding letting their bodies brush against each other as they walked. Now that he appeared to finally be ready to talk to her, she didn't want him distracted. When they were both seated, she asked again, "Why didn't you talk to me about this curse story?"

"For years, my father forbade anyone to speak of it. The subject was painful."

"He himself lost three young wives."

"Aye."

"Yet he made a bargain to marry his oldest son to an O'Donnell. If he was so sure that his family was cursed, how did he reconcile that with his conscience?"

Cormac frowned. "I'm not sure he ever did. As I say, he refused to speak of it. But I reckon he thought it would be a risk worth taking if it would end the generations of fighting between our families."

Claire leaned back on her hands. "We'll never know for sure about your father, since he's no longer with us, but what about you? I take it you believe in this so-called curse."

Cormac nodded. "Aye, Claire, I do. I agreed to the marriage to end the feud, but by the rood, I've struggled to keep myself away from you. Only . . ." He stopped.

"Only what?"

"Only I had no idea how difficult it would be, especially living with you side by side each day, watching you transform this household with your determination and hard work."

She smiled archly. "So it was my hard work that attracted you?"

He laughed. "Not exactly, but it wouldn't be gentlemanly to list all the things that were driving me wild as I watched you each day."

"You did want me, then?" she asked softly.

"Good God, woman, does a drowning man want air?"

She sat in silence, considering his words. She should be angry, she decided. For weeks he'd made her think that something was wrong with her, that somehow she wasn't good enough to share his bed. Now it turned out he was trying to save her life. All because of some mawkish legend.

"Why didn't you just come to me and explain, before the wedding? Or at least once your father wasn't around to swear you to silence?"

"I believe I knew what your reaction would be. You're such a practical, no-nonsense person, Claire. I suspected you wouldn't let an ancient curse determine the course of your life."

"No one should," she said. "Look at the trouble all this has caused."

"Aye."

His sigh of remorse gave her a little pang, and she knew that she was beginning to forgive him. She felt the curse to be foolish, a jumble of old stories about perfectly natural childbirth mishaps through the ages. But Cormac obviously felt it was real. And perhaps that was understandable. He had, after all, lost a mother and two stepmothers.

"So what happened today?" she asked gently. "What changed your mind?"

He sat gazing into the fire. "I'm not sure. Perhaps 'twas the place."

"Perhaps 'twas Cliodhna, the faerie lady in the stone."

He smiled. "The mysterious lady who was never there and then was. Maybe she appeared today to warn us."

Claire shook her head. "I think she was there to give us her blessing."

He raised his gaze to her face and nodded. "Aye, I think you're right. It felt more blessed than cursed, didn't it?"

She was relieved at his easy agreement. Of course it had felt blessed. It had felt perfect and wonderful, and she only hoped that now her husband would forget any notion he ever had about some old family curse.

She grinned. "How did it feel?" she teased. "Hmm. I'm having a little trouble remembering."

He caught her change of mood immediately, and seemed equally glad to leave behind the discussion of the curse and all the problems it had caused them.

He hooked an arm around her waist and drew her near him. "Fie on you, milady. Is my lovemaking so easily forgotten?"

She tipped her head to look laughingly up into his eyes. "Well, it has already been several hours now."

He jumped up, lifting her along with him, and strode quickly over to the bed, depositing her none too gently. "Then mayhap 'tis time for another session. I wouldn't want you to forget what you've learned."

This time she slipped out of her own robes before he had undressed and moved next to him in the bed. She was as eager as he to feel his touch again along the length of her bare skin. For several minutes she lay still and let him caress her with hands and fingers and lips. Then she boldly flipped on top of him.

He lay still beneath her, surprised. "So you've turned the tables, eh, minx?" he said, giving her bottom a light swat.

"Sometimes a woman has to take her own measures," she replied, whispering low. She finished by swirling her tongue along the edge of his ear, which elicited a groan of pleasure.

"You're a fast learner, *chara,*" he growled, flipping her back on the bed to put himself back in control.

Claire closed her eyes and reveled in the feeling of his body on top of hers. The coarse hair of his thighs rubbed her smooth legs. His rock hard chest gently flattened her stiffened breasts.

"I think I'm remembering," she said, her voice catching as his fingers found her moist folds.

He laughed, but soon neither of them had the breath to speak or laugh as she parted her legs and he entered her. Once again her world was lost in the incredible waves emanating from her core. Both lovers were less tentative than they had been in the afternoon. His thrusts were deeper, surer. Her response was more uninhibited as she wrapped her legs around him and waited for the climax.

She was soaring. Up and up and up until she had almost reached the heights she sought. Then, incredibly, he pulled away. She gave a cry of protest. Cormac kissed her hard, then said, "Sweetheart, I'm sorry. Give me a minute."

She realized that he had withdrawn from her in time to lose his seed outside her body, just as he had that afternoon. The idea was like a dousing of cold water. Desire drained from her as the sweat cooled on her body.

After a minute or two, Cormac took her in his arms and apologized again. "I'm sorry. Let me help you finish."

She shook her head, feeling shaky and strangely insulted. "Nay, 'tis not necessary."

He didn't argue, just held her, cradling her tenderly. After several moments, he kissed her forehead, then spoke in a low voice. "Chara, I know that you think my reasons foolish, but if we are going to make love, it will have to be this way. I'll not take a chance on losing you. Until the first year has past, I'll not fill your body with my child. Not if I can help it."

She was quiet for so long, he finally spoke again. "You do understand that 'tis for you I do it this way?"

"For me? Ah, Cormac, I think 'tis not for me, but for yourself. 'Tis the fear of loss that you carry from your childhood. If it were for me, then you would ask me what I think, what I want." She rubbed a hand over her stomach. "This is my body. I should have some say in whether or not a child is to be born of it."

Now it was his turn to be silent. Finally he said, "I'm not trying to take away your say, Claire, but you must trust me on this."

She could tell from the tone of his voice that she was not going to sway him. He had her welfare at heart, however misguided. She decided to try another argument. "In this modern age, they say that lovemaking is to be enjoyed by the woman as well as the man. Am I to go unsatisfied for a whole year?"

"I promise you that will not happen," he said, sounding relieved that she had hit upon a problem he could solve.

She normally would have been more shy in discussing such things with him, but her indignation was overruling her modesty. "I hadn't yet, um, *finished* when you pulled away."

He pulled her against him more closely. "Nay, but we're not done with this night's work."

"Aye," she said, "I think we are." The discussion had left her with no further desire for lovemaking.

He nuzzled her neck. "I may be able to convince you otherwise. There are ways of achieving pleasure that have nothing to do with making a baby."

She had only a vague notion of what he was talking about, but his words and his husky tone were making the flutters begin again in her belly.

"I don't think—" she began.

He stopped her words with his mouth on hers, and after several deep kisses, her body was approaching the heightened state it had reached before he had pulled away from her.

"Now, sweetheart," he told her, "just relax and let it come." His mouth was at her breast, laving her nipple in warm rhythmic strokes while down below his hand found the sensitive nub of her private place. She lay back and let him minister to her, her total being focused on the feel of his tongue circling her nipple and his fingers tantalizing her. In mere moments he had pushed her over the top and her body quaked in climax.

She kept her eyes closed. The waves turned to ripples, then subsided. Her breast felt chilled as he withdrew his mouth. She took in a long, ragged breath.

He was right, she thought, her mind still hazy. It *had* been pleasure, though somehow it wasn't the same as earlier when he had been sharing it with her. She felt a little embarrassed.

His lips touched her nose, then the tip of her chin. She let her eyelids flutter open.

He was smiling at her tenderly and with a hint of

teasing. "You see, *chara*, lovemaking comes in many forms."

"I liked the original way we did it," she said, trying to keep the observation from sounding like a pout. After all, he had taken pains to please her.

He didn't seem in the least offended by her complaint. "So did I, princess. Though I also enjoyed watching your face just now."

Now the embarrassment was definite. "That's what I mean. I'd understood lovemaking to be a mutual thing."

"It was mutual—you were taking the pleasure and I was giving. It's one of the ways it can work, and 'tis an erotic thing for both sides."

Claire paused a moment to consider his comment. She was new at this, she realized, and she did have a lot to learn. Perhaps Cormac was right. "And can it work the other way? With me giving the pleasure while you take?"

Cormac appeared to choke. Recovering, he said, "Aye, princess, it can. But 'tis a lesson that will wait for another time. I believe you've had enough for one day."

She wondered if he was going to leave her and return to his own bed, and she was curiously reluctant to let him go. His warm body felt comfortable and right next to her. "Will you stay here?" she whispered.

He pulled her more firmly into his arms and whispered, "Princess, a team of prize mules could not pull me from this bed tonight."

When she woke up the next morning, he was gone. For a moment, she wondered if she'd dreamt the whole thing—the amazing afternoon at Cliodhna's Glen, then the revelations about the curse, and finally the nighttime lovemaking and falling to sleep in Cormac's arms. But it was no dream. She could still see the indentation of his body next to her in the soft mattress. She fancied she could still feel some of his warmth. Stretching like a contented kitten, she snuggled down for another few minutes in bed, letting her mind linger on the memories.

It was almost midmorning before she got down to the dining hall for some breakfast, feeling guilty for slacking off on her duties first yesterday and now today.

Eileen was waiting for her. "Is it true?" she asked, standing up with her hands on her hips as if ready for a fight.

"Is what true?" Claire asked mildly. She was determined not to let anything ruin her happy mood.

"Everyone's buzzing with the news that the master of the house finally spent the night with his bride."

Claire supposed that she shouldn't be surprised. Living in such close quarters, people seemed to know everyone else's business. Still, she would have liked to keep her new experience to herself awhile longer.

"Aye," she admitted. "Though I don't know why a husband and wife sleeping in the same room should be such a cause for commotion."

"It's cause when the husband has sworn he will never bed his wife lest the Riordan curse kill another bride."

Claire waved her hand. "Eileen, don't let yourself be carried away by foolish superstitions."

Eileen looked unpersuaded. "Are you sure, Clairy?" she asked. "Mayhap you and I should go back to O'Donnell House until the year has passed."

Claire was searching the table to see what remained of breakfast. After no dinner the previous night, she was starving. Most of the food had been eaten or removed, but she found a berry tart. She picked it up and began munching the edges without bothering to sit down first. "I'm not going anywhere," she said between nibbles. "My place is here with my husband." She met her sister's worried eyes. "But mayhap 'tis time for you to go home, Eily," she suggested gently. "I warrant Father is lonely with the boys gone."

"Aye, 'tis time for me to go back, but now I'm not sure I should leave you."

Claire laughed, her mouth full of the sweet pastry. "Leave me to the mercies of my husband? Nay, sister, I'll be fine. Things are beginning to turn out just as they should."

"But you will be"—Eileen gulped back threatening tears—"you'll be careful?"

Claire licked her fingers, finishing off the tart to the very last morsel. Then she gave her sister a slightly sticky kiss on the cheek. "I'll be careful, and I'll be fine. Let's finish breakfast, then I'll make arrangements for someone to escort you back home."

Cormac had ridden Taranis all day with little rest, but the big horse didn't seem to notice. They came back to the stables just as the sun was setting. Cormac asked Aidan to give the stallion a good wipe-down and headed slowly toward the house.

The hard riding had not helped, he realized. He still felt as guilt-ridden and confused as he had in the morning when he had awakened to find Claire's soft body nestled beside him. In the course of one day, all the resolutions of a lifetime had flown.

He told himself that he could be careful. Lovemaking didn't always have to result in pregnancy. He would continue to stay away from her as much as possible, and when that became unbearable, he would exercise control. That way, perhaps they could survive the year living in the same household without risking her life.

He had a flash of memory—the lifeless body of Rhea, Niall's mother, the woman he himself had come to love as a mother. His father had brought him to his step-mother's deathbed to say his farewells. Her skin had already begun to turn oddly gray. *This is death,* he remembered thinking, *this gray nothingness.* Last night Claire's body had been flushed rosy pink in the aftermath of their loving. He shuddered.

He would stay away from her, he vowed. He couldn't undo what had already been done, but he could avoid further risks. This night he would move back to his own bed.

Claire had shed a couple of tears as she watched Eileen ride away down the road, accompanied by Niall and Dermot. The banter of the two men had helped make the parting easier, but once they had ridden out of sight, it felt lonely.

But as she wandered back through the grand hall, she gave herself a shake. Moping was unproductive. It was fine to miss her sister. She and Eileen had had many wonderful childhood years together, but life brought changes, and she now had a husband to provide companionship.

At least, she hoped she did. She'd seen nothing of Cormac all day, and he'd left no word for her, which was disappointing after their closeness of the previous day. But she knew that their lovemaking represented a momentous step in their relationship, and she was not about to let things drift back to the way they had been before.

All day, she'd noticed sly glances from the servants. As Eileen had said, behind her back they were probably busy discussing their master and mistress's new intimacy. None of Cormac's brothers or cousins had been rude enough to make any comment, but she imagined that they were involved in their own speculations about exactly what had gone on behind the closed door of her chamber last night. The thought made her cheeks burn.

With sudden resolution, she went out the back door of the house and made her way to the kitchens. Molly was kneading bread. She had flour up past her elbows and a dusting of it covering most of the rest of her.

"Ye look especially rosy today, milady," the cook said with a wink.

"Thank you," Claire said evenly, ignoring any deeper implications of the compliment. "I'm sorry I wasn't around for consulting all day yesterday."

"Aw, milady, I was happy to see it. I was telling my Rolf this morning that I knew things would work out between ye. Young lovers just need time off to themselves."

Normally Claire would have thought it improper to be discussing such personal matters with a servant, but Molly was so obviously well-intentioned that she relented and gave the round little woman a smile. "I believe you may be right, Molly, and, aye, I think things are working out between Lord Cormac and myself."

"I'm so happy for ye, milady. Those boys have been in such sore need of a woman here. Ye've brought sunshine to this place, and I daresay ye've brightened Master Cormac's life as well."

The cook's warm words stayed with Claire all day and helped to make up for the lack of word from Cormac. Since she'd essentially taken Molly into her confidence, it was easy to explain that she'd like to have a special meal served that evening in her chambers.

"A romantic supper for two," Molly had exclaimed. "Ye'll have to have oysters."

Nancy had mentioned something about oysters as well, and neither Eileen nor Claire had understood her meaning. "Why oysters?" she asked Molly.

When the cook had explained that oysters were supposed to enhance lovers' desires, Claire's cheeks had turned pink, but she had approved the menu choice.

Lordy, she thought to herself, as she went up to her room to dress for the evening. Molly had been almost as knowledgeable about bedroom arts as Nancy. Did every female in Ireland know tricks of seduction except for the O'Donnell sisters? Perhaps it was what came from not having a mother during those years when she and Eileen were growing into women.

She was beginning to worry. Cormac had still not come home, and she hoped she wouldn't be sitting by herself with her tureen of oyster stew. If Riordan Hall had been buzzing today, that would surely be good fodder for tomorrow's gossip.

She looked out her big window. The days were growing shorter with the approach of winter. Surely he wouldn't stay out long after dark?

She finished dressing and had wandered out twice asking for news of him. Niall and Dermot had not come back from taking Eileen, and Eamon was nowhere to be found, so she'd been forced to ask the servants. But there'd been no word.

The dining hall was dark, since there were not enough people around to warrant a formal supper. Claire went back up to her room for the third time, resigned to finishing as much as she could of the oyster stew so that Molly's efforts would not go totally to waste.

She sat at the table that she'd had set up in front of the fire and lifted a spoonful of nearly cold soup to her mouth. Before she could swallow it, the door opened and she heard a voice saying, "I hear you've been asking for me."

Fourteen

She almost dropped the spoon. Recovering, she answered a little stiffly, "I asked where you had gone. I assume 'tis a normal question for a wife to ask about her husband."

He grinned at her and walked over to drop a kiss on the top of her head. Pointing to the place setting at the other side of the small table, he asked, "Is that for me?"

She nodded, though she wasn't yet mollified. His casual attitude made all her careful plans seem a little ridiculous.

"Good," he said, sitting across from her. "I'm famished. May I?" he asked, taking the ladle from the bowl of soup. At another nod from her, he served himself a bowl of soup, then sniffed it. "Oysters?" he asked, one brow lifting slightly.

"Molly made it," she said quickly.

"Bless her," he said with a smile, lifting his spoon.

Claire had forgotten about her own plate. She watched him eat in silence for several minutes. Apparently he had told the truth about being hungry since he quickly finished one bowl of stew and served himself another. Finally he looked up and said, "You're not eating."

She took a couple of token bites, but her appetite had fled. Somehow, this was not the romantic meal she had imagined when she'd awakened with such hope this morning. Except for the light kiss when he'd come into the room, he seemed little different from before they had made love. If oysters were supposed to boost the fires of desire, she saw no signs of it. Perhaps she should try conversation.

"Were you visiting farms today?" she asked.

He scooped the last two spoonfuls from his second bowl, then sat back with a sigh. "For a time. Mostly I was riding Taranis into a sweat, trying to forget about a certain beautiful woman who has somehow managed to begin haunting my every waking thought."

Claire's stiffened shoulders relaxed. This was more like what she had had in mind. "How impolite of her," she teased.

"Aye," he agreed with mock indignation. "I believe I just may have to give the wench a good talking-to."

"What will you tell her?"

He stood up and pointed to her bowl. "First I'll tell her that if she's going to eat any more supper, she'd better do it quickly."

Claire looked up at him through lowered lashes. "And if she says she's had enough supper, thank you?"

He reached for her hand and pulled her from the chair. "Then I'll tell her to come closer so that I can let her feel the tortured state she's had me in all the infernal day."

He slid his arms around her and lifted her into a tight embrace that left her with no doubt about the state of his body. "I'm not sure that would be the way to dissuade her," she protested.

He chuckled and lowered his mouth to hers. "Who said anything about dissuading?" he murmured.

Cormac's resolutions to keep his distance from Claire had pretty much fled before he even reached the stable yard. He could almost feel the increased humming of his body as he got nearer to Riordan Hall. When he'd walked into the dark dining hall and had been told by a servant that the lady had ordered dinner in her room for them both, the humming had turned to an incessant throb that still pulsed through him as he held her against him.

He'd be careful, he swore to himself. He'd not do her harm. But he had to have her again. Even if it doomed them both.

"I didn't really need the oysters," he whispered in her ear. "I've been past ready for this all day long."

"So have I," she whispered back.

He led her to the bed, then stopped beside it. With his thumbs pressed gently under her jaw, he tipped back her head and thoroughly explored her mouth with his own, stoking the fires that were already flaming in them both. "I've waited for this all day, too," he said, pulling back for a moment. "I've gone around in a daze, thinking about this mouth." His fingers smoothed her moist lips.

She turned her face up for more, but soon kissing was not enough and they started ridding themselves and each other of their clothes, laughing as they tangled with the laces. "When you didn't send word, I thought you were regretting your decision," she told him. "I thought you were letting that curse notion take over our lives again. I'm glad I was wrong."

He saw no point in telling her that he'd never stopped believing in the curse. He'd merely made a compromise with his own conscience to make love to her without allowing himself the ultimate completion of the act. He supposed that in a way it was fortunate that the Riordan brothers had early on been targets of some of the more worldly women of the surrounding area, which meant he'd learned plenty of ways to satisfy a woman. He didn't think Claire would be disappointed. His body flared in anticipation.

She slipped into bed and moved over, making room for him to join her. "Not so far away," he protested, scooping her back with one arm as he got in beside her. "I don't intend to let you go before morning."

Claire giggled with happiness. "Perhaps I should have eaten some of those oysters after all."

"You won't need them, sweetheart," he promised, and proceeded to massage her body with slow circles from neck to toe.

At first, Claire lay passive, letting his warm hand stroke her into passion. Then she lifted her head and pushed him back on the mattress so that she could run her fingertips the length of his broad chest, up and down his thighs and, finally, around the tip of his erect shaft. He could only take the exquisite sensations for a few short minutes, before he grabbed her wrists, turned her on the bed, and positioned himself above her. She moaned with readiness, and almost as soon as he had entered her she clutched his neck and he felt her violent shudders. Her instantaneous response triggered his own, and he barely managed to escape in time to keep from exploding inside her.

They both lay still for several moments afterward. Claire was the first to speak. "So Molly was right about the oysters," she said. "We were both so"—she searched for the words—"*ready.*"

He laughed. "As I told you, I'd been ready all day. That's the way it is with men. All we need is the mere thought of our fair lady and our tool begins to respond."

"I believe women think about it, too, though perhaps our bodies are not quite so directly connected with our thoughts."

"It can be a curse at times." The word *curse* seemed

to echo in the room. Cormac quietly rephrased his observation. "It can be inconvenient."

"Is it still the curse that makes you pull away from me, um, before . . . you know . . . ?"

"Aye, and in spite of your dismissal of the notion, I'm not convinced that there is nothing to worry about. So we'll have no more discussion on the matter until we're an old married couple—one year from now."

His insistence on limiting their lovemaking left Claire curiously vexed, even though this time he had been able to fully satisfy her before he had felt it necessary to leave her. It was almost as if some perverse female instinct wanted him to be so carried away by her that he would forget all other considerations.

It was foolish, she told herself, letting him pull her back into his arms. He reached down to gather the covers up around them.

"Sleep well, princess," he told her.

"You, too," she answered.

Within minutes his even breathing told her that he was doing exactly that, but it was a much longer time before her own spinning thoughts let her drift off into slumber.

"You look tired, brother. Mayhap you should let me do the hard work today," Eamon joked to Cormac as the two walked up to the stables, where they'd agreed to help Aidan with the horseshoeing. The big farrier didn't really need their assistance, but the brothers had participated in the event since they were boys. As youngsters, they'd found the process fascinating, and now that they were grown, it had become a custom for one or more of them to be present on shoeing day.

"I can work circles around you," Cormac scoffed. "Especially since you've taken to spending so much time in the library like some kind of damn priest. You're fast going soft on us."

Eamon was unoffended. He'd always been the book learner of the three and had endured his brothers' jibes about it his whole life. He flexed his arm. "I can still take you down three out of four falls."

"Aye, but only when I'm drunk."

The banter was typical, but as usual, underlying it was mutual caring. "Seriously, Cormac, you look haggard. I trust 'tis only your new sleeping arrangements causing you to miss your rest. You're not feeling ill, are you?"

Cormac was slow to answer, but finally said, "Nay."

"I warrant a new husband with a wife as beautiful as Claire has a right to be tired come morning."

The matter was too private to confide, even to Eamon, but his brother had a discerning eye. Cormac *was* tired. It had been over a week since he and Claire had begun to make love, and their evening sessions had been full of passion, tenderness, and excitement. Yet each night he became more worried about his own ability to control himself. What if he slipped? If he'd been unable to bear the thought of losing a bride he had yet to know, it was now a thousand times more unthinkable. He could not lose Claire now that he had come to know her determination and spirit and now that he had experienced loving her.

No matter how hard she had worked during the day, each night she was eager for him, ready to learn and to explore the heights their passion could reach. It had become a household joke that they could barely stand to finish their supper before they disappeared up the long stairway and down the hall to their room.

"I'm not tired, Eamon," he said finally.

They were almost up to the stables. Eamon stopped walking and put a hand on Cormac's shoulder to hold him back. "But there is something wrong, isn't there?"

Again Cormac waited a long time before answering and finally said, "Nay." His whole life he and Eamon had shared problems, but this was one he'd have to deal with himself.

"Is it that you're worried about the English?"

Cormac looked up in surprise. He'd almost forgotten that they'd received a message that morning from Sean Riordan reporting that General Bixleigh had received reinforcements in preparation for an all-out attack on the rebels.

"I don't like the thought of this country being overrun by English troops," he said, "but I don't expect to lose sleep over the matter. 'Tis no concern to Riordan Hall."

"It will be if Sean and the other northern Riordans join forces with the English. Then it will be our kin fighting fellow countrymen."

"I hope Sean and the others will stay out of it," he agreed. The rest of the way to the stables they discussed the possibility of war, which to Cormac seemed a much less volatile topic than his own domestic dilemma.

"Ye seem happy enough, milady," Molly said kindly. "A bit tired, but that's to be expected with a new bride." She leaned across the kettle of hot wax that she was ladling into candle molds. "It gets easier, dearie," she added in a conspiratorial whisper.

Claire smiled. "I appreciate the concern, Molly, but I'm just fine."

"He's treating ye kindly, then? Men can be beasts sometimes."

Kind was hardly the adjective Claire would use to describe how she'd been treated during the past week of long, amorous nights she and Cormac had shared. It was hard to imagine that Molly, now entering a comfortable old age with her Rolf, would even remember the kind of lightning passion she and Cormac had found together.

"Aye, Molly, he treats me well."

The old cook beamed. "I always knew that Cormac was a good lad. Sometimes when he was little I'd worry about him. He seemed to brood more than natural for a young'un. 'Twas losing his mum and stepmums that way, I warrant. I was afraid it might leave him scarred for life."

Perhaps it had, Claire thought. She'd still been unable to persuade Cormac to make love to her completely, and she began to fear that she never would. It was the only cloud in their newfound happiness.

"I say, have you heard from yer sister, milady?"

Molly was evidently repeating the question for the second time. Claire forced her thoughts away from Cormac and answered, "Aye, she's happy back at home with my father."

"With yer father and your brothers, right?"

Claire had told no one at Riordan Hall that her brothers had ridden north to join the rebels. Since the English general had stayed here, she didn't feel the revelation would set well with the Riordans. "My brothers are away at the moment," she said.

"Ah, then I bet your father especially misses ye, lass. 'Twas right for Mistress Eileen to go back to him."

"Aye."

"I trust yer brothers have gone south, not north. That's where the trouble's likely."

"What trouble?" Claire asked.

"Didn't ye hear about Master Sean Riordan's letter?"

"Nay."

"He says that English general has fresh troops sent right from London. They're determined to clear out the nest of vipers that are causing problems across the northern counties."

The candle mold Claire was steadying wobbled, spilling wax on the dirt floor. Claire forced herself to concentrate on her task, but she asked, "Nest of vipers? Is he talking about the rebels?"

"Aye, the O'Neill himself. They say he eats small babies for lunch and when they come across anything that has a royal seal, he personally pisses on it, beggin' yer pardon, milady."

"So the English have sent more troops to fight against O'Neill?"

"That's what I'm telling ye. They say they're going to wipe the rebels out—down to the last man."

The news about the English reinforcements dominated the conversation at dinner. The table was full. As many of the Riordan kin as possible had come to join the brothers to discuss the new developments. Claire kept mostly quiet, other than to offer that she didn't see why it was that men always got so worked up when battle was discussed.

The Riordans regarded her with the amused tolerance men reserved for women in such matters, then continued talking.

"The rebels haven't a prayer," Niall said. "Bixleigh's troops are seasoned and have much better arms—muskets and cannons with plenty of powder. O'Neill's men are fighting with knives and rocks."

"Aye, but they know the countryside," Eamon pointed out. "And they're fighting for their homes and their families."

"Why don't they ask their families if they want to be fought *for?*" Claire asked. "I warrant most of them would rather see their men home safe and sound. Who cares if Elizabeth wants to call herself queen of all the Isles? Everyone knows that the land belongs to those who live on it and work it."

None of the men could see her logic. " 'Tis a matter of principle, *chara,*" Cormac told her.

Though it warmed her that he now felt comfortable enough to show their changed relationship by using endearments in public, his condescending tone irritated.

She still felt it later that night when he finally left behind the talk of war and joined her in their room. She'd almost considered pretending to be asleep, but decided that would be foolish, especially since it would deprive her of their nightly pleasure as much as it would him. Instead she sat upright in bed, waiting for him, pondering the question of whether she should tell him that her brothers were with O'Neill.

She didn't think that he would report the O'Donnell family loyalties to the British, but she had to keep in mind that Riordan kin were supporting the English. And Cormac had always been adamant about the allegiance he owed to his kin. In the end, she decided it was best to wait and say nothing. She knew that Cormac had little respect for Bixleigh, and there had been no mention of anyone at Riordan Hall joining forces with the English.

He looked a little unsteady when he finally came to bed.

"It appears that talk of war makes men thirsty," she observed wryly.

He gave a sheepish grin. "Aye, the ale pitchers were all dry by the time we left the table," he admitted.

She shook her head. "I suppose I may as well have gone to sleep, then. I daresay you'll not want more than sleep yourself this night."

His slightly tipsy grin became wolfish. "I had the very same thought climbing the stairs just now." He paused to strip off his doublet and shirt in one exaggerated gesture. Then he came over to the bed and leaned on it with both hands. "But the sight of a beautiful woman in my lair has changed my mind."

She looked at him with a doubtful expression. "I'm thinking sleep may be the best plan."

His gaze had slipped to where her nightclothes revealed the tops of her breasts. "Nay, princess," he said. "I'm not that drunk."

In a minute he was naked and had joined her in bed, his mouth beginning the by-now familiar slow arousal of her body. The irritation that had been prickling at her all evening vanished, and she willingly returned his embrace. His mouth hinted of liquor, but the flavor was not unpleasant. In fact, she soon found herself squirming, ready to feel his deeper touch.

She tried to move into an inviting position, but he held back. "*Chara,* much as I want to, I'd not risk taking you that way tonight. I'm afraid in my current condition, my control is not what it should be."

Her irritation returned in an instant. She knew her pique was unreasonable. He was trying to protect her, but her body was clamoring for some kind of release, and she couldn't believe that he was denying it.

He studied her face, then laughed. "Don't scowl, sweetheart. I don't intend to leave you unsatisfied. 'Tis time I showed you some of those other tricks I told you about."

He pushed her gently back against the bed and resumed kissing her skin, moving from her neck to her breasts and, this time, continuing down along the soft curve of her stomach. His hands massaged her thighs, encouraging her to open to him, as he moved higher, closer to her private core. His thumbs found her there, gently parting her to allow access to the warm stroke of his tongue.

She gasped in pleasure at the incredible new feeling. He was utterly gentle as he moved his mouth over her, sucking lightly, then licking, then sucking again. Her fingers gripped the bedclothes. She lay awash in wave after wave of sensation. His fingers moved inside her, and his mouth now focused on her sensitive nub. She cried out as he brought her to a wracking climax.

He moved quickly up her body and softened her cries with his kiss as he murmured, "Hush, sweetheart, you'll have the entire hall awake thinking that I've murdered you."

She could neither move nor speak.

"I haven't, have I?" he asked after a moment, but his voice was thick with amusement.

She managed to shake her head weakly.

"Well, good. I'm sorry, I should have given you some warning about the intensity of that particular practice."

"Aye," she croaked. "You should have."

He laughed. "I'm glad you liked it."

He gathered her in his arms while she took a few more moments to recuperate. Finally she asked, "But what about you?"

He shook his head. "I took my pleasure this night watching you, sweetheart. You are so beautiful in passion."

She already knew that he did like to watch her, and had finally lost her shyness at the thought.

"But you didn't have . . ."

" 'Tis not always necessary, sweetling, especially when one has had more ale than warranted."

This was new to her. As much as she had enjoyed what he had just done to her, she missed the feeling of bonding they had when they made love.

"It was lovely," she said softly, "but I think I prefer when we do it together."

"Aye. This way is not better, just a different kind of pleasing."

He seemed to be drifting off to sleep, but the intense stimulation had left her wide awake. "Did you men manage to solve the dispute while you finished off the ale?" she asked.

His voice was groggy, but he answered her. "Dermot is a hothead. He thinks O'Neill and his men are going to make the English come down on all of us so hard that the whole country will end up a battlefield."

"Of course, he has more at stake. His own brother is with Bixleigh. 'Tis logical he should speak against the rebels."

"Aye, especially now that Bixleigh has appointed Sean to be his special commander."

Claire had not heard this report. "You mean he may fight with him?"

"He *will* fight with him if the rebels don't surrender. This time the English are apparently determined to bring peace to Ireland, no matter how many Irishmen they have to kill to do it."

Distressed, Claire went up on an elbow and looked down at Cormac, whose eyes were already closed. "If there is fighting with the rebels, will Dermot join his brother?"

"If there is fighting, I reckon every able Riordan will join Sean."

Claire's throat closed. "Including you?"

He opened his eyes and regarded her gravely for a long moment. "Aye, princess, including me."

She didn't speak for a moment. Then she said, "You'd leave Riordan Hall?"

"The fighting is in the north. You'll be safe enough

here. And you have your brothers nearby if you need help."

Claire closed her eyes and lay back on the bed. Her brothers were nowhere near. They were north with Shane O'Neill. And from the sound of things, her husband might soon be facing them on the field of battle.

Fifteen

It was Claire's first visit home since she'd moved back to nurse Rory. As usual, the few O'Donnell servants were delighted to see her. Fiona, their childhood nurse, had greeted her with tears in her eyes.

"The house is not the same without ye, dearie," she'd said, giving Claire an embrace.

Eileen had come down to greet her and stood waiting patiently while their old servant fussed over her sister. But when Fiona had bustled off to be sure the cook was preparing one of Claire's favorite dishes for supper, Eileen took Claire's arm and said, "Walk with me in the garden, love. I've something to tell you."

Claire had been looking around for her father. She had sent word of the visit and couldn't imagine that Raghnall would not have made a point to be there to greet her. "Where's Father?" she asked Eileen, while letting her sister lead her out the side door to the gardens.

"He's not here. That's what I need to talk to you about. I'm afraid you'll find it upsetting."

Claire stopped walking and closed her eyes. "He hasn't gone to join them, has he?"

"Aye. He said if his three sons are going to fight to keep Ireland free, the least he can do is stand with them."

Claire opened her eyes and looked at her sister with a big sigh. "He's nearly sixty years old."

"Aye, but Father was never one to acknowledge the possibility of aging."

Claire looked around at her flowers. Except for the seasonal changes, the garden looked the same, and as always, it gave her a sense of peace. "Didn't you try to talk him out of it?" she asked her sister. But she knew that Eileen could have argued all day and all night and it wouldn't sway Raghnall once he'd made up his mind.

"Of course I did. I called him a blithering fool."

Claire laughed in spite of herself. "You didn't!"

"Aye, and a few things beyond that. But he was set on going, Clairy. He says that withering virgin that sits on the English throne has no business calling herself queen of our country."

The O'Donnells had always been independent and fiercely protective of their small tracts of land. She understood her father's reasoning. She just couldn't understand why he felt that he himself had to go fight. "War is for young men," she said aloud.

"Well, our young men are in it now, and our old one as well," Eileen replied. She motioned to the bench by the rose arbor and the two sisters sat side by side, staring ahead miserably, the beauty of the flowers surrounding them temporarily forgotten.

"I wish you'd been here, Claire," Eileen said after a moment. "Together we may have been able to convince him."

"Nay, if he was set on going, nothing would have altered it. We'll just have to hope that the matter is settled peaceably after all."

Eileen looked stricken. "Oh, Claire, you've not heard?"

"Heard what?"

"It was the news that made Father decide to go. The English troops and the traitorous countrymen who support them have begun attacking rebel camps. A number of Shane O'Neill's men have already been killed."

"Seamus, Conn, and Rory?" Claire asked, holding her breath.

"We know nothing more. Father said he would send word as soon as he finds them."

"Oh, Eily, what a coil this is!" Claire felt as if her heart were being squeezed by a giant hand. Cormac's cousin Sean was undoubtedly among those "traitorous countrymen" Eileen had mentioned. And if the fighting had started in earnest, Cormac and his brothers might be riding to join them before long.

"Aye," Eileen agreed glumly.

The sisters sat lost in their own thoughts for several minutes, then finally Claire said, "I'll just have to stop him from going."

Eileen looked confused. "He's already gone, Claire. I told you. He left two days ago."

"Not Father—Cormac. I'll have to stop him from going."

"Going where?"

"North to fight."

"Is your husband planning to join the rebels, too?"

Claire met Eileen's eyes. "Nay, the Riordans' kin are supporting the English. Cormac would be fighting with Bixleigh."

Her sister's jaw dropped. "Lordy, Claire."

"Aye," she agreed. "If I don't do something, I may very well have my husband killing my father or my father killing Cormac."

"What can you do? Cormac appears to be every bit as stubborn as Father."

Claire agreed with her sister's assessment. Desperately, she tried to think of things that would keep Cormac back at Riordan Hall. Only one possibility came to mind. Claire jumped up from the bench. "I'm sorry, Eily, but I'm going to have to cut short our visit. There's only one thing I can think of that would make Cormac stay here, but it's a plan that will take some time to accomplish. I'll just have to hope the news about the fighting doesn't reach Riordan Hall until I can make it happen."

"What are you planning?" Eileen asked.

A glint of determination lit Claire's eyes as she answered, "First of all, I need to have another visit with Nancy. Do you want to come?"

Eileen smiled for the first time since Claire's arrival. "For more of her advice? I wouldn't miss it for the world."

"Let me get it straight, Mistress Claire." Once again Nancy had chosen to perch on a table instead of using one of the benches in her comfortable quarters above the taproom. "Ye and yer husband have been having at it every night now for—how long?—a fortnight?" At Claire's nod, the barmaid continued. "But he's mortal afeared of filling yer belly, so he leaves the thing half done."

Claire sat with her cheeks flaming and wished she hadn't invited Eileen to share this discussion, but it was too late now, and the stakes were too high to worry about modesty. "Aye," she confirmed. "I need to know what I can do to, um, get with child."

"Of course, you ladies know that if he's wigglin' around inside ye, eventually ye could end up with a babe, even if he doesn't let go full bore."

Eileen and Claire both swallowed hard, but nodded as if such wisdom had been common talk over supper at

O'Donnell House. Her voice weak, Claire pressed, "The thing is, er, I can't wait for eventually. I need this to happen soon."

Nancy was dressed for the evening in a shockingly low gown. Every time she leaned toward the two sisters, it appeared that her ample breasts were in danger of tumbling out of the lacings. She grinned wickedly. "Well, ye could always call upon another candidate to accomplish the job. Husbands are rarely any the wiser." At the sisters' horrified expressions, she put up her hands and added, " 'Tis not necessary if ye're squeamish about such matters. Ye can make yer man lose control easy enough. Women have been doing it for centuries."

Put that way, it sounded like an underhanded tactic, and Claire had a moment of doubt, but then she thought about the possibility of her husband and her father meeting each other in war, and hardened her resolve. "That's what I want, Nancy," she said firmly. "I need to know everything you can tell me about how to make a man forget himself and lose control."

Eileen sat to one side on a stool, her eyes as wide as penny cakes.

"It helps to start with a bit of tongue swirling right at the tip, if you know what I mean."

Claire and Eileen looked at each other. It was obvious that Nancy had already lost them both. The barmaid gave a slightly exasperated cluck of her tongue and said, "Nay, you're not with me? Ah, ladies, it appears that we'd better start with basics."

Eileen and Claire leaned forward, determined to catch every word.

Cormac, Niall, and Eamon were somber as they rode back to Riordan Hall from the home of the Clearys, a neighboring family who was planning to join the Riordans as they headed north to the fighting. Dermot Riordan had already left, taking a few other of their kin along with him. During the meeting at the Clearys' it had been agreed that the rest of the Riordans, along with the other loyalist families—the Gallivans, the Mitchells, and the Sullivans—would gather at Riordan Hall tomorrow and leave together from there.

"People would understand if you decided not to go, Cormac," Eamon told him as they helped Aidan stable their horses. The horse master had greeted them with news of Claire's early return from O'Donnell House. "You've a new wife who's eager for your company."

"What kind of leader lets his men go off to war while he stays at home?" Cormac asked in reply. "Do you think Father would have ever let us go fight without standing at our side?"

"He would have been leading the charge," Niall confirmed.

"It seems a harsh thing for Claire," Eamon protested.

"I may send her back home to her father," Cormac said. "I haven't decided. We'll have to discuss it tonight."

"She doesn't know we're leaving?" Niall asked.

Cormac shook his head.

"I don't envy you that discussion, brother." Niall grinned at Eamon. "Mayhap we should vacate the hall for the evening lest we get caught in the crossfire."

Eamon remained serious. "I don't envy you, either, Cormac. Her family's sympathies are with the rebels, I believe. This will not set well with her."

Cormac put a bucket of oats in Taranis's stall, then started walking toward the door. "Aye, but she'll just have to understand."

"We should have ridden through Kilmessen to buy her a little present or something," Niall muttered.

"I'm not worried," Cormac said. "Claire and I have begun to understand each other. I can handle this. I'll see you two in the morning."

He strode quickly down the hill toward the house. His brothers exchanged dubious glances. "What's your prediction, brother?" Niall asked.

Eamon shrugged. "I've met few women as feisty as Claire. We'd do well to stay clear of the north wing tonight."

"I think you're right. What's more, it's our last night here. What do you say we head into Kilmessen? Surely we can find a couple of comely wenches who would like to brighten up our last night at home before we head off to battle."

Eamon shook his head at his wild younger brother, but he smiled and agreed. "I'll say one thing. We'll likely be welcomed more warmly than Cormac will, once he's told Claire he's leaving."

Claire had hurried to get home by dinnertime only to be told that Cormac and his brothers had not yet returned from a meeting they had had at a neighboring manor. The delay allowed her time to settle the butterflies in her stomach that had begun as she had listened to Nancy's careful descriptions of how to be irresistible to a man. This time the tavern maid's instructions had been much more intimate than a recipe for talc.

She ate lightly, then tried to relax by wandering out to the vegetable garden to pull weeds in the waning light of the day. She hoped Cormac would not be too late since she was determined to put her plan into effect that very night. She couldn't afford to delay. It might take some time for her to actually become pregnant and, of course, it would be some weeks before they would know. She could only hope that word from the fighting in the north would be very slow in coming and that she could keep Cormac here at Riordan Hall in the meantime.

The fast fall twilight came and went and there was still no sign of them. She wandered around to the kitchens to wash off the garden dirt, then went up to her room to wait.

It wasn't long before she heard his footsteps. The mere sound of them set the butterflies jumping again. What would he say if she tried to do some of the things that Nancy had suggested? Would he think her a wanton? Perhaps, but if it would keep him home from the fighting, she was willing to risk it.

"You've retired early, princess," he said as he came into the room.

She threw aside the embroidery hoop she'd been absentmindedly stabbing without much purpose. "Nay, I've not retired. I was waiting for you." She smiled and held her face up for a kiss as he came over to where she was perched on the bed.

"Waiting for me? That has a nice sound to it."

She pointed to the fire. The nest of cushions in front of it had become their own special place. Tonight she'd readied it with some wine and a platter of cheeses and dried fruits. "Shall we have some wine and you can tell me about this important meeting that kept you all away so late?"

He seemed to avoid her gaze for a moment, and he said, "I'll take the wine, but I'd rather hear about your day. I was surprised to see you back. I thought you'd planned to stay a couple of days with your family."

"I changed my mind."

"How is your sister? And is Rory now completely recovered from his wound?"

For a moment she wondered what he would say if she

told him that Rory was with Shane O'Neill, along with her other brothers and her father. Perhaps that would be enough to keep Cormac neutral in the conflict. He had kin on one side, but *she* had kin on the other. The best solution for them all would be for the Midland Riordans to stay home.

But as soon as she had the thought, she dismissed it. The conflict between the O'Donnells and the Riordans was too fresh. Rory had killed Cormac's father. If anything, knowing that the O'Donnells were taking up arms with O'Neill might hasten his decision to join the fight. It would be a chance for the Riordans to take their revenge in honorable battle.

Her original plan was still the best one, she decided. Cormac was so terrified by the idea of her being pregnant, she was confident that he would not sign on to fight if he knew she was in that precarious state.

"Rory has recovered well," she answered finally. "And Eileen is fine, though she claims to miss me."

He gave a frown of sympathy. "Of course she does. Perhaps you can go back for a longer visit soon," he added, with a hint too much of casualness.

Before Claire could analyze the meaning of his suggestion, he pulled her up and over to the pillows. "Are you going to feed me, woman," he asked, "or shall I begin to ravish you at once?"

Claire laughed. This was going to be easy, she reassured herself. And it was the right thing to do. She and Cormac were in love. Every new exploration of their passion had led them to new delights. This would simply be one more extension of the happiness they had found together. Once the baby came, healthy and strong, he'd be grateful that she had inveigled his cooperation.

"I shall feed you first," she replied, "and then you can

ravish me. Or, who knows? Mayhap 'tis I who shall ravish you tonight."

He lifted an eyebrow at her bold answer and bent to kiss her before taking a long drink of his ale. "That would be novel," he said. "I don't think I've ever been ravished before. Certainly not by a princess."

Their teasing quickly became physical and soon they both had discarded their clothes and lay naked in the warmth of the fire, stroking each other without impatience in the fashion of lovers who had grown familiar with each other's bodies.

Finally Claire decided that the time had come to try her new knowledge. She traced a finger down Cormac's flat stomach and into the nest of hair below. His manhood had already sprung to life. Taking a deep breath, she leaned over to encircle it with her mouth. She was unsure of how hard or how soft to suck, but Cormac's moans of surprised pleasure reassured her that she was doing it more or less correctly.

She looked up for a moment to see his face. His eyes were closed and he looked lost in bliss. "Is this good?" she asked him softly.

"Ahhh, sweetheart," he breathed. "You have no idea."

She smiled and went back to her task, using her hand as well as her mouth to heighten the sensations. Finally she tasted salt at the back of her mouth, just as Nancy had told her.

'Tis almost the moment, Nancy had said. *It's all easy from there.*

Pulling away, Claire moved quickly to straddle him, then guided him into her moist and ready sheath.

Cormac groaned. Every bit of feeling in his entire body had pooled into his loins. He'd been unprepared for her exquisite ministrations. According to the ribald talk of the old men of the family, such attentions were usually given only by women who were paid for the service. But this had been Claire's mouth around him, Claire's tongue teasing, her lips pressing the most intimate part of him.

Her thighs held tight as she rocked against him, building the fever with each stroke. He reached for her shoulders to pull her down on top of him in a crushing embrace. "Forgive me, *chara*," he whispered as he pulsed inside her, deep and long and uncontrolled.

"God almighty," he said after a long moment.

Claire lay collapsed against him, their bodies still joined. Tears she didn't remember shedding wet her cheeks and his chest.

When she could think again, she had a brief moment of triumph. She'd done it. With a little help from Nancy, she'd accomplished her goal. But her triumph was tempered with worry. Other than his one outburst, which she wasn't sure whether to interpret as an oath or a prayer, Cormac had remained silent. He still held her, but his arms had stiffened.

Her tears had dried. The moisture on her body had cooled, and she shivered, in spite of the fire. She had known that he might be angry. It was a risk she had been willing to take.

"You're cold," he said, his voice tight. "We should get into bed."

He *was* angry, she decided. Well, so be it. When he held their baby in his arms, he'd forgive her.

She moved away from him. "Aye, the evenings are getting chilly." The weather was the last thing she wanted to talk about, but his tone had become so frosty that she couldn't find the right words.

They were both silent as they climbed into bed, but when they were settled, he reached for her. The gesture was enough to make her risk asking, "Are you angry with me?"

"Angry, lord, *chara*, how could I be angry with such a generous and passionate lover? Nay, 'tis myself I'm angry with. I wasn't careful tonight as I have been up until now, and the consequences may be disastrous."

"Would it be so very terrible?" she whispered. "Wouldn't you like me to give you a son?"

"I'd like nothing more," he answered, "but not at the cost of your life."

His answer relieved her. As long as she was sure that he, too, would welcome a baby, everything was all right. "Well, 'tis too late to worry about it," she said contentedly, snuggling into his arms.

"Aye, it does no good to close the barn door once the cows have escaped. But perhaps after all it's a good thing that I'm leaving. Being apart from you may be the only way I can be sure that this won't happen again."

She pulled away in alarm. "What do you mean, *leaving?*"

He tugged her back again. "I'm sorry, princess, but tomorrow we're gathering the loyalist families of the Midlands and riding north to Bixleigh's camp. Fighting has broken out, and they are going to need our help."

Tomorrow. Claire felt sick. Even if she were already with child, there was no way she would be able to tell for at least three weeks when her next cycle was due.

"And if I ask you to stay?" she asked.

"Don't ask it, sweetheart. These are my people, and my duty is to be at their head. If my father were alive, he'd not shirk from being there."

She debated again whether to tell him that her family was with the O'Neill, then decided against it. She could not in good conscience provide him with information about what he would be calling the enemy. Not when that enemy was her own family.

"I want you to go home to your father while I'm gone," he said. His tone became light as he kissed the tip of her nose and said, "It will keep you from missing me."

Desperately, she tried one more plea. "You yourself said there may be consequences of our lovemaking tonight. Isn't that reason enough to stay? What if I am already with child?"

She could hear the guilt in his voice as he answered, "If you are with child, then God help me, *chara,* for I may have doomed us both."

Amazing herself, she managed to get through the morning without a tear. Perhaps it was the presence of all the strangers, crowding the yard in front of Riordan Hall, that kept her emotions in check. Or perhaps it was the anger that simmered as she watched the preparations for battle.

The men acted as if they were going to some kind of a tournament or village festival, not to a deadly fight from which many may not return. She didn't understand their jovial good spirits and dark humor. One of the horsemen had an effigy of Shane O'Neill skewered on the end of his lance. Another had a skinned rabbit with an *O* carved on its belly. The poor creature dangled from a miniature noose hung over the man's saddle horn.

Everywhere men were testing their weapons or strutting to show off new armor or wrestling in typical male tests of skill. Claire was jostled and bumped as she made her way through the crowd, looking for Cormac. Finally she spotted him at the little stone armory.

"You should go inside, *chara,*" he said. "There's no need for you to be out here."

"I wanted to be here to say good-bye," she said. She felt utterly dispirited and exhausted as well. After Cormac had told her his news, she'd lain awake most of the night. All her plans had been to no avail. Cormac and his brothers were riding into danger, and there was nothing she could do about it.

"I doubt it will take long to finish this business," he told her, his voice consoling. "You go back to O'Donnell House, and I'll be riding there to fetch you before you know it."

Two men who had fallen into a wrestling match suddenly tumbled into them, nearly knocking her off her feet. They picked themselves up, murmuring apologies, and ran off, but Claire felt a sob rise in her throat.

"Give me a kiss, then go on inside, princess," Cormac said again, more gently. "I need to see to my men and I don't want to have to worry about you."

She nodded, trying not to let the tears fall as he brushed her lips with his. "Take care of yourself, *chara,*" he said, then he put his hands on her shoulders and pushed her gently in the direction of the house.

Sixteen

Claire was in for a surprise when she arrived back at O'Donnell House with the news of Cormac's departure. She'd expected to find the place nearly empty, with Eileen wandering the big rooms missing their brothers and father. Instead, the house was full to the rafters.

"The rebel families sent word that their womenfolk and children were to join together here," Eileen explained, as Claire came in through the front door and looked around in confusion.

"They're *living* here?" she asked. "All these people?"

Eileen laughed. "Aye. 'Tis quite a lively crew. At last count, I believe it was twenty-two women and some three dozen children."

"Good Lord, Eily."

"I know, but we're making do. Everyone helps, and they all brought along food when they came."

"How long will they stay?"

Eileen shrugged. "I don't know. The men thought it would be safer for us all to be together. I suppose they'll be here until the war is over."

In the side parlor a group of children were playing soldier, bouncing on the furniture and firing pretend muskets. From upstairs, Claire heard the sound of two babies crying at once. "Perhaps I should go on back to

Riordan Hall," she said. "You don't need one more body to house here."

Eileen threw an arm around her. "Don't be silly. The more the merrier. Besides, we can use another pair of hands caring for the babies." She leaned to whisper in her sister's ear. " 'Twill give you practice for the day you get one of your own."

Claire gave a weak smile. "Now that Cormac has gone with the others, I can't be sure that day will ever come."

"It will, Clairy. Soon enough the men will tire of their rough-and-tumble war games and they'll be back here wanting their soft beds and soft women."

A train of children suddenly barreled out of the parlor, weaving in and out between the two sisters. Claire smiled as Eileen tried to gently steer them back into their makeshift playroom.

"I hope you're right, Eily," she said finally. "This war can end none too soon for me."

They received no word about the fighting—from either side. At least the days at O'Donnell House passed quickly. With such a household, there was always food to prepare or linens to clean or children to tend. At night, after all the youngsters had finally gone to sleep, the women sat around the great room fire and talked of how they missed their normal lives in their own homes with their menfolk by their sides.

Claire enjoyed their company, but she missed having special time alone with her sister. Eileen had not asked Claire about her final night with Cormac after the two sisters had gone to visit Nancy, and Claire hadn't spoken of it.

In any event, Claire had begun to think that her efforts to become pregnant against Cormac's wishes had been wrong. Now that Cormac had officially joined the Eng-

lish side, he couldn't leave the army, even if he wanted
to. If she discovered that she was with child, she would
be left to deal with the matter all by herself.

Still, she couldn't help counting the days until the end
of the month, waiting and wondering. In spite of her
guilt, some part of her still hoped that Cormac had
planted a permanent part of himself inside her, especially
now that he was in peril.

As much as the matter was in her thoughts, it was still
a surprise when her always regular monthly flow did not
appear. A day or two later, she started to have some
unsettled feelings in her midsection. Amazing as it
seemed, when they had just come together that one time,
it appeared that her plan to have Cormac's baby had
succeeded.

The two sisters had escaped to their rose arbor bench
for a little bit of quiet.

"Some days I feel as if I'll go mad if we don't get
some kind of word soon," Eileen said.

"Not hearing is probably a good sign, Eily," Claire
reassured her. "If there had been any mishap with any
of our kin, they would have sent the news."

Eileen gave her sister a sharp glance. "Usually I'm
the calm one and you the worrier. What's making you
so calm these days?"

Claire flushed. "I'm worried, too, of course, but worrying won't get the food cooked or the beds changed."

Eileen didn't want to be steered off the subject. She
turned around on the bench and leaned toward her sister
to ask insistently. "Nay, Clairy, something's *different*
about you. You walk around singing and half the time
look as if you're off somewhere in another world. It's
not like you."

Claire's suspicion about the pregnancy had grown to

a certainty, but so far she'd told no one. Circumstances being what they were, she'd felt it would be better to go as long as possible without worrying anyone else about her condition. But she should have known that she'd not be able to keep such a thing from Eileen.

"Ah, Eily, you're right. There is something different about me, but I don't want you to worry about it."

Eileen bounced on her seat. "Mary Claire O'Donnell, why didn't you tell me?"

Claire smiled. "I'm telling you now, aren't I?"

"But you—" Eileen stammered excitedly. "I thought you and Cormac had never. . . . There wasn't time after we talked to Nancy. . . ."

"Apparently there was time," Claire said with a smile.

"Oh, Claire!" Eileen slid over to give her sister a hug. "Does Cormac know?"

Claire shook her head. "Nay."

Her answer sobered Eileen. " 'Tis not the best of times for such a joyous event. It doesn't seem fair."

"Nay, it doesn't seem fair, Eily, but I reckon babies come when they come."

"Aye." Eileen took her sister's hand and gave it a squeeze. "And no matter what's going on with the rest of the world, we'll be sure this little one gets a warm welcome."

Weeks turned into months, and still there was little news from the north. The O'Donnell House garden was show-ing signs of spring. The women had settled into a routine that was busy and pleasant enough, even though every-one knew that they were all just marking time until their men could come home.

The routine was broken abruptly when one day Eileen came sailing down the stairs, heading for the door.

"It's Seamus!" she called to Claire, who was seated

in the middle of the parlor floor playing a game of nones with three little cousins.

Eileen disappeared out the front door, and Claire rushed after her, in time to see her brother, Seamus, ride up to the O'Donnell stables. Both sisters ran down the stone path to meet him.

Their immediate fear—that he had come with bad news—was relieved when he smiled at them and lifted each of them off their feet in a big bear hug.

"Ah, Mussy, 'tis good to see your face," Claire said.

Seamus grinned at her use of the old childhood pet name. "And you, sister. It appears that married life has not been so tough on you. I swear you bloom brighter than the roses in your precious garden yonder."

She laughed. Of all her brothers, Seamus had always been the one with the pretty words. "You look wonderful yourself, Seamus, though I'll not say that war favors you, for I'll never admit that anything good can come of it."

Seamus's smile died. "You have the right of it, sister. 'Tis an awful thing—there's no other description."

"But Father is well?" Eileen asked. "And Rory and Conn? Were you all together?"

"Aye, all were well when I left. Father joined us as soon as he arrived. We all argued that he'd be better back here taking care of O'Donnell House and the women I understand you have gathered, but we couldn't convince him."

"He's so stubborn," Claire said with a little stomp of her foot.

"Aye, and his oldest daughter is not at all like him," Seamus said with an ironic grin.

He hadn't asked what she was doing back at O'Donnell House, which made Claire wonder if he already knew that Cormac had joined the fighting on the opposite side. They had a lot to discuss, she realized, but it could wait until he'd had time to recover from his long ride and eat something.

"Are you hungry?" she asked.

"Starving. Anything in the barnyard that's not moving is in mortal danger," he teased.

"It's so good to have you back, Seamus," Eileen said, her eyes filling with tears.

Seamus threw an arm around each of his sisters and the three walked linked all the way into the house.

Shane O'Neill had succeeded his father, Con Bacach, as the chieftain of the O'Neills of Ulster by engineering the death of his major rival, his own half-brother, Matthew. His supporters knew that he was utterly ruthless in his pursuit of power, yet when he had traveled to London the previous year to try to negotiate a peace, it was said that Queen Elizabeth had been quite taken with his proud manner and Irish charm.

The fragile peace had not lasted, and this time the English were determined to put an end to the O'Neills' dominion. It appeared that General Bixleigh had a personal stake in the defeat of the famous rebel. O'Neill had belittled the general in front of the queen and Bixleigh had never forgiven him. He seemed to take out his grievance on every poor farmer they encountered who may have even the slightest connection to the O'Neill side.

"He's gone too far this time," Eamon said as he ducked inside the tent he shared with his brothers and cousin Dermot. "These people fed some of O'Neill's men when they passed through here, and now Bixleigh wants to lay waste to the whole farm. It's outrageous."

Cormac was lying on his bedroll, staring at the canvas ceiling above him. His thoughts had been on Claire.

They'd had no word from home, so he had no way of knowing if she was well. Or if his last night with her had produced the disastrous results he so feared.

" 'Tis an old principle of war, Eamon," he said. "You defeat the enemy by cutting off its supplies. Especially an enemy like O'Neill's men, who seem to melt into the landscape any time we get near enough to fight."

"It's just a humble farm, Cormac, inhabited by women and children. How would you like it if Claire were left without food by an invading army?"

Cormac sighed and boosted himself up from his bed. He was as fed up with Bixleigh as his brothers were. When he'd traveled to London with his father, Cormac had met many fine English soldiers, brave men who were interested in the welfare of Ireland as well as their own country. But Bixleigh was different. Cormac had decided that at heart the man was a coward, and, like many cowards, it made him eager to test his power on people who were defenseless against him. He didn't envy his cousin the close association he'd had with the man for so many months. "Did you speak with Sean?" he asked Eamon.

"Nay, Sean's been sent out with the group of men who were to head to Derry. That's why I came to you. There's no one left to talk any sense into that madman."

Serving under Bixleigh had become increasingly difficult for all the Irish troops, and the Riordans were no exception. Bixleigh's pursuit of Shane O'Neill sometimes bordered on maniacal, and he didn't seem to care what damage was done in the meantime. He'd as much as said that if he had to destroy all of Ulster to root out the rebels, he'd do it.

"I'll talk to him," Cormac said. "Where's Niall?"

"He went with Sean and Dermot."

It was just as well, Cormac decided as he made his

way across the encampment to the commander's large field tent. His little brother's outspoken manner had already gotten him into trouble with the English general. This was better handled with diplomacy.

"It looks like we're too late," Eamon said bitterly. He pointed beyond the general's tent and Cormac could see that a distant grainfield was aflame.

"Good God!" Cormac exclaimed. "That could set the whole countryside on fire."

"I tell you, Cormac, the man's a lunatic."

They watched as the fire reached the end of the field, jumped the small ditch separating it from the next, and continued blazing. "It's coming this way," Cormac said.

"Aye, and it's heading for those farmhouses as well."

They ran to Bixleigh's tent, but as Cormac reached for the closed flap to enter, he was stopped by an English orderly. "I'm sorry, sir," the young soldier said. "The general's at his prayers and is not to be disturbed."

Cormac pushed the man's arm away. "He'd better be praying that this entire camp doesn't burn to the ground when that wildfire spreads," he snapped, then shouldered his way inside.

Bixleigh was kneeling at the edge of his camp cot, a Bible clutched in his hands. He turned and glared at Cormac when he entered.

"I'm busy at the moment, Riordan," he said.

"I can see you're doing your best to escape the flames of hell, General, but unless you get some men out in that field quick, you'll have real flames licking at your heels any minute now."

The Englishman looked alarmed. "What's happened? The fools were only supposed to burn the fields," he said.

"Evidently your men forgot to tell that to the fire,

General, because it's jumped the ditch and it's heading here."

Bixleigh scrambled to his feet. "Well, don't just stand there, man. Go do something. Stop it."

"Fires don't take commands, sir, even from a general. We'll need every soldier here to set up a bucket brigade between the fields and the river."

"Can you put it out in time?"

"If we act quickly."

Bixleigh's shoulders sagged with relief. "Do whatever has to be done, Riordan. I'm grateful to you."

Discussion about why the fire was lit in the first place would have to wait, Cormac decided. First they had to put it out. He turned to leave, then stopped as Bixleigh sat down on his cot. "I said every soldier, General," Cormac told him. "That means you, too." He stalked over and picked up the slop pail at the foot of the general's cot, then shoved it at Bixleigh's chest. "Here's your bucket," he said. "With all due respect, General, start hauling."

"It sounds dangerous, Seamus," Claire told her brother. She was sitting at one end of the big window seat the O'Donnell children had always thought of as their own special place. Seamus sat at the opposite end, and they both had their feet tucked up under them as if they still were those children of long ago. They'd had to wait until everyone else in the house had gone to bed, but finally they were alone in the front parlor.

"Faith, Clairy, war is a dangerous game. None of us ever thought otherwise. But if I don't meet the Spanish ship, we won't know where to get the gold. O'Neill needs that money. We'll be lost without it. As it is, the English have ten times our armaments."

"Yet you say that English troops have taken control

of the port, expecting some kind of transfer of funds."

"Aye, but I won't be collecting the money there. The Spaniards knew Dublin would be guarded, so they made a secret landing north of here and unloaded the gold. I just need to make a connection with the Spanish captain to pick up the map of where they left it."

"And carry that map with you back north?"

"Aye. I'll be meeting Conn and Rory and some others. We'll go for the gold together."

"What if you're stopped by English troops? The map will be incriminating evidence against you."

Seamus grinned, untwisted his folded legs and pulled off one of his boots. "Which is why one of O'Neill's cobblers made me this special pair of boots." He twisted the heel to reveal a secret compartment. "The map will be safely tucked away where no one would think to look."

Claire leaned forward to examine the boot more closely. When Seamus handed it to her, she moved the trick heel back and forth several times. "It's ingenious," she admitted. "But I still don't like the idea of you riding straight into an English stronghold all by yourself."

"Better by myself than with a group of us. A group might be pegged as rebels. A lone sailor trying to sign on with one of the captains in port won't cause much notice."

Claire knew she wouldn't dissuade her brother from his assignment. "Be careful, Seamus," she pleaded.

"Aye, aye, sister," he answered crisply with a grin and a mock salute.

She sighed. How much more danger would her family and Cormac's family have to face before this conflict was over? "Are you sure this is worth it?" she asked. "From where I see it, Shane O'Neill is just as power hungry as the queen, and neither one of them has the good of the people in mind."

"You're wrong, Claire. O'Neill's tough, but he's a good man. He's not looking for power for himself, but to free Ireland from the English yoke."

"Didn't he kill his own brother to become chief?"

Seamus looked uncomfortable, but he said, "He does what he has to for the good of his land."

"I'll never understand it," Claire said. "Isn't it absurd for men to think that the best way to protect their wives and children is to get themselves killed?"

She'd had the same question often in the past, but now that she had a new life growing inside her, it had taken on extra meaning.

"Women have a different view of things, Clairy. This is particularly hard for you having men on both sides."

"Aye." Eileen knew that the Riordans had gone to join Bixleigh, and Claire had decided to tell Seamus, too.

"Don't worry, love. I don't intend to get myself killed."

"Soldiers rarely do intend it," Claire observed dryly, "and yet they die."

"Not this soldier." He grinned at her, then jumped up from the seat. "But I may fall asleep on my horse tomorrow unless I get to bed."

"Will you stop back here after you meet the Spanish captain?"

"Probably not. I want to get the information back to the others as soon as possible."

"I hate to see you go so soon, Seamus. I miss our talks."

He reached over and ruffled her hair. "I do, too. I suppose you and Eily could ride with me tomorrow over to the coast. I'd leave you before I went to search out the Spanish ship."

"I'd like that," Claire agreed.

• • •

"I've met with the queen, and I ‚ell you she does want a fair settlement. I can't believe she's aware of the havoc Bixleigh's causing here." Sean Riordan was addressing a group of the loyalist families who were meeting in secret to discuss their growing dissatisfaction with the English commander. Bixleigh's treatment of the simple people in the countryside surrounding their encampments was getting increasingly intolerable. That morning he had ordered a twelve-year-old boy hung for sneaking into camp and taking a meat cake from the food supplies. It was the final straw for many of the loyalists, and Sean had called for a meeting in the forest away from camp.

"Whether the queen is aware of it or not, it's happening," Niall said, "and I don't think we can sit by and let it continue." The three Riordan brothers sat at the head of the gathering along with Sean.

"A number of the families here have already said they were leaving, Sean," Cormac pointed out. "As his liaison, I think you'd better suggest to Bixleigh that he think about withdrawing and urging the queen to try to negotiate with O'Neill and the other northern earls."

"He's not interested in negotiating," Sean said wearily. "He wants O'Neill's head, and nothing else seems to matter to him."

Niall added, "He told his men that if he had to send a bunch of bloody Catholics to hell in order to get their leader, it would make the world a better place."

There was a murmuring in the group. Most of the families, including the Riordans, were Catholic just like the rebels.

"I think the man may be unbalanced," Eamon declared. "He reads his Bible all day long, then comes out and orders the death of a child with as much emotion as asking for a pint of ale."

"So the question is, what are we going to do?" Cormac asked.

An older man with a bushy white beard stood at the back of the group. It was Brian Cleary, the Riordans' neighbor. "I don't know what you all are going to do, but the Clearys are going home. And I think the Mitchells are, too."

The man on his right nodded. "Aye, the Mitchells are for home."

Sean put up his hands. "Wait a minute, lads. I know things haven't gone as we had planned, but if our alliance falls apart now, it will be trouble for all of us. The rebels aren't likely to look kindly on the families that opposed them, and from the reports I hear, O'Neill can make Bixleigh look like an altar boy. I doubt any of you want him coming after your loved ones in retribution."

This brought a moment of silence. Then Brian Cleary asked, "What would you have us do?"

"I'd like time to talk with some of Bixleigh's junior officers. Some of them are good men. They may know how we can work around him or let London know how he has abused his command here."

"I vote we give Sean the time he needs before we make any further decision," Cormac said. "In the meantime, we'll make sure that none of the locals get in Bixleigh's way."

"I'm with Cormac," Eamon added, and one by one the men of the circle nodded in agreement.

"It's not fair, Seamus," Eileen pouted as she, Claire, and Seamus rode toward Dublin. "You told Claire what this great mission of yours is, but you won't tell me."

"It's not to tease you, Eily," he answered. "I shouldn't

have told Claire, either. The fewer people who know about this, the better."

"I wouldn't tell anyone," Eileen argued.

"Nay, but if anything should happen to me, they may come to question my family. I want you to be able to honestly say that you don't know anything about what I was doing."

It was a bright day and they'd had a pleasant ride all morning. Now they could see the rooftops of Dublin down the hill below them and the masts of the harbor beyond. It was time for Seamus to leave them, and both sisters were dreading the parting.

"This thing can't last forever," Seamus reassured them. "Father, Conn, Rory, and I will be back raising a ruckus at the house before you know it. You'll wonder why you ever missed us."

Both sisters had tears in their eyes as he leaned from his horse to embrace each in turn. "Be careful," Claire whispered in his ear.

He nodded. "I want you two to go straight home. There are English troops billeted in town and I'd not have them catch sight of my beautiful sisters."

Then with a wave he was gone.

The ride back was much quieter.

"Do you think you were right not to tell him about the baby, Claire?" Eileen asked after a few moments.

"Aye. It would just worry him, and worry Father once Seamus returned north and told him. There's nothing they can do about it up there."

"It might stop them from wanting to kill your baby's husband," Eileen pointed out grimly.

"I'm afraid not. Men don't appear to think that way."

"I only hope everyone will come out of this safely and that's it's over soon."

They both were worried about Seamus and the others,

but Claire's thoughts also were occupied with her child. What would Cormac's reaction be? she wondered. And when would she see him? She had not told her brother of the pregnancy, but didn't the baby's father have a right to know about it? She thought about it all the way home, but short of writing the news in a letter that could end up in anyone's hands, she could see no way to let him know.

They were almost back to O'Donnell House when they heard a horse coming up fast behind him. They turned in unison. "It's Seamus!" Eileen cried.

They stopped their horses and waited, smiling, but their expressions changed when it became obvious that their brother was listing in the saddle and appeared to be barely holding on.

"What's happened?" Claire asked as he drew near enough to hear. But even as she asked the question, she gasped. The entire right side of Seamus's doublet was stained bright red. "You're hurt!"

Seamus nodded, but didn't speak. His face was deathly pale, and as his horse finally reached theirs, he closed his eyes and tumbled to the ground.

Claire had stayed with Seamus while Eileen rode to the house for help. By the time they'd managed to bring him back and carry him up to one of the upstairs chambers, his breathing had become so shallow that Claire sometimes had to put her fingers on the side of his neck to be sure that his heart was still beating.

Her own heart felt as if it were being ripped in two, but she didn't have time to waste on herself. Willing herself to stay calm, she directed Eileen and Fiona to help her strip off his clothes and wash away the blood so they could see the nature of his wound. The blood appeared to have come from a musket ball that had gone all the way through his shoulder. Fortunately, it seemed to have missed his heart and lungs. But the loss of blood and his white face concerned her.

"It's still seeping," she told Eileen. "Keep this cloth pressed against the wound while I get my medicines to make a poultice."

They worked quickly and by the time the wound was dressed and bound, they were rewarded by the return of some color to his cheeks.

Even so, it was morning before he regained consciousness. In spite of all the extra women in the house, many of whom had offered to relieve her, Claire had insisted on sitting with him through the night herself, wiping his forehead, holding his hand. It had seemed like an endless vigil, and there had been plenty of time for her to wonder if she would ever hear his voice again.

"Claireeey." His voice was slurred, but the sound of it made Claire's heart leap.

"I'm here, Seamus," Claire answered as relief flooded through her.

"I . . . have . . . to . . . ride north."

"Nay, Mussy, you're wounded, and you've lost too much blood. I fear it will be awhile before you're up on a horse."

"Have . . . to," he said again.

She squeezed his hand. "What happened to you?"

"English . . . soldiers."

"They caught you meeting the Spanish captain?"

He nodded.

"Thank God you were able to escape."

He tried to lift his head, then sagged back. He said something, but she couldn't understand the words. When she looked at him blankly, he tried again. "Boot!" he said. "Where . . . boot?"

Fiona had taken away his bloody clothes, but his

boots were standing by the wall. She pointed to them, and he gestured for her to bring them to him.

She lowered her voice. "So you got the map?"

"Aye," he said weakly. "Boot."

"Seamus, there's no way for you to take it north now. You can't even sit up. How would you expect to ride?"

He finally seemed to realize that she was right. "Have to find someone . . . to go," he panted.

"One of the servants?"

"Nay."

She understood his reluctance. This was not the kind of job you paid someone to do. It was a job for someone who was dedicated to a cause. She hesitated. She was not dedicated to the cause of Shane O'Neill, but she was dedicated to her brother, and she could see that he was getting more agitated. If a substitute could not be found for his mission, he would shortly insist on going himself, even if the effort killed him.

"Where are you supposed to meet Conn and Rory and the others?" she asked.

"Straight on the North Road. Iron Horse Inn." Claire had heard of the popular coach stop just south of Ulster. It wouldn't be hard to find.

She felt torn. She had two lives to think of now, not just one. But as long as she didn't have to go into the actual area of fighting, she couldn't see that riding to the inn would be that dangerous.

Then, too, Cormac was north, and some instinct was telling her that she needed to be closer to him. Perhaps after delivering the map to O'Neill's men, she could find the English encampment and see him.

The whole idea was mad, and if her father had been here, he would never have let her attempt it. If Seamus were thinking clearly, he'd probably forbid her from going as well. But her father was with the rebels, and

Seamus lay gravely wounded. There was no one to stop her.

"I'll go," she said.

Seamus shook his head with as much vehemence as he could muster. "Can't . . . let you."

"I hardly see that you have a choice, Mussy. You yourself said the fate of the rebels lies in the gold, and there's no gold without the map." She walked across the room and picked up his right boot, then tapped the heel. "I'll take it," she said again. "It's not that difficult. I'll simply ride north, find Conn and Rory, give them the map, and be back here practically before anyone misses me."

Seamus closed his eyes and groaned.

"You might as well not waste your energy arguing," she told him. "You need all your strength to get well."

His eyes opened and he looked at her, his expression full of admiration. He spoke slowly to get all the words out. "If O'Neill had a hundred men like you, Clairy, the English would already be back in London licking their wounds."

She smiled at him and said, "I'll need instructions." Then, looking down at the boot in her hand, she added, "And I'll need to borrow some of your clothes."

Seventeen

"*Our reports tell* us it will be at a place called the Iron Horse Inn, General," Lieutenant Grenville said, keeping his voice low.

"That's where the gold is?" Bixleigh asked.

"Nay. A messenger is coming to tell them where the Spaniards left the gold, somewhere on the coast. The rebels are meeting at the Iron Horse and will ride to the coast from there once they have the location."

Bixleigh was seated at his field desk, which he'd had placed under a tree at the edge of camp in order to be away from the smoke of the cookfires, which he said made him sneeze. He looked around to see that his conversation with the young lieutenant was not being overheard. "Take as many men as you need to set up an ambush," he said.

"Aye, sir. The Riordans are the best fighters. . . ."

"No loyalists. Take only Englishmen. These Irish don't have the stomach when it comes to dealing properly with their own countrymen."

Grenville hesitated. "Does that mean the rebels are to be—"

"Killed, aye. With luck we'll rid the world of a whole nest of Catholic vermin with this night's work."

"Sir, it may be better to keep them alive. Otherwise, we may never learn the location of the gold."

Bixleigh huffed and began waving at the man in an agitated fashion. "On second thought, Grenville, it appears that you are losing the stomach for this venture, too. I just may have to go after those papist traitors myself."

"You, sir?"

"Aye." He rubbed his hands together with a look of relish. "Aye, they won't be expecting us. It should be an easy kill, and it's been awhile since I've had some good sport."

Grenville looked slightly sick. "Do I have your permission to go then, sir?"

Bixleigh was looking across the clearing to where Cormac and Eamon Riordan were helping with preparations for the noon meal. He narrowed his eyes as he stared at the two Irishmen. The lieutenant waited at attention in front of his desk. Finally the general turned to him and said, "I want you to give an assignment to the Riordans, the Clearys, and the Mitchells."

"Aye, sir."

"Tell them I want them to scout the Farlach Woods. Order them to search it thoroughly and bring back a report in two days."

"The Farlach Woods, sir? They're likely to ride right into O'Neill's stronghold."

"We're not sure the stronghold is there, so you needn't mention the possibility to them. If they run into O'Neill, why, then we'll have the information we seek, won't we? In the meantime, they'll be out of our hair while you take care of this little matter of the rebel gold."

Grenville frowned. "They've only about forty men. O'Neill may have over five hundred at his base camp. It would be suicidal to—"

"Did I ask you to give your opinion of how I disperse my troops, lieutenant?" Bixleigh roared.

Over at the camp, heads turned in their direction.

"Nay, sir." Grenville clamped his lips tightly and made no further comment.

"Then you are dismissed. See to it that my orders are carried out."

The young lieutenant, his face strained, turned sharply on his heel and headed over to where the Riordans and the other loyalist families were camped.

Seamus had barely stayed conscious long enough to give Claire complete instructions about how to reach the Iron Horse and what she should do to find Conn, Rory, and the other rebels there.

"If there's any sign of English troops, our men'll stay in the woods behind the inn," he'd told her, struggling to get out the words. "The tavern keeper, a man named John Black, will tie a black kerchief on one of the hitching posts. 'Tis your signal to skirt the inn and keep riding."

"Then what do I do?"

"Don't worry—Conn and Rory will find you."

"Will they recognize me? They'll be looking for you."

"They'll recognize my horse for sure." He'd given a weak smile. "And, Clairy, I'm sorry, but you don't make much of a lad."

She'd decided to wear some of Rory's clothes, since he was the smallest of the O'Donnell brothers. She'd found a floppy hat to tuck up her long hair, and had dirtied her face. When she'd viewed herself in the looking glass, she'd decided that she made a passable young man. The boots were the biggest problem. They were huge for her slender feet, but there was no time to work out another solution for keeping the map safe, so they would have to do.

"I think I'm a rather dashing fellow," she'd argued, but Seamus was too weak for teasing.

"Don't get close . . . to anyone . . . until . . . reach . . . Iron Horse." Then he'd fainted, and Claire had been forced to entrust him to the care of Eileen and the other women and start her journey. Even if she rode hard all day, it would be close to nightfall before she reached the inn. In spite of Seamus's assurance, she wasn't sure that her brothers would recognize her in her male attire, much less in the dark.

She'd had no trouble throughout the day, managing to stay away from the few other travelers she'd encountered. Eating food she'd brought from home, she skirted the roadside taverns along the way. By twilight, she was sure that she must be getting close. Her back ached from the long day riding astride. Every now and then she put her hand along her stomach and whispered an apology to her unborn child. "Not much farther, little one," she said now.

If all was well, soon she'd be resting in a warm, lighted tavern with her brothers. She closed her eyes briefly and let herself picture the thick slab of beef that was no doubt roasting on a spit in the Iron Horse kitchens, waiting for her arrival.

It was nearly dark, but she could make out a rambling wooden structure up ahead that had to be the tavern. A coach and at least four horses were tied up at the front. The hitching posts extended around the far end, so she couldn't see the total number of horses on hand. She didn't immediately recognize any of the animals as O'Donnell horses, but she was still too far away to see clearly.

Please let there be no black kerchief, she prayed silently. Now that she was almost at her destination, she felt as if she could not ride another mile. Seamus's mount was tired, too. The stocky sorrel had kept a steady pace all day without complaint, but its head was beginning to droop.

She boosted herself in her stirrups, trying to see the entire front of the inn. The hitching posts were in the shapes of little horse heads, and there was definitely no black cloth at the first three. Her spirits rose.

The coach blocked the next few posts from view, which meant she couldn't be sure there was no warning flag without riding practically right up to the tavern door. Still some distance from the inn, she pulled the sorrel to a stop.

With a hand on her stomach, she asked her little traveling companion, "What do you think? Should we risk it?" So far, not even a flutter answered her, but the communication gave her a curious satisfaction.

She moved a little closer to the building, veering off the road on the far side. If there was trouble, she didn't want to be spotted from inside. Once again she tried to see around the big coach. Wouldn't the tavern keeper have put the flag on the first post? she reasoned. That post was definitely clear.

She waited several more minutes, trying to make up her mind. She saw no suspicious activity whatsoever around the inn. It had gotten increasingly dark. "I think everything's all right, little one," she whispered. "Shall we give it a try?"

She left her horse tethered to a tree across the road and approached the inn cautiously, but the closer she got without a mishap, the more she became convinced that she'd find Conn and Rory inside, waiting for her by a blazing fire with a mug of hot rum. She smiled in the darkness.

The inn was surrounded on two sides by a wide wooden porch that separated the hitching posts from the inn door. As she made her way carefully around the end of the coach, she searched the row of horses and still saw no sign of Conn and Rory's mounts. They could be around the back, she decided. Then she turned her head back toward the front and froze. Knotted around the tiny horse head nearest the coach was a black kerchief.

She was still staring at the signal when the door to the inn burst open and a shadowy group of men appeared from around the other side of the inn. Before Claire could even think about trying to escape, she was seized by countless hands, hauled off her feet, and carried into the inn. Once inside, her captors dumped her on the wooden floor. Her hat came off and her long hair tumbled down.

"It's a woman," one of the men cried.

She lifted her head, blinking to get her eyes accustomed to the sudden light. Then she heard an oily voice that she couldn't fail to recognize. "Well, well, well, it appears we've caught a real fish this time."

She looked behind her. Sitting in a captain's chair at the end of a long table was General Bixleigh, the man who had dined at her table back at Riordan Hall. He stood and walked over to her with a leering smile that made her lose any hope that he didn't remember her.

"Good evening, General," she said with as much dignity as she could muster, sprawled as she was in male clothes on the floor.

She thought she detected a quick glint of admiration in his eyes before he said, "You're not receiving me in your parlor this time, *Lady* Riordan."

There was a low murmur among the soldiers scattered around the taproom, and she could see that the name was familiar to them. Claire felt a swift pang of despair.

Not only had she herself been caught on a mission for the rebels, her connection to Cormac was out in the open. The English might hold him as responsible as her for this night's work. And what about the baby inside her?

She forced herself to rally. Despair would not solve her dilemma, and it would not help her child. As calmly as she could, she sat up, brushing herself off. "It appears this time I've come to you, General, but I'm glad you remember that you once received hospitality in my home."

Bixleigh leaned toward her so closely she could smell his fetid breath. "That was before I knew that you were a *traitor,* madam."

She stayed silent while she looked around the room for any sign that her brothers or others of O'Neill's men had been caught. As far as she could tell, there were only English in the room. The men were eating dinner and seemed to be liberally helping themselves to the numerous pitchers of ale scattered around the tavern tables. It didn't appear that they had had any kind of showdown with armed rebels, which meant that the only evidence they had against her was that she had showed up at an inn.

"Traitor, General?" she asked coolly, standing up. "I don't know what you're talking about."

Bixleigh frowned. "I suppose you're going to tell me that you didn't know that a number of O'Neill's men were scheduled to be at this tavern tonight."

She looked around. "Really? How frightening. Where are they?"

Bixleigh's soft face started to turn red. "You're not going to talk your way out of this. What are you doing here? Why are you dressed in men's clothes?"

"Why, General, I thought to spend the night since I'm

afraid to travel after dark. As to the men's clothes, it was the only way I could think of to travel safely so that I could reach my husband, who is, I believe, at your camp."

"You were coming here to find your family—who are a bunch of bloody rebels!" Bixleigh shouted. A vein pulsed under his left eye.

"I came to find my husband, who is here in the north, as you know, General, lending support to the forces of Her Majesty the Queen."

The rest of the soldiers were listening avidly to their exchange, and Claire felt that she had a good deal of support on her side. She wasn't sure how many of them believed her, but it wasn't important. As long as they didn't have any evidence, she was sure that Bixleigh wouldn't dare act against the wife of one of the most important loyalists in the country.

"I'm sorry if I interrupted you, General. Do you know if there is a room available for me here?"

"The only room available for a rebel wench is a prison cell," Bixleigh snarled.

"I'd watch my language if I were you, General. When I tell my husband how you've treated me, you may lose every Irishman you've been able to win to your cause. What do you think your queen would think of that?"

A man with an apron, who had been standing in the doorway to the back room, stepped forward. "I'm John Black, milady, and I'm the proprietor of this place." He gave her a significant little nod.

"Ah, good," she said, turning her back on Bixleigh to address the innkeeper. "I'm in need of a room for the night."

Bixleigh appeared to be hesitating, as if her cool demeanor were causing him some doubt about her guilt, but he wasn't ready to give up. "Hold!" he said. "You'll answer my questions before you go anywhere."

He put his hand on her shoulder and spun her around so forcefully that she stumbled, her feet becoming entangled in her oversized boots. As she struggled to stand straight again, the heel of the right boot doubled over and snapped off. She looked down in horror to see the Spaniard's map tumble to the floor.

Bixleigh's eyes lit with a fanatical gleam as he pushed her out of the way, knocking her to the ground, and reached for the folded paper. John Black took a step toward Claire, but was held back by a uniformed soldier who held a musket across his chest.

"This is it," Bixleigh said triumphantly, scanning the paper. Then he frowned. "There are no names written on it. We'll have to go back and get one of the damned Irishmen who is familiar with the coastline." He chuckled and looked down at Claire with a cruel smile. "Coming to see your husband, eh, my little rebel whore? I wonder what the noble Lord Riordan will say when he learns that his wife is a bloody spy for Shane O'Neill."

Claire heard the general's words through a haze. She had a more pressing concern—when Bixleigh had pushed her to the floor, a sharp cramp had begun in her abdomen.

She curled up, both to ease the pain and as a kind of instinctive protection of the life inside her. *Dear God,* she prayed silently, *don't let me lose my baby.*

John Black, still blocked by the soldier's musket, watched her, his eyes anguished. "She's hurt," he said.

Bixleigh was trying to make some sense of the map. He glanced at Claire, then gave a wave of dismissal. "Take her back to camp. We'll truss her up and give her as a present to Lord Riordan. He can have his whore for one final night before we hang her for treason."

Claire felt herself being seized by each arm and

dragged up. Sharp pains stabbed at her midsection. "Please," she said weakly. She was ready to beg for her baby's life, but as she was considering her words, the front door of the tavern exploded open.

Suddenly there were men everywhere—jumping down from the rafters, bursting out from the big side cupboards, pouring over the ledge of the back window. One even popped up from what had appeared to be a barrel of ale.

Within seconds, every English soldier was subdued. With a rush of joy, Claire recognized Conn and Rory among the newcomers. John Black had taken the musket from the soldier who had been holding him and was now pointing it at Bixleigh himself.

"Whoa!" Rory said. "We'll have a fine prize to take back to O'Neill tonight."

Conn was more interested in his sister than in the general. He went immediately to her side. "Are you all right, Claire?" he asked. "And, by the way, what in blazes are you doing here?"

Claire could not muster a smile. The cramping seemed to be subsiding a little, but it had her badly frightened. "Seamus couldn't make it." At Conn's concerned look she continued, "Nay, he's going to be all right, but he took a musketball in the shoulder retrieving that." She pointed to the map, still in Bixleigh's hand.

Conn reached over to the general and relieved him of the paper. "You'll have no need of that where you're going, General," he said.

Now that the commotion was over, Claire realized that there weren't as many of the rebels as she had thought. The English soldiers outnumbered them two to one, but the rebels had been prepared and had had the advantage of surprise.

"How were you able to set a trap that way?" Claire asked her brother.

"We had help on the inside," Conn said, giving John Black a conspiratorial wink.

Conn seemed to be in command of the rebel contingent. He looked around the room. "We don't have enough men to take prisoners," he said, "especially not when we'd be risking my sister's safety." He directed his men to begin tying up the soldiers. "Bixleigh's the one we want," he told them. "We'll leave the others here."

As he turned to give further instructions, Bixleigh lunged forward and grabbed Claire around her waist. He pulled a dagger from his belt and held it at her throat. "Don't move, O'Donnell, or she's dead."

Conn stood still, his eyes on the point of the knife pressed into Claire's flesh. "Hurt her, Bixleigh, and we'll roast you over a slow fire. There are too many men here for you to go up against."

Bixleigh was backing toward the door, dragging Claire along with him. "You forget that we outnumber you, and if you want your sister to live, you'll begin untying my men now, nice and slow with no tricks."

He was nearing the entrance and reached behind himself to open the door. Claire took advantage of the momentary loosening of his grasp to kick at him backwards with all her might. Bixleigh let out a great yelp and released her. She ducked to one side to give the rebels a chance to take him, but the general brandished the knife, keeping them back long enough for him to spin around, leap from the porch, and disappear into the darkness. Seconds later they heard the sound of a horse riding away at a fast gallop.

"Let's catch him," Rory said, beginning to run to the

door, but Conn stopped him. "Nay. The gold is more important."

He turned to Claire, who was clutching her middle. "Do you think Bixleigh will remember how to find the gold?" he asked. "Is there danger that he might send his troops to the hiding place?"

Her head was spinning. The final wrench pulling herself from Bixleigh's grasp had seemed to tear something right across her middle. But she managed to say, "They couldn't read it. They don't know the coastline."

"Well, these men do," Conn said, pointing to a group of four men waiting by the door. From their dress, they looked as if they may have been fishermen. "You'll ride to the coast to fetch it, as planned," Conn told them. "The rest of us will go back to base camp. And you, Clairy, will hie yourself back to O'Donnell House where you belong."

"Bixleigh knows about me," Claire gasped. The pain was searing. "He might come after me there."

"That's a chance we'll have to take," Conn said. "I want to see you safe back at home."

Her mind wasn't making sense anymore. She knew somehow that she needed help, that there was no way she could ride unaided back to O'Donnell House, but she didn't seem able to communicate her state to Conn. Instead, she started obediently toward the door. "Back home," she said, her voice hollow. Then her eyes rolled back and she fell to the floor in a dead faint.

When she opened her eyes, she had no idea where she was. She lay on a wide cot and the ceiling above her was made of roughly cut logs. Her first thought was of the baby, and her hands went automatically to her stomach. The pains had stopped, she realized. Had she lost it? she thought in sudden terror. But then, as she pressed her hands on the area, she felt a faint fluttering. Was it her imagination? She pressed again, and this time there was definitely an answering movement, like tiny wings beating inside her. Tears of relief stung her eyes.

"The babe should be fine, mistress," said a voice at her side. "But you should stay still for a day or two." It was the innkeeper, John Black.

He regarded her with such a gentle expression that she forgot to be embarrassed at the intimate comment coming from a virtual stranger. "How . . . how did you know?" she asked him.

"Women have a look about them. You get to know it when 'tis your profession. I suspected it even back at the inn when you arrived in breeches."

She was confused. "Aren't you the innkeeper at the Iron Horse?"

"I'm whatever Shane O'Neill needs me to be at any given moment, but by profession, I'm a doctor. I practiced in Dublin for many years, and I daresay I've helped my share of babies into the world."

Claire sent up a silent prayer of thanks. Who would have thought that in spite of her risky adventure, she would end up in the hands of a physician? "Where are we?" she asked. "And where are my brothers?"

"We're at the rebel camp, mistress, and your brothers have gone to give a report of this night's work to the O'Neill. I assured them that you would be fine and that I would stay here by your side."

" 'Tis very kind of you, Master Black."

He smiled. "Black's not my real name, but John is, so why don't you use that?"

"I shall, if you will return the favor and call me Claire."

"I doubt your brothers will approve, Claire, but I thank you for the privilege."

She looked around at the neat little room. "This is not what I had expected the camp to be like."

"You're in one of the more luxurious guest suites," John said with a smile. "But 'tis not a bad place. If a man can no longer live in his own home, this is not a bad substitute for a spell."

She wondered why it was that John Black could no longer live in his own home, and why he had had to take a false name, but curiously, she felt too lethargic to ask him.

"I've given you some sleeping powder," he explained, as though reading her thoughts. "It will keep you calm for the next few hours. You need to give that little one time to settle down again."

She gave him a warm smile. "I felt him. He was moving inside me."

"That's a good sign. You're a strong woman, Claire, and even more important, you have a tough spirit. I see no reason why you shouldn't be able to have a healthy baby. That is, unless you plan more adventures like the one you had today."

She shook her head. "Nay. I'd not have done it if it hadn't been so important to my brothers." She suddenly remembered. "My father, too. Is he here?" she asked, starting to sit up.

John Black shook his head in reproach and gently pushed her back down on the cot. "I said quiet, Claire, and I meant it. You and that little one have been through a lot tonight. I don't want you getting up from that bed for two or three days. Your father was here to see you earlier, but O'Neill sent for him. I expect both he and your brothers will be back soon."

She relaxed, feeling happy and sleepy. "They don't know yet," she said.

"I suspected as much, and I've not said anything. I

thought you should be the one to tell them."

"Thank you." She closed her eyes and had begun to drift to sleep when she heard the door to the shelter open. She opened her eyes to see her father standing over her bed. For the first time she could remember, his eyes were misted with tears.

"I'll never forgive Seamus for sending you into such danger," he said.

She shook her head. "Nay, don't be angry with him. In the first place, I insisted, and in the second, he was nearly out of his mind from the wound himself. I doubt he clearly understood what was happening."

"Ah, well, Dr. Black says you're going to be fine, so I warrant there was no harm done. And you brought the map."

"Aye."

"They're calling you a hero, daughter."

"A tired one," she said. Whatever the doctor had given her was starting to take effect. As happy as she was to see her father again, she couldn't keep her eyelids from closing.

"You need rest, and I'd not bother you except that I felt you should have some warning."

She forced her eyes open. "Warning?"

"I was just meeting with the O'Neill. He's had word from some of the loyalist families that they want to parlay with him. It appears that they may have come to their senses at last."

"Loyalist families?" Claire asked, trying hard to understand her father's words through her haze.

"Aye. Cormac's with them, of course."

She couldn't make sense of it. "What about Cormac?" she asked.

"He should be here any minute. The loyalists are being escorted into camp right now."

Eighteen

Cormac had expected to be impressed with the legendary rebel leader, but he hadn't anticipated that he would instantly like the man as well.

Shane O'Neill was nothing of the ruthless, baby-eating fighter he was portrayed to be by the English propagandists. Though he was a big man, he moved with a kind of natural grace that made you forget his size. His manner of speech was cultured. He laughed easily and treated his men with unmistakable warmth, to which they responded with unquestioning loyalty.

The contrast with the English general was striking, but the loyalists were not interested in a personality contest between leaders. If they were to switch alliances, it would be because they had found a better cause for the sake of their families and their country.

It was after midnight, and the meeting between the loyalist and rebel leaders had dragged on for two hours. They were inside what looked to be an old barn that had been incorporated into O'Neill's base camp. Claire's brothers were among the group of rebels sitting behind O'Neill in the crowded building, but Cormac hadn't spoken with them. When he'd arrived, he'd thought he had also seen Raghnall O'Donnell, but as he scanned the group he couldn't find him.

When he'd first learned at the English camp that

Claire's family was with the rebels, he'd felt a swift stab of disappointment. Why hadn't she told him? he wondered. There had been passion between them almost from the moment they first saw each other, but before he had had to leave her, he thought they had finally begun to enrich that passion with feelings of trust and understanding.

Of course, he realized how difficult it must have been for Claire to have her loyalties split in such a fashion. She was close to her family, and she'd grown close to the Riordans. It must have been terrible for her to realize that the two families could meet each other in battle. Still, he wished she had confided in him so that he could have tried to provide her with some measure of comfort.

"All we want is to be left alone to raise our families and work our farms," O'Neill was explaining. His voice was a ringing bass that carried high into the rafters of the old barn. " 'Tis nothing more than I was promised by the queen herself. Now we have foreign troops burning our fields and killing our women and children. We want them gone from Ireland forever."

Cormac waited for Sean to speak for them. After all, it had been Sean and the other northern Riordans who had pulled the family over to the British side.

"Ireland is poor and weak while England is rich and strong. As subjects of the queen, we are protected from being overrun by the French or the Spanish," Sean pointed out.

"But we are overrun by the English," O'Neill answered with a wise smile. "What matters who is wearing the boot if it's stomping on your neck, cutting off your very breath?"

Sean looked weary, as if he knew that he had taken his kin down a mistaken path and now had a long way to go to make up for it and find the true road. "Our families no longer have the stomach for this fight, O'Neill, but neither will we take up arms against our former comrades."

"I understand your position, Riordan. Obviously, I'm happy to know that the English are losing your support. I hope the day will soon come when not a single Irishman will aid their cause."

"What we want from you is a guarantee that if we withdraw from our alliance with Bixleigh and return to our homes, there will be no reprisals for past grievances on either side."

"I can't promise to control every one of my men at every hour, Riordan, but if you agree to act no more against us, I swear I will set the example and embrace you as my brothers. You have my word." The red-haired rebel let his gaze drift over the row of loyalist leaders, making the same silent promise to each.

When Sean remained silent, Cormac spoke. "I, for one, am willing to give this thing a try. From what I hear, the word of Shane O'Neill is good." The other Riordans nodded agreement.

O'Neill shot him a glance of approval. "As is the word of a Riordan, from what I hear." He stood. "It's late; shall we clasp hands on it tonight and work out more details in the morning?"

One by one the men got to their feet, stretching after the long negotiating session. O'Neill offered his arm first to Sean, then to Brian Cleary, who had been sitting at Sean's side. Then he came up to Cormac.

"Your father was a good man, Riordan," he said, as the two men clasped forearms. "I see the family has a worthy leader to succeed him."

Cormac was unexpectedly moved by the rebel's words. "I intend to try to be half the man he was," he said.

"And from what I hear, you've gotten yourself a wife worthy of such a man."

This was a surprise. How did O'Neill know about Claire? Perhaps from her brothers and her father? "Er . . . aye, sir," he answered uncertainly.

"She's a spirited one, they say. A lady who knows her own mind."

"Aye, sir." O'Neill had definitely heard about Claire from some source.

"So perhaps you'll not be too surprised to learn that she is here."

O'Neill could not have taken him more off guard if he'd driven a fist into his stomach. "Here? You mean here in this camp? Claire?"

"Aye. I suppose you'd like to be taken to her."

"What's she doing here? I thought she was at O'Donnell House. How long has she been here?"

"I expect your wife would be the best one to answer your questions, Riordan."

Cormac forced himself to calm down. Shane O'Neill had more important things to do than stand and listen to him babble. "Of course, I'm sorry, sir."

"Not at all, son. I hope you have a happy reunion." The rebel leader's smile was kind. Cormac looked into his eyes, and saw there the reason why so many had followed this man.

He smiled in return. "Aye, sir," he said.

Cormac's initial reaction to the news that Claire was here in this very camp had been sheer elation, but as he followed the young man O'Neill had assigned to take him to where his wife was staying, he'd begun to have doubts. What did her presence in camp mean? He'd convinced himself that Claire hadn't told him about her family's involvement with O'Neill because her loyalties had been torn, but perhaps he'd been wrong. Perhaps she'd known all along that her loyalties lay with the rebel cause. He'd had no word from her in all the long weeks since he'd left her at Riordan Hall.

"She be in there, sir," said his young guide. "But I do believe she's still with the doctor."

Cormac looked up in alarm. "The doctor?"

"Well, John Black, sir. He be a doctor some of the time."

"Is she hurt?"

"I don't know, sir. I reckon. She didn't seem to be conscious when her brothers brought her here."

Cormac's ears pounded. *Let her be all right,* he prayed. Questions of loyalty could wait.

The guide pointed to a small wooden structure at the edge of the trees. "They took her in there, sir," he said.

Cormac quickly thanked the man and walked up to the building, his stomach rolling.

A small oil-paper window showed a light inside. He opened the door without knocking. Across the room he could see her on a cot, apparently asleep. She looked pale, but appeared to be breathing normally. Cormac felt the fear drain out of him.

A man he didn't know was sitting on a low stool beside her bed, and Raghnall O'Donnell sat on a bench against the wall. He stood when Cormac entered.

"Is she well?" Cormac asked, keeping his voice low.

Raghnall nodded his head at the third man, who stood as well and came over to Cormac, extending his hand.

"I'm John Black, sir. I've been tending your wife."

At Cormac's suspicious look, the man smiled and said, "In another life, I was a physician. I think your wife will be fine, but she's had a bit of roughing up, and I've told her she needs to rest for a couple of days."

"Roughing up?"

Raghnall answered. "It was the English beast, Bix-leigh. The bastard flung her to the ground. 'Tis a wonder he didn't break her neck."

Cormac felt a flood of red hot rage. "Is she hurt?" he asked John Black.

The doctor seemed to hesitate a moment, then shook his head. "She's uninjured," he said, choosing his words.

That was all Cormac wanted to hear. "Good. I'll let her sleep, then, and tomorrow we can ride south. I want her out of this place."

Black frowned. "Perhaps you didn't hear me, Riordan. I said your wife needs rest. She should stay in bed for at least the next two days, preferably three."

"You said she wasn't hurt."

"Aye, but—"

Cormac was tired after his long day and not in the mood to be told by another man what his wife should be doing. "I hardly think her welfare is being served by allowing her to stay in the middle of a rebel stronghold, Doctor. The sooner we leave here, the sooner she will be safe at home. She can rest up there."

The two men stood facing each other, a crackle of antagonism between them. Finally, John Black said to Raghnall, "O'Donnell, if you don't mind, I'd like a few words with your son-in-law in private."

Raghnall looked surprised, but he nodded and left the room. When the door had closed behind him, Black said, "Your wife can't travel just yet. You'll have to consider that doctor's orders."

Cormac bristled. "You don't know Claire. If she's not hurt, she'll be ready to ride tomorrow. She's not a woman to let grass grow under her feet."

Black smiled. "I've gathered that. I'm not questioning your wife's spirit, Riordan, I'm merely telling you that she's taken some abuse. She needs time to recover, and *so does the baby.*"

For the second time that night, Cormac felt as if the wind had been knocked out of him. He stared at the doctor, speechless.

"I take it you didn't know."

Cormac shook his head.

Black shrugged. "Perhaps your wife was not sure of her condition when she last saw you, but I can't believe you're surprised by the news. When a healthy woman marries, babies are usually not far behind."

Cormac's eyes were on Claire. Her pale features suddenly took on a more sinister meaning. Fingers of dread crept up his neck. "Tell me the truth, Doctor. Will she live?"

Black cocked his head in confusion. "I already told you, sir, she's fine. But she experienced some cramping after the events of this evening, which is not a particularly good sign. She needs to stay prone to be sure the pregnancy is continuing in a normal fashion."

Cormac walked over to the bed and put his hand on Claire's forehead. "She feels cold," he said. Her breathing was so shallow it was almost impossible to see. She was lying straight and motionless, covered by a single blanket. His mind flashed to the image of his stepmother, Rhea, the last time he had seen her, still and beautiful in the long sleep of death.

John Black shook his head. "She's just sleeping. I've given her a draught. But if you continue to touch her, she will wake up," he added pointedly.

Cormac stepped back from the bed. He felt helpless and angry at the same time. This was his fault, of course. In spite of his best resolutions, he'd done the very thing he'd sworn never to do. His bride was pregnant, another victim ripe for sacrifice to the relentless gods of the Tara hills.

"Go find yourself a place to sleep, Riordan," the physician said. "You look exhausted. I'll stay by her side tonight just in case."

Cormac shook his head. "Nay," he said, his voice dull. "Thank you, Doctor, but Claire is my wife. I'll stay with her."

The first thing Claire saw when she opened her eyes was Cormac's grave face, bending over her. She had wanted to stay awake to see him the previous evening, but whatever John Black had given her had been too strong. She had fallen asleep, apparently for the entire night.

She'd dozed before she even had time to decide what she would say to him. As she looked up at him, she still wasn't sure what to say. Did he know about the baby? Did he know about her mission for the rebels? Was he angry?

He didn't appear to be. His expression was tender. "Thank God, princess," he said. "This had been the longest night of my life. How are you feeling?"

"I feel fine," she said, instinctively moving her hands under the blanket and down to her stomach. Cormac followed the movement with his gaze, and she realized that he *knew*. " 'Tis the little one I'm worried about," she added with a shy smile.

She could see a hard swallow make its way down his throat. "May I?" he asked, and at her nod, he slid his hand under the covers and placed it on her rounded belly.

There was a look of sheer wonder on his face, but he said nothing.

"Did John tell you?" she asked finally.

"Aye, *John.*" Now there was irritation in his eyes. "A

man I've never met knows more about my own wife than I do."

"I could hardly have known about this when you left, Cormac. If you recall, it had just happened."

"You should have tried to get word to me."

She nodded in agreement. "Aye, I should have, but knowing the way you felt, I didn't want to burden you with the knowledge."

"It's not proper to keep such a thing from a husband, Claire, burden or no."

Claire sighed. "Perhaps you're right. I'm sorry. I wish I could have told you myself."

"That's behind us now," Cormac said, though she sensed that the hurt would linger a spell. "The important thing is to get you well so that we can all ride back to Riordan Hall."

"You're coming home!"

"Aye. Most of the loyalist families have withdrawn their support from the English. The only thing that would make me go back to their camp would be in order to find Bixleigh and give him the thrashing he deserves."

Claire sat up and put her arms around his neck. "Forget Bixleigh. I don't care about him. The only thing I care about is that you'll be home again. Your brothers, too?"

He carefully pulled her arms from his neck and pushed her gently back down. "Don't excite yourself, *chara*," he admonished. "Niall has decided to stay here and join the rebels, but Eamon will be riding south with us."

"What of your cousins?"

"Sean and Dermot and the other northern Riordans are here with us. We've all seen Bixleigh for his true colors, and have no more stomach for it."

She beamed up at him. "I'm so glad. Do you think

the English will leave now?" Her true happiness would be if the conflict were over so that her own brothers and father could go home as well.

"I doubt it. Bixleigh is fanatically stubborn."

Her smile faded. "I wish all my family could come home."

Cormac grew serious. "It must have been hard for you to know that your husband and your family were on opposite sides." He took her chin gently so that she'd be forced to look at him. "You could have told me, sweetheart."

The tears that seemed all too ready to come these days misted her eyes. "I couldn't betray my own father and brothers. Blood is everything, you once said. Remember?"

"Aye. But you and I share blood now, too." He nodded toward her rounded stomach. "In this little one here."

She gave him a watery smile. "Will you forgive me for risking the babe's health? If I hadn't ridden north with the map, Seamus would have tried to go himself, and could have killed himself in the process."

There was a glint of pain in Cormac's eyes as he answered, "I've come to accept that my bride is going to do what she feels is right, whether I approve or not. The rest is up to the fates."

Claire pulled herself up to give him a kiss on the cheek. "If you've forgiven me for my adventure, then I believe the fates have, too, my fretful husband. I'm in fine fettle, and so is your son, from the strength of these kicks."

She lay back down and moved his hand over her belly, watching as his worried expression was replaced with one of awe. "I can feel it!" he said.

They grinned at each other. " 'Tis a boy," Claire declared proudly. "Another brawny son to carry on the Riordan line."

Cormac's grin died, and he removed his hand from her. "Aye," he said. "Another brawny Riordan boy."

Claire knew instantly that she'd said the wrong thing. She sighed. It was something that only time would cure. When the day came that she could rise whole and healthy from her birthing bed and put a strong son in his arms, Cormac would lose that haunted look forever.

"Do you know if they have gone to fetch the gold?" she asked, changing the subject to distract him.

Cormac sat back and appeared to relax. "Nay, but as a matter of fact, we former loyalists brought a present with us to camp that might help hurry this conflict to a swift conclusion."

"A present?"

"Aye. In fact, Sean should be giving it to O'Neill right about now."

The tensions of the previous evening seemed to have dissolved in the morning light. At cookfires all over camp, rebels and former loyalists joked and laughed together as though the weight of battle had never separated them.

The Riordans had been invited to breakfast with O'Neill and his inner circle. Cormac had sent regrets, since he was not leaving his wife's side, but Sean, Dermot, Niall, Eamon, and the others sat around the O'Neill cookfire, sharing thick slabs of bacon and oat porridge.

"We'll be heading back to our homes today," Sean told the rebel leader, who had already downed an entire plate of bacon and was reaching for more.

"I could use men like you and your cousins," O'Neill said. "I'd be proud to fight beside you, if you'd change your minds."

Sean shook his head. "Our homes and families need tending, and most of our men don't have the heart to fight against men who were formerly our allies. Niall, here, is staying."

O'Neill glanced at the youngest Riordan. "And 'tis very welcome you are, son," he said.

"However, we do have a gift for you that may make up for not being able to fight by your side."

O'Neill looked surprised. "A gift?"

"Aye," Sean said with a wide grin. The others were smiling, too. "Eamon, Dermot, do you want to bring it over?"

The two stood and then disappeared inside the tent they had shared for the night. When they emerged, they were pushing a big chest. Together they dragged it toward the fire. It was obviously heavy.

"Here you are, O'Neill," Sean said with a flourish of his arm. "Spanish gold. Specially delivered."

"Our gold!" O'Neill cried. He lumbered to his feet and walked over to the chest. Then he pulled the latch and flipped open the top. For a moment, everyone in the circle was quiet, staring at the gleaming metal.

One of O'Neill's lieutenants gave a low whistle. "This could turn the tide," he said.

O'Neill himself lifted a bar out of the chest and hefted it. "Pretty, isn't it?" he asked with a grin. He turned to Sean. "I guess the question is, how did you boys come by it?"

"It appears that while Bixleigh was off chasing your map, a few of his men on a scouting party had already seen the Spaniards putting it into a secluded little harbor north of Balbriggan. They watched the Spaniards bury the gold, waited for the Spanish ship to leave, then rode in and dug up the chest. We ran into them heading back to camp with it as we were riding out. Since we already knew that we were coming to make our peace with you, we decided it would be a nice idea to 'liberate' it."

"A very nice idea," O'Neill agreed. "I'm in your debt, Riordan." He looked around the circle of smiling men. "That means all of you. If you are ever in need, remember that Shane O'Neill pays his debts."

She'd dozed again, and this time when Claire awoke, Cormac was gone and John Black had once again taken a place by her bed.

He answered her unspoken question. "I forced him to go get some sleep. He hadn't slept for two days."

She nodded, understanding, though she was disappointed. She hadn't been able to stay awake to talk with her husband long enough to find out his true feelings about the baby. She hadn't had time to go into explanations about her trip to the Iron Horse and why she had never told him about her family's connections with the rebels. There were so many things left hanging between them, and now that she knew that the baby was going to be all right, she couldn't wait to get all their misunderstandings cleared up.

"I don't imagine he'll stay away long," John Black said, amusement twinkling in his eyes. "He was none too happy to leave you here."

"I appreciate all your help, Doctor. You must be behind on your sleep, too."

"I've never been much of one for sleeping, Lady Riordan. There's always been too much else to do."

She noticed that he had reverted to a more formal mode of address, and she didn't question it. John Black had been there for her when she had needed him, and she would never forget it, but at the moment she had to concentrate on her husband.

As if in response to her thoughts, the door opened and

Cormac came in, looking much the better for his few hours of sleep. He smiled when he saw that she was awake. "How's the patient?" he asked the doctor.

"I believe she's better now that you're here," he answered, standing and relinquishing his post to Cormac. "I'll leave you two alone."

After he'd left, Cormac took Claire's hand and leaned close. "Now *you* tell me—how's the patient?"

"She's fine, though she's worried about what her husband is thinking."

Cormac gave a brief laugh with little humor. "Thinking about what? About how he almost lost his wife last night? About how in hell he could have been so selfish and stupid as to put her in this condition in the first place? About why she was in disguise on a mission for the rebels when she knew she was putting not only herself but her child at risk?"

Claire looked away. "Aye," she said softly. "I'm worried over what he's thinking about all those things." She turned back to him. "Except for the selfish and stupid part. 'Twas not you who determined what would happen with us that last night. I seduced you."

This elicited a small smile. "You did, eh?"

"Aye. With tricks I learned from Nancy."

Cormac looked dumbfounded. "Nancy, from the tavern at Kilmessen?"

Claire nodded. "The same tricks I used to convince you to make love to me in the first place."

Cormac shook his head as if to clear it. "What nonsense is this?"

"I went to Nancy for advice about how to make myself irresistible. Eileen went with me."

"Your sister?" Cormac groaned. "Good lord, what were you thinking?"

Claire gave a rueful twist to her mouth. "I wanted us

to be together. I needed to know how to make you want me."

"By the rood, sweetheart, you didn't need any of Nancy's tricks for that. I've wanted you since the first moment I saw you standing by the hill at Tara. I wanted you so desperately that I couldn't trust myself to be near you. It was torture."

She frowned. "Truly?" she asked.

"Truly. When I finally made love to you it was because I could no longer stop myself. I felt as if I were about to explode every time I looked at you."

"It wasn't the talc or the sweetwaters?"

He threw back his head and laughed. "It wasn't the scents or the oysters or anything but you, my adorable and desirable wife."

Though it made her feel better to hear him admit that he had wanted her from the beginning, Claire wasn't sorry that she had enlisted Nancy's aid. The outspoken, warmhearted tavern maid had taught her things that would enhance both her own pleasure and her husband's.

"I'm glad you find me desirable," she said, her voice dropping. "In fact, if you can find a bolt on that door, perhaps you'd like to reassure me on that score right now."

Cormac looked horrified. "Good God, woman, are you daft? You're supposed to be in bed."

She grinned impishly. "I wouldn't have to get out of bed."

"*Resting* in bed," he said firmly. "I don't intend to come within two yards of you."

"Too bad. I still have a few of those tricks of Nancy's that I haven't showed you yet."

He groaned. "Behave yourself or I'll have your father in here to deal with you."

Her smile faded. "I wish they were going home with us, too."

Cormac grew sober as well. "Aye, but I don't think it will be long now. The English are now outnumbered and, thanks to the Spanish gold, will soon be outgunned."

She had been relieved and pleased last night when he had told her the story of their liberation of the gold, even though it meant that all her efforts to bring the map north had been for nothing. "The ladies of O'Donnell House will have to wait awhile longer for their men's safe return," she said with a sigh.

He reached for her hand and squeezed it. "Aye, but for the Riordans this war is over. You and I are going home."

Nineteen

By the time they'd been back at Riordan Hall for a fortnight, Claire was starting to wonder if she had dreamed those passionate times she and Cormac had shared. While he was solicitous of her health, sometimes almost to the point of annoyance, he had kept his word about staying away from her. He had moved back to his room in the distant south wing and did not so much as kiss her good night. In some ways it seemed as if they had gone back to those miserable days when she had first come to Riordan Hall.

He had never chided her about risking their baby's life on a mission for men who were at the time his enemies. But she felt that her actions stood like a silent barrier between them.

Then, too, she was lonely. After the weeks of camaraderie with all the women at O'Donnell House, Riordan Hall seemed big and empty. Eamon and Cormac were busy setting things to right on the estate after the long absence. Niall had stayed with the rebels. Sean and Dermot had gone to their home in the north. She missed having someone to talk to, Claire realized as she left the kitchens after visiting Molly for the fourth time that afternoon.

Sometimes it seemed as if her only companion was the unborn child inside her. She'd had no more of the ominous cramping she'd had that night at the Iron Horse Inn, and the baby now regularly made himself felt with kicks and flutters. Once after supper when the kicking was especially strong, she'd put Cormac's hand on her stomach to feel the movement. She'd seen the same look of awe on his face that he'd had when he'd first done so at the rebel camp, but after only a few seconds, he pulled his hand away, as though he were afraid of hurting her.

She sighed and, instead of heading back toward the house, turned in the direction of the stables. Aidan was alone, cleaning.

"Do you know where Lord Riordan and his brother have gone today?" she asked him.

"I believe they intended to ride to the Clearys' for news of the rebellion, milady," he answered, putting aside his rake.

The Cleary estate was a good ten miles. She'd be lucky if they were back by suppertime. She looked at the western sky. There was an hour or so of daylight left.

"I think I'll go for a ride, Aidan," she said, heading inside the stable. "Will you please help me saddle Lucifer?"

The stable master looked glum. "I'm sorry, milady, but I can't do that."

She looked around in surprise. "Why not?"

"Master Cormac's orders. I'm not to let you take out a horse. Not any horse, much less Lucifer."

Claire was dumbfounded. "I rode all the way from Ulster."

Aidan looked decidedly uncomfortable. "I'm sorry, milady. He made me swear."

Claire reckoned she could saddle the horse without assistance if she needed to, but she didn't want to put kindhearted Aidan in a bad position. "Don't worry about it then," she said with a forced smile. "I'll straighten this out with my husband tonight and come again tomorrow."

"I'd be grateful, milady," Aidan said, obviously relieved.

She turned around and headed down the hill, getting angrier by the step. He avoided her company, left her alone all day while he rode about the countryside, and now he had forbidden her to have the same freedom? It wasn't fair, and she'd told Aidan the truth. One way or another, tonight she intended to straighten things out with her husband.

As she had anticipated, Cormac and Eamon did not arrive home in time for supper. In fact, she had retired to her room and there still was no sign of them. She stood for nearly an hour by her bedroom window, before she saw them ride up to the stables. She continued watching their shadowy figures as they made their way to the house. She hadn't bothered to leave food out for them in the dining hall. If they were hungry, they'd have to seek something out in the kitchens.

Cormac usually came to bid her good night. She waited another half an hour, but there were still no steps coming down her hall. He had probably decided that the hour was too late and she may be asleep. But she wasn't the least bit sleepy.

Once before she'd managed to find her way in the darkness to his room. He hadn't been there, but she had the feeling that tonight he would be. She lit her candle in the glowing embers of her fire and started resolutely toward the south wing.

By now she knew the castle well, and it wasn't difficult to make her way through the dark corridors. The difficult part was deciding exactly what she was going to say when she arrived. She finally gave up trying to prepare and decided to let the conversation take its own course.

He was in the process of taking off his shirt as she opened the door. He looked over at her in surprise. "Sweetheart," he said, "I thought you would be long asleep."

"Nay." She walked toward him. "My bed is too lonely for sleep."

He looked wary. "I should call one of the servants to build up the fire."

She shook her head and walked closer. "That's not the kind of fire I'm looking for," she said. She knew that her nightrail had slipped lower as she walked, nearly revealing the tips of her breasts.

Cormac took a step backward. "Lord, Nancy and her bloody lessons. Such things should be outlawed."

Claire smiled, and she didn't have to remember any of Nancy's advice to make the smile inviting. She had already begun to feel the stirrings of desire as soon as she found herself alone with him in the darkened room. "I reckon it's a bit late for that," she said.

"I reckon," he said.

By now she knew the signs. His voice was altered. Beads of sweat had sprung out along his temples. His eyes had turned dark.

She was within inches of him when she stopped. "I've missed you," she said.

"I'm here with you every day."

"We live in the same house, but that's not what I mean." She moved imperceptibly closer. "Don't you want to kiss me?"

He groaned. "I want you to go back to your own room

like a good girl and leave me to figure out how I'm going to get through another long night."

Irritated, she took a step backwards. "There's no reason for either one of us to have to figure out how we're going to get through a long night alone. You're my husband."

"I don't want to risk . . ." he began.

She continued on as if he hadn't spoken. "And I'm your wife. We belong together. If I have to spend the next four months lonely and miserable, sleeping alone and forbidden to even ride my horse, then I may as well leave here and move back to O'Donnell House with the women. Women understand that childbirth is a natural process. At least there, I won't have people treating me as if I'm made of glass instead of flesh and blood."

Cormac was watching her lips as she spoke. When he didn't say anything in response to her outburst, she put her hands on her hips and said, "Well?"

"You asked me if I wanted to kiss you. The answer to that is aye, I do." Then he took a step forward and pulled her into his arms.

It had been so long, the heat was instantaneous. Claire moved against him and tipped her head slightly to allow him access to the depths of her mouth.

"I don't want to hurt you," he murmured.

"You won't," she reassured him, and shrugged off her robe, leaving her neck and shoulders bare for his kisses.

Once more he asked for reassurance. "This won't harm the baby?"

"The baby will tend to itself," she told him. " 'Tis I who need tending at the moment." Boldly, she reached down to pull off her nightrail and stood before him naked.

His eyes flared as he looked at her. Her body had grown more lush. The curve of her stomach was still small, but her breasts were fuller and the nipples more pronounced.

"I'm changing," she said, suddenly shy about what his reaction might be to her now-obvious condition.

He gazed at her a long moment, then said slowly, "You're the most beautiful thing I've ever seen."

The words melted her like warm honey. She put her hand against his rough cheek. "I love thee, Cormac Riordan," she said.

"And I thee, *leannan,*" he whispered, using the ancient term for sweetheart.

They led each other to the bed, and while Cormac discarded his clothes, Claire watched him with brimming eyes. *This is how it should be,* she told herself. *This is the fullness my heart has sought.*

Then they were tumbling together on Cormac's bed, remembering the feel of each other's skin, the touch of each other's hands. Cormac's lovemaking had a new quality of reverence that Claire found incredibly touching and utterly erotic.

When he entered her, he did it with exquisite slowness, watching her face to be sure that each inch of depth was causing her pleasure and no pain. By the time he was fully within her, she was the one that was urging speed, moving beneath him in a nearly frantic rhythm, seeking both his release and her own.

She arched her back, and he hissed an oath as they thundered to completion.

Afterward she lay underneath him with a feeling of total peace. All the misunderstandings of the past few days were forgotten. With words and with body, Cormac had said that he loved her. It was all she needed.

Abruptly, he moved off her and sat up. "I'm crushing you," he said, concerned.

"Nay."

"I may be crushing the babe, then," he argued. "We shouldn't be taking these chances, sweetheart."

She was too sated and happy to be upset by his abrupt change of tone. She realized that Cormac would never be comfortable with her pregnancy until she had had a healthy baby and put all his curse fears to rest. "My love," she said. "I'm fine, and I intend to stay fine. Now if you would just settle back down here beside me, we can both get some badly needed sleep."

He was still looking down at her with a worried frown. "Are you sure you're all right?" he asked.

"Aye. In fact, I'm decidedly *more* all right than I was before I came to this room tonight."

Her grin finally made the frown leave his face. He lay back down and pulled her into his arms. "Ah, princess," he said, "so am I."

She had broken his resistance in the matter of lovemaking. Cormac had moved back into their shared chamber, and most nights he could be convinced with very little effort to share satisfying, if somewhat careful, passions. But in every other matter, he continued to guard her like a gaoler with a prize prisoner. She chafed under the restraints and his constant worry, but she tried to remind herself that he had seen three mothers die. He was a strong leader for his people, a fiercely loyal kinsman, and a tender lover, but he was beyond reason on this one point.

Finally the time came when even she agreed that it would be wise for Cormac to move back to his own room, though her awakening body still seemed as needy as ever for his attentions. The baby was due in less than six weeks, and the best advice she could glean from the women servants who had given birth was that further relations would not be considered decent.

The lack of Cormac's company at night made her even more restless. She'd argued with him tirelessly about the horseback riding, but in this he would not relent. The problem was, she felt wonderful and seemed to have more energy than ever before in her life. She'd organized the servants to clean the hall from top to bottom. She had mended sheets until she thought she would scream.

"I need a change, Molly," she told the cook one morning after Cormac and Eamon had ridden away for yet another trip to the far reaches of the county, saying that they would be gone two or three days.

Molly gave her a look of motherly sympathy. "Poor lamb, once the baby comes ye'll have more than enough to keep ye busy. Ye'll be longing for these times back again."

"That may be, but right now, I'm suffocating." She was occupying herself by throwing peas, one at a time, into a kettle of boiling water. "There's not even much point in cooking. Everyone's gone."

"Fine by me," Molly said with a grin.

Claire straightened up with sudden resolution. "I'm going to go see Eileen. She's been there shouldering the responsibility for all those women ever since Seamus went back up to join O'Neill, and I bet she'd welcome a visit from her big sister."

Molly looked doubtful. "The master has forbidden ye to ride, mistress. How would ye get there?"

"There's nothing wrong with me, and a gentle ride along a smooth road is not going to hurt me any."

"But with the babe almost due—"

"All the more reason," Claire interrupted. "Once it arrives, who knows when I'll next be able to visit O'Donnell House? This is the perfect chance to go. I could ride over today and return tomorrow before Cormac and Eamon get back."

Now that the plan had come to her, she was filled with enthusiasm at the idea of seeing Eileen again. And of riding.

"Aidan won't let ye, mistress. I heard him swear to Master Cormac that he'd tie you down afore he'd let you up on a horse."

"Men!" Claire declared, then she gave Molly a sly look. "I'm going to need your help, Molly dear," she said in a cajoling tone.

"Oh, no, mistress. Master Cormac'll boil me in my own soup pot."

"He'll do nothing of the sort. All I'm asking you to do is invite Master Aidan down for a piece of your berry tart. While he eats it, I'll scoot up to the stables and get a horse."

The round cook gave a big sigh, resigned to the fact that she could refuse her adored mistress nothing. "Ye will be careful, dearie?"

"I'll go sidesaddle and I'll take a gentle little mare, not Lucifer. I'll be just fine."

Molly shook her head. "Ye better be back afore the master or there'll be hell to pay."

Claire jumped up and planted a big kiss on Molly's cheek. "Thank you, Molly. He'll never even know I was gone."

Cormac was glad that he and Eamon had finished their business early. He hadn't wanted to leave Claire, even though things were not the easiest between them at the moment. He knew that his close scrutiny of her every move was irksome to her, but he couldn't help it. Every time he was away from her, his mind began to paint scenarios of her beginning the pains of birth without him. Somehow, he had the feeling that if he could be beside her to lend her his strength during the ordeal, she would have a better chance surviving.

In any event, it made him feel better to be with her. He resolved that after today, he would put off any further trips until the baby was born. That way he would be sure to be at her side when she needed him.

Aidan was waiting for them at the stables, as usual, but Cormac could tell immediately that the normally cheerful stable master was upset about something. He jumped from his horse. "Claire—is she all right?" he shouted.

Aidan's grim countenance seemed to confirm his worst fears. Hellfire and brimstone, he should never have left her, he berated himself. "Is it the baby?" he asked.

"I'd never have let her go, Master Cormac," the big man stuttered. " 'Twas that conniving Molly and her pies that did it."

Cormac could make little sense of the man's babbling. He moved close to him and gripped the edge of Aidan's leather apron. "What has happened, Aidan? Just tell it to me slow."

"She's gone, Master Cormac. Came right on up and took herself a horse without a by-your-leave."

"She went riding?"

Aidan nodded miserably.

At least it was not as bad as he had feared. He knew that Claire had been dying for a ride for weeks. Like a naughty pupil, the little minx had taken advantage of his absence to satisfy her wish.

He looked up at his brother, who had not dismounted. Eamon grinned at him. "Looks like we're going out riding, eh, brother?"

"Do you know where she was heading?" he asked the stable master.

Aidan nodded unhappily. "O'Donnell House."

"All the way to O'Donnell House? How long ago did she leave?"

"She left yesterday, sir. Without a by-your-leave."

Cormac muttered an oath.

"Come on, Cormac," Eamon said. "We'll head over there after her."

"You'd better take care of the other matter first," Aidan said.

"What other matter?" Cormac asked.

"He's waiting for you at the hall, sir. 'Tis that lieutenant from that English general, Bixleigh. He says he has something important to tell you."

Eamon looked at his brother. "Do you want me to go talk to the man?"

Cormac shook his head. "Nay, if Claire left yesterday, a few more minutes is not going to make much difference. We'll see the lieutenant together, and then we'll ride to O'Donnell House."

Eamon looked down at his brother's face, which was set in grim lines. "She's going to be fine, Cormac," he reassured him with a smile. "It's just that you happen to have a wife who is more than a little independent."

But Cormac's tense expression didn't change. "I have a wife who doesn't need the Riordan curse to kill her off. She's hell-bent to do it all by herself."

Then he turned and stalked down the hill.

Lieutenant Grenville had apparently come alone. In his agitation over the news about Claire, Cormac hadn't stopped to wonder what the English soldier could be doing here without an escort, but Grenville answered the question immediately.

"I've come on my own, gentlemen," he said, standing as Cormac and Eamon walked into the parlor where he was waiting. "So before I go any further, I should tell you that, at the moment, I might be considered a fugitive from Her Majesty's justice."

Cormac regarded the young man with surprise. Grenville had always seemed to him to be the model soldier. "I suspect there is more to be told, Lieutenant," Cormac said mildly, as he and Eamon took seats opposite the man. As anxious as he was to get on the road to find Claire, Cormac had a sense that the Englishman had something important to tell them. The young officer looked haggard and tired.

"Have you eaten, Lieutenant?" he asked. "Shall I send for some food?"

Grenville waved off the suggestion. "I don't need to eat, Lord Riordan. I need to talk to you."

Cormac leaned back in his chair. "We're listening."

"Sir, I believe you know me to be a good soldier, or at the very least, a loyal one."

"Such has been my impression, Lieutenant. I'd always considered Bixleigh lucky to have you."

The young man let out a long breath. "Since that night he went to the Iron Horse Inn and all the loyalist families left, the general has become increasingly irrational. He stays in his tent praying and muttering about Catholics all day long. His orders have been odd and"—the lieutenant paused—"*cruel.* 'Tis the only word for it, sir."

Cormac had seen enough of Bixleigh's mean streak to understand what the lieutenant meant. He leaned toward Grenville and said gently, "Yet it's not an easy decision to go against your commanding officer."

Grenville shook his head, his lips tight. "Nay, 'tis the hardest decision I've ever had to make, but this final notion of his was simply too much."

"What notion?" Eamon asked.

"He's here in Meath, and he's brought a platoon of men with him."

"What's he doing here?" Cormac asked. "O'Neill's still in the north, isn't he?"

"Aye, little by little he's chipping away at us. His men appear suddenly, attack, then slip back into the rough terrain where we can't seem to follow. We've endured month after month of it, and the troops have become increasingly demoralized."

"And Bixleigh has become increasingly erratic," Cormac added.

"Aye. Now the general has come south to attack the women of O'Donnell House. He says if the rebels won't come out of the woods and fight, he'll strike them a blow where it hurts. He'll kill their women."

Eamon and Cormac both straightened up in horror at the lieutenant's words.

"But that's monstrous," Eamon exclaimed. "They're totally defenseless."

"Aye." Grenville looked miserable. "That's why I'm here, sir. I couldn't let it happen."

Cormac had already jumped to his feet. Claire was at O'Donnell House. "How many men does Bixleigh have with him, Lieutenant?" he asked.

Grenville stood as well. "Not more than fifty. He's anticipating a slaughter, not a fight."

Claire is at O'Donnell House, Cormac's brain shouted at him again, but he couldn't let himself think about that right now. "Eamon, we'll round up every man we can here and start for O'Donnell House at once. You ride to get the Clearys and send Aidan for the Mitchells. Meet us there as soon as you can."

"I'd like to go with you," Grenville said.

"You're a fugitive, Lieutenant," Eamon pointed out.

"Aye, but I'd like to go. I didn't become a soldier to massacre women and children."

Something in his words clicked in Cormac's head, but he didn't have time to stop and consider why. He began running toward the door and shouted back over his shoulder, "Come along, then, Grenville. But hurry!"

Twenty

There had been no time to even think about defending themselves. The women of O'Donnell House had been gathered in the big solar at the back of the house, working on their tapestry, when suddenly doors were slamming, men were yelling. They could hear the sound of heavy boots running through the halls and then they were there—English soldiers in full uniform, crowding the room and seizing the women, dragging them off their seats and holding them captive.

Eileen and Claire were caught as off guard as all the rest. Claire was able to land a couple of healthy kicks to the soldier who grabbed her from behind, but all it got her was a painful stranglehold around her neck.

Restrained as she was, she was helpless to do anything, and all the others seemed to be in the same straits. Immediately she chided herself for not having been prepared. It had always seemed as if the fighting was far to the north and couldn't affect them. They'd never thought to worry about how vulnerable the women were with no male protection.

She looked around, trying to see if she could recognize anyone from when the troops were staying at Riordan Hall. In particular, she hoped to find the nice young lieutenant, Grenville, who had been kind to her. But none of the men looked familiar.

Then her gaze went to the doorway. Finally there was a familiar face, but it was the last one she wanted to see.

Bixleigh spotted her at once. "I see we have an added bonus," the general said with relish, walking in her direction. "I hadn't dared hope that the famous rebel spy, Lady Riordan, would be here at O'Donnell House."

"What did you hope to find, General?" Claire asked with disgust. "There are none here but helpless women and children. Have Her Majesty's forces fallen so low?"

Bixleigh appeared unperturbed by her words. "Her Majesty's forces are the best and bravest in the world, Lady Riordan, and as such, we fight with whatever weapons we think best."

"What bravery is there in fighting against defenseless women?" she asked.

Bixleigh smiled broadly and his beady black eyes glowed. The man was unbalanced, Claire realized with a sinking heart. There was no way to try to reason with a madman. She looked around the room at the other soldiers, many of whom were holding captive other women. Surely some of these men must see that their commander had lost the thread of reality?

She searched the crowd again, desperately looking for Lieutenant Grenville. Even months ago at Riordan Hall, she had thought that he had been embarrassed about many of his commanding officer's actions. But Grenville was nowhere to be seen.

She called out to the room in general. "Look at us, gentlemen! We are women. There are children in this house. Don't any of you have mothers back in England? Wives? Sisters? How can you follow this man when he declares war on such as us?"

Some of the soldiers looked uncomfortable, but none spoke up to support her, and they continued holding their women prisoners.

She turned back to Bixleigh, who appeared pleased at her outburst. "What are you planning to do with us?" she asked.

His smile looked even more demented as he said, "Why, I'm going to kill you, Lady Riordan. One by one. I believe I'll save you for last, so that you can watch the others go."

Claire looked around in amazement. Wasn't it clear to his men that something in Bixleigh's mind had become unhinged? "Don't do this thing," she pleaded, trying to catch the eyes of the soldiers who stood nearest. None of them moved.

Suddenly they heard the sound of shots outside. Bixleigh's head came up like an animal scenting danger. "Are our troops surrounding this place?" he shouted at the soldier who stood guard at the door.

"Aye, sir," the man answered. "We should have the entire area covered."

There were more scattered shots, and Bixleigh's face started to turn red. "Kill them," he sputtered, throwing his arms around wildly. "Kill them all immediately."

The soldiers who were holding women looked at each other, their faces reflecting confusion and misgivings.

"Your commander is no longer sane," Claire said in a loud, ringing voice. "Don't listen to him."

Now there was a definite sound of fighting, some of it coming right outside the room. Bixleigh dashed over to one of the windows and threw open the shutters. Claire couldn't see clearly, but she could hear the shouts, English accents mingled with Irish.

Bixleigh turned back to face the men in the room. "Draw your daggers and slit their throats. That's an order," he yelled. "I'll run through the first man to disobey."

None of the soldiers made a move toward his dagger.

Around the room a number of women dropped to the floor or stumbled sideways as their captors released their hold. Bixleigh began brandishing his sword and screaming. Claire could see the spittle flying from the sides of his mouth as his words became incoherent.

Then, suddenly, they were there—Cormac, Eamon, the Clearys, the Mitchells. All at once, the room was crammed with Irishmen. Claire sagged with relief as the soldier holding her took his arm from around her waist and put his hands in the air.

From the far side of the room, Bixleigh pulled a pistol from inside his coat and leveled it at Claire. "I'll shoot her!" he shouted. "Everyone freeze or I'll shoot Lady Riordan."

Cormac was halfway across the room to her, but he stopped dead. The room grew quiet. "It's over, Bixleigh," he said. "Drop the pistol and you'll be able to head back to England. No one else will be hurt."

Bixleigh took two steps closer to Claire. "She's a dead woman if anyone moves," he said again.

Claire could see the strain in Cormac's face. His gaze was on the pistol in Bixleigh's hand. It looked as if he was calculating whether he could get to it before Bixleigh could fire. It would be a risky move. If Cormac dove for the gun, it could kill her. Or it could kill him. *Don't try it,* Claire begged silently.

Suddenly there was a movement at the back of the room. One of the English soldiers released the woman he'd been holding, drew a dagger and sent it whizzing across the room toward Bixleigh.

The general fell backwards to the floor, the soldier's knife protruding from his neck. Around it bright red blood gushed out like a water pump.

Claire looked in amazement from the fallen Englishman to the soldier who had thrown the knife, a stout man with a completely bald head.

He looked straight at her. " 'Twas what ye said about me mum, mistress. 'Twarnt right to come after women this way. Me mum's all alone back in Bristol, and I'd kill any man who would touch 'er."

"Thank you," she whispered. Her limbs felt incredibly weak and she grasped a nearby chair for support.

Cormac was at her side in seconds, lifting her, holding her against him. "Are you all right, love?" he whispered.

A rush of joy went through her at his endearment. She'd expected that he would never forgive her for once again risking the life of their child. She didn't know how he had found out about Bixleigh's raid or how he had gotten here just in time to save them. All she knew was that he was there, and he still loved her.

Then the pain began, stabbing through her like a hot knife. The last thing she was aware of was Cormac's lips meeting hers in a kiss.

"The way I see it, brother, 'tis time for the Riordan curse to be lifted. If we were cursed centuries ago for participating in the massacre of helpless women and children, why couldn't we be blessed now that we were the ones who rode to the rescue of the women at O'Donnell House?"

Following the raid, Cormac had had the same notion. Could this be the reversal of history that the ancients had been waiting for? But he had been reluctant to give voice to the thought, and somehow hearing his brother speak the words didn't help. It made it seem irreverent, since Eamon had never much believed in the curse in the first place. "I don't want to talk about the curse," he snapped.

"Don't get surly. Your wife's in labor and you're up-set, but it won't do any good for you to take it out on me. Brothers have to stick together in times like these." He slapped Cormac on the shoulder. "You're about to become a father, lad."

"Or a widower." Cormac sat on the grassy edge of the pond in Cliodhna's Glen, staring gloomily into the still water.

They hadn't let him stay with her. When Claire had fainted at O'Donnell House, just as the fight with the English was ended, Cormac had picked her up and taken her to a bedchamber. While his men were dealing with the suddenly docile English soldiers, he had hovered around Claire anxiously, asking questions and making suggestions while the O'Donnell women gently worked around him to take care of Claire.

"You're driving us all to distraction, Cormac," Eileen had told him finally, her firm voice reminding him of her sister's. "Get your brother to take yourself off for a ride somewhere. Nothing's going to happen here for hours yet."

"But she fainted," Cormac had argued. "That's not normal, is it? Someone needs to ride for a doctor who can tell us if she's all right."

"The midwife from Kilmessen is here, and we've got a house full of women. This is going to be the most assisted birth since Anne Boleyn bore the queen."

In the end, Eamon had dragged him off to the stables, and Cormac had agreed to take a ride to Cliodhna's Glen, both because it would remind him of the time he'd brought Claire here and because it had always seemed to him such a magical place. He and Claire could both use some magic right about now.

"Come with me, Eamon." Cormac jumped up, no

longer able to stay still. "I'll show you something strange Claire and I found."

Eamon stood, and Cormac led him around the end of the lake to the little stone ruin. "How many times did we play inside here as children?" he asked his brother.

"Countless. Sometimes we were pirates and sometimes kings. Or buccaneers sacking a city on the Spanish Main. It was our fort."

Cormac managed a smile. "Aye. And how many times did you see a lady inside our fort?"

Eamon looked blank. "A lady? Why, never. 'Twas just us three."

"Well, I don't mean a real lady, but look." He ducked inside the building and moved to one side so that Eamon could see the carving on the far wall.

Eamon squinted into the dark space and gave a low whistle. "I'll be damned," he said.

"I would have sworn there was no such carving when we were young," Cormac told him.

"I would, too."

"Yet it looks old. See how certain areas are worn with age?"

Eamon looked mystified. "Could we have missed seeing it?"

"I don't know how, but we must have. I suppose young lads aren't too observant."

Eamon looked doubtful about his brother's explanation. "You were never one to miss a thing, Cormac. I don't know. I can't explain it."

Cormac squirmed out of the little building. "Nor can I," he said, standing.

"Perhaps it's Cliodhna come to visit her special place," Eamon said after a moment.

"I thought you didn't believe in faeries."

"I don't, but"—Eamon shrugged—"this is Tara. Who knows what may happen here?"

"Aye," Cormac said slowly, looking around the little glen.

"Well, if 'tis Cliodhna, I warrant she's come to bring good news and tell us that the Riordan curse has been lifted forever."

Cormac shivered. "I told you not to speak of it."

Eamon looked at Cormac's stricken face. "I'm sorry, brother. I'd thought to cheer you. Claire is tall and strong and healthy. You say that you believe in the magic of this place. Faith, what it's telling me right now is that Claire will bear you many children and live to hold your grandchildren in her arms."

"I hope to God you're right." Once again he felt a shiver up his spine. "Let's go back," he said. "I want to be with her."

Eamon looked across the clearing at the pink western sky. "Aye, and it's time. It's almost dark."

They made their way around the pond and headed toward the break in the trees that would lead them out of the clearing and back to their horses. Cormac turned around for a last look at the ruin before they left.

"Look!" Eamon said, pointing to the darkening sky.

Cormac followed the direction of his hand. A great bird was silhouetted in the sunset. As they watched for a moment, it appeared to be flying directly toward them. "God help me, Eamon," he said in a strangled voice. "It's a black swan."

Neither spoke for several moments as the graceful creature glided toward them, big and dark against the glowing sky. "It's just a swan, Cormac," Eamon said finally. "Nothing more."

Cormac nodded, his throat too full to speak.

They turned to leave the clearing again, but as they

neared the trees, Eamon clutched Cormac's arm and said again, "Look!"

They turned back to see the swan heading toward a landing on the smooth pond behind them. "Cormac," Eamon said, his voice triumphant. "It's not black."

Cormac stared at the water where the big swan had touched down in a perfect landing. Now that it was near, they could see that its feathers were not dark at all. They were a beautiful, snowy white.

"Don't tell me to stay away any longer," Cormac told his sister-in-law as he and Eamon came back in the front door of O'Donnell House. "I intend to be with my wife, and your team of midwives will just have to put up with my help."

" 'Tis not your help we object to, brother, it's the pacing and the moaning and the never-ending questions. I swear, you're worse than an old lady."

Eamon looked as if he were trying not to laugh.

Cormac didn't smile. "That may be," he said, "but I'm going to her."

Eileen shrugged and stepped aside so that Cormac could climb the stairs. When he had disappeared down the hall, she gave Eamon a look of helplessness. "Babies are born every day, you know," she said.

Eamon grinned. "Aye, but not *Cormac's* baby."

She returned his smile. "He'll make a bonny father," she said.

"That he will," Eamon replied.

Cormac's heart began to beat faster as he walked toward the door of the birthing room. As Eamon had said, Claire was strong, but she'd been through one too many adventures on the way to this moment. When she'd slumped in his arms earlier, her face had been deathly pale. It had been nearly a half hour before she had regained her senses, and by then her labor pains had begun in full force.

And it was happening too early. The baby should not have come for another month. He'd heard all kinds of dire things that happened when births began before their time.

He should have chained her to her bed, he thought with a surge of anger. Knowing how prone she was to do things her own way, he should have stood guard over her twenty-four hours a day. He was a Riordan. He may have doomed her to this moment the day he married her, but if he'd been more vigilant, perhaps he would have been able to defy fate.

His hand shook as he reached for the latch of the door. Then he heard it. A reedy wail. The blood drained from his face as the cry became louder and more insistent.

He pulled open the door. Claire, drenched with sweat, sat half upright in the bed. She looked over at him, her face radiant, then she looked down to the bundle she held in her arms. "Come, husband," she said. "Come and meet your son."

Occupied with the birth of his son, Cormac had given over the responsibility for dealing with the captured English to Brian Cleary. Once their commander was dead, the young soldiers had proved cooperative. Most of them were homesick and unhappy and relieved to have been saved from a campaign that they found unmanly and repugnant.

At Cormac's suggestion, Cleary had sent word north to O'Neill to inform the rebel leader about Bixleigh's death and ask for suggestions about what to do with the five dozen or so English prisoners who had been herded into a makeshift camp on the Cleary property.

Cormac had put in a special request for John Black to be among the contingent of rebels sent south to deal with the matter. Though Claire insisted that she was recovering well from the birth, Cormac hovered over her like a brood hen, worrying every time she grimaced at an odd pain.

"Having a baby hurts," Claire had told him with some indignation, "especially when 'tis a strapping big boy like the one you bred, sir. I've a right to wince a little when I take a seat."

But Cormac wanted the doctor to examine her, just to be sure. Niall's mother, Rhea, had lived a full month after Niall was born before she had died.

He tried not to remember that fact as he sat in the bedchamber at O'Donnell House watching Claire nurse their child, four days after the birth. The color was back in her cheeks, and there was a new tenderness in her expression as she looked down at the baby. The mother and child were so beautiful together, it almost hurt to look at them.

He also was trying not to remember that it was exactly a year ago today that he and Claire had been wed at Tara Hill. By legend, if the Riordan curse was to claim another victim, it would happen before the sun went down on another day.

Claire looked up from her nursing. "I want to name him Ultan, after your father," she said.

Cormac swallowed hard. "Aye, 'tis a proud name."

She nodded, then made a little face as if in pain.

Cormac jumped up from his chair and went to the bed. "What's wrong?" he asked.

Claire shook her head with a sigh of forbearance. "Nothing's wrong, my love. 'Twas just an extra strong tug from young Ultan, who's proving to be as lusty as his father."

Cormac looked a little embarrassed. "Oh," he said, and sat back down again. "Still, I wish the doctor would arrive."

Claire laughed. "I need no doctor to tell me that I am perfectly well. In fact, I'm ready to leave here. I want us to go back to Riordan Hall."

Cormac shook his head. "I don't want you riding that far. Aren't you happy here with your sister and all the other women?"

"Of course, I'm grateful to them all for all the help, but I'm a little tired of being buzzed around like the queen in a hive. I'm ready to have Ultan to myself for a while in our own home."

"Not just yet," Cormac answered firmly.

Claire frowned. "If you recall, the last time you forbade me from my horse, I ended up—"

"I recall very well where you ended up, minx," he said crisply. "If you weren't the mother of my child, I'd consider giving your backside the paddling it deserves for that bit of foolishness."

Claire stuck her tongue out at him, but then said, "Seriously, I'm quite recovered. I feel that if I have to lie here much longer, I'm going to turn into a turnip."

He laughed. "How about if I take you for a short ride—just over to Cliodhna's Glen?"

She gave a little jump of excitement, causing a gurgle of protest from the child at her breast. "Would you? It would feel wonderful to be in the sunshine again."

"Will the baby be all right?" he asked.

"With two dozen mothers to tend him? I should think so."

"Good," he said with a smile. "We'll go tomorrow afternoon."

•   •   •

It was one of those rare fall days when it seemed that nature had relented and let summer back out for one last warm glow. Claire and Cormac rode slowly side by side. He'd made her pick the most plodding animal in the O'Donnell stables, but nevertheless she was *riding*. She gave a sigh of pure contentment. Her baby was peacefully sleeping under the vigilant eyes of Eileen and a whole line of other volunteers. Her husband was beside her, watching her with eyes that brimmed with pride and love. As they mounted the hill that looked down over the mounds of Tara, she decided that the world could simply not be any sweeter.

Cormac seemed to read her thoughts. "Happy, *chara?*" he asked.

She nodded. "Thank you for bringing me here today." She pointed down at the temple ruins, where they had pledged their vows. " 'Twas just a year and a day ago that we were wed here in this place."

He nodded, but didn't speak. They left their horses tied on the hill as they had on their previous visit and, hand and hand, walked through the circle of trees into Cliodhna's Glen.

"Let's visit the faerie spirit," Claire suggested, tugging him toward the pond.

They walked around to the ruin and Cormac said, "Be careful going in there now. Don't hurt yourself."

She grinned at him. "You forget, Cliodhna is a benevolent spirit. She won't let me be hurt." She went down on her knees and crawled inside.

After a long moment of silence, Cormac said, "Are you all right, sweetheart?"

Claire was looking at the inside wall of the stone house in amazement. "What happened to her?" she asked finally.

"What do you mean?" Cormac crouched down and poked his head in beside her.

"The lady's gone."

"She can't be. I just showed her to Eamon the other day."

"Well, she's not here." Claire ran her hand over the smooth stone wall. "There's no carving at all."

Cormac crowded in next to her and moved his hand over the wall, dumbfounded. "It's impossible."

Bewildered, they both eased out of the little house. Claire peeked in one last time to be sure her eyes hadn't been playing tricks. The far wall was bare.

"She's left us," she said finally. "You swore that she wasn't here when you played in this place as a child. Maybe she came just for a short time. Maybe she wanted to bring us a message or watch over us."

"Aye," Cormac said slowly. "Perhaps she did. Perhaps it was to protect you this past year that she came."

Claire laughed. "Lord knows I've needed protection a time or two." She didn't really believe in otherworldly spirits, but she had to admit that she could make no possible sense of a carving that appeared and disappeared in solid stone. She leaned into the doorway of the house again and shouted, "Thank you, Cliodhna."

Cormac reached for her hand as they began to make their way back around the lake. The sun had already sunk behind the tops of the trees, and the clearing was growing dark. Cormac had a faraway look in his eyes as he looked out over the water.

"Eamon and I saw a swan here the day Ultan was born," Cormac told her.

"A swan? They are rare. Was it one of the Riordan black swans?"

Cormac gave her an odd look. "It came at us against the sunset, so we thought it was black, but when it landed, we could see that it was white as snow."

They had reached the far side of the pond. Claire smiled and went up on tiptoe to give him a kiss on the cheek. "Ah, my superstitious husband, perhaps now you will believe that I haven't brought tragedy into your life."

He drew her into his arms. "Sweetheart, you have brought me warmth and tenderness and happiness such as I'd never known existed."

"Not to mention a son," she added.

He looked down at her tenderly. "Aye, you've also brought me a son."

She looked around with a sigh. A gentle breeze had begun rustling the leaves on the trees around them and sent little ripples along the silvery pond. "It will still be awhile before I'm fit again, but do you think Cliodhna will mind if we come back here someday soon and make love by her pond?"

Cormac smiled. "I don't think she'll mind at all, *chara.*" Then he lowered his mouth to hers for a long kiss.

Epilogue

Tara Hill, 1564

The new English general looked almost fragile seated across from the robust rebel leader as the two began the negotiations that were to end the conflict, this time for good.

"Is he really a general?" Claire whispered to Cormac. The Riordans and the O'Donnells had joined many other neighborhood families at Tara Hill to watch the peace parlay.

"Aye, princess, he's a general, and close to the queen, they say. His appearance may not be much, but he's a good man, as unlike Bixleigh as fire and water."

Claire resisted shuddering at the name of the man she had last seen lying mortally wounded at her feet. "I'm happy that he's reinstated Lieutenant Grenville."

"Aye, he's a captain now. General Fairmont could have picked no better man as his adjutant. It's just one of the wise decisions he's made."

"Such as bringing the queen's full pardon for the rebels."

"Aye, and setting a zone for the English troops."

They couldn't hear the discussion, but they knew they

would get the details later from Niall. In the year since the defection of the loyalists, the youngest Riordan brother had become one of O'Neill's most trusted aides. He sat just behind O'Neill at the conference table.

Claire juggled Ultan, who had grown restless in her arms as they stood watching the proceedings. "Now that he's learned to run," she whispered, "he wants to be on his feet all day long."

Cormac reached over and plucked the baby from her arms. "I have to agree with you, son," he said. "Meetings are dreary. You and I would rather be out riding the hills, wouldn't we?"

"One-year-olds do not go out riding, Cormac," Claire said firmly. Just last week, to Claire's horror, he had put Ultan up on Dian, the colt whose hoof she had nursed, and led them around the stableyard.

"Your mama worries too much, doesn't she, Ultan?" he teased.

Claire rolled her eyes. "This from the man who once threatened to chain me to my bed the next time I was with child."

He leaned over and kissed her. "That was before I understood that we have a charmed life, you and I."

She rubbed her fingers over the white swan emblem she had embroidered on Ultan's little dress. "Aye, that we do," she said.

They'd momentarily forgotten about the political discussions going on behind them, but Cormac turned back to look as O'Neill and General Fairmont stood and shook hands. Niall got up as well, smiling, and after a couple of words with O'Neill, he made his way over to them.

"The negotiations are proceeding satisfactorily, I take it?" Cormac said.

"Aye, more than satisfactory. They're giving us

everything we wanted," Niall said. He sounded exultant. "And what do you think, brother? I'm off to London."

"London!" Cormac and Claire said at once.

"Aye, to the court of Queen Elizabeth herself. O'Neill's made me and John Black his special envoys."

Claire looked at her husband to see if there was any sign of envy over his brother's opportunity, but he had the same peaceful, content expression on his face that he'd had for most of the past year. "How exciting for you, Niall," she said.

He smiled at her, then, dropping a kiss on the baby's black curls, he said, "Your uncle Niall will have a lot to tell you, Ultan, my lad, and I'll bring you back a remembrance from the court of the queen."

"Just bring yourself back safely," Claire said.

Niall nodded, then drifted off again to rejoin the men who were standing around in small groups going over the day's progress.

"So your baby brother is heading to London," Claire said softly.

"It will be good for him," Cormac said. "He's always been a bit too restless to be happy staying at Riordan Hall. Now that the fighting's over, he'll be needing another adventure. London sounds like it will be just the thing for him."

"I just hope he's careful. Niall sometimes acts before he thinks, and I've heard that the queen's court can be a risky place."

Cormac grinned. "What I've heard is that the queen's ladies are the most beautiful in the world, and that should suit Niall just fine."

"The most beautiful in the world, eh?" Claire repeated with a little huff.

He grinned and kissed her on the mouth. "Of course, the people who say that have never been to Tara."

She licked her lips at the familiar taste of him, then leaned her head back with a little purr of contentment.

"So that's the way you're thinking, is it, *chara?*" Cormac's voice lowered. "Perhaps while the men are taking a break you and I should wander up the hill to Cliodhna's Glen."

Several times in the past year they'd made good the promise they'd made a year ago by sneaking away to the secluded clearing to make love under the open sky. Each time they'd looked in the little stone house, but the mysterious carving had never returned.

Claire looked at Ultan, who was still being bounced in his father's arms. "I'd like nothing better, but our lad here is getting too adventuresome to be left wandering while you make me forget everything else in the world."

He grinned at her. "You do tend to get lost in the moment, love," he said. He looked around the clearing and spied Eileen, talking with Eamon and the rebel physician, John Black. "Wait just a moment."

She watched as Cormac walked over to Eileen, spoke to her briefly, then transferred Ultan to her arms. He came back over to her quickly and seized her hand. "Come on, we don't have much time. Ultan will be hungry before long."

He began pulling her up the hill toward the clearing as she protested, "Cormac, we can't. Everyone will know what we're up to."

He stopped, turned around, and pulled her into his arms for a thorough, lusty kiss. "They will now," he said, then he continued to pull her up the hill.

They were both breathless and laughing by the time they reached the break in the trees and moved into the clearing. "No time for niceties, sweetheart," he said. "Off with that pretty frock."

She was as anxious as he, and in a flurry of laces and

petticoats, they soon lay entwined on the soft grass, skin to skin. They joined their mouths and their bodies in eager passion that flared quick and hot. In just a few short moments, they were spent, and lay side by side looking up at the soft white clouds that floated overhead.

"I think Cliodhna approves of us," Cormac said after a moment.

"Aye," Claire agreed happily. "I'm sure she does, else we couldn't be this happy."

Cormac boosted himself up to give her another kiss. "Now who's the superstitious one?" he asked.

" 'Tis not superstition," she protested. " 'Tis merely appreciation for our own private guardian spirit."

Cormac leaned on his elbow and looked down at her. "Ah, *chara,* I do love you."

"I'm glad," she said.

He frowned. "You're supposed to say that you love me, too."

She laughed. "I love you, silly lad."

"I'm glad," he said with a grin. "And may I say that you look mighty tempting lying there with nothing on."

She gave a little stretch. "I feel tempting as well."

He looked at the sun to gauge the time. "Um . . . just how soon do you think Ultan will need your attentions?"

She grinned and held up her arms. "Not for a little while," she murmured.

He lowered himself to her, his mouth seeking hers, while once again they lost the world in each other's arms. The white clouds swirled above them in lazy patterns, and Cliodhna's laughter echoed through the trees.

Irish Eyes

From the fiery passion of the Middle Ages
to the magical charm of Celtic legends
to the timeless allure of modern Ireland
these brand-new romances will surely
"steal your heart away."

The Irish Devil by Donna Fletcher
0-515-12749-3

To Marry an Irish Rogue by Lisa Hendrix
0-515-12786-8

Daughter of Ireland by Sonja Massie
0-515-12835-X

Irish Moonlight by Kate Freiman
0-515-12927-5

All books $5.99